DEATH ON THE SUMMIT

A RITCHIE AND FITZ SCI-FI MURDER MYSTERY

KATE MACLEOD

1

MURDINA RITCHIE HAD RIDDEN the Intergalactic Railway to the far-flung planet of Oymyakon twice before, but this third time was very different from the first two.

She was coming back from a mid-year vacation. That was definitely new.

And hard for her to forget, even for a moment. Her skin was tanned a golden color that startled her every time she caught a glimpse of her bare arms. Not only was the tone different from her more usual pale flesh of a space station dweller, it felt like she had actually caught sunlight within it. Like her body felt warmer to the touch, even though she was no longer in the sun.

And the salty, not quite briny ocean smell still clung to her hair, its waves now a shade lighter but also curlier.

She thought she remembered her childhood well, all the endless days out in the wind under the sun, frolicking in lakes and streams. But just two short weeks under the sun on the ocean world of Epsilon 20 had her feeling like her whole body had been transformed. What had she lost moving from Buennagel to the overcrowded space station that had been her home through most of her adolescent years?

Well, the very first thing she had lost was her own father. She should probably forgive herself for not noticing the other, littler changes.

"Are you getting maudlin on me?" Moreau asked her, nudging Ritchie with her elbow. They were moving down the endless corridor of the train's sleeper cars, hunting for their compartment.

"No," Ritchie said.

"Not that I'd blame you. Oymyakon is going to feel twice as cold, wet and miserable now that you've spent the last two weeks in perfect bliss," Moreau said. Her skin was as ivory-pale as ever, but her long blonde hair hung loose down her back, spinning in tendrils that inter-mixed with the colored strips of fabric that decorated her latest vaca-tion outfit. And she had yet to put shoes on, even though they had now left the beach behind and boarded the intergalactic train. She was even more still in vacation mindset than Ritchie was.

"I'm not getting maudlin," Ritchie said. "I was just thinking this is my first time on an intergalactic railway train that wasn't departing from Intergalactic Transport Depot Delta-Gamma-Delta. Which I wouldn't think would really matter, but this is clearly a very different train."

Moreau looked around, as if unsure what Ritchie was referring to. Like she didn't even see the replicators installed in every open compartment they passed, or feel the thick lushness of the carpet under their feet, or smell the light fragrance to the air like jasmine was growing just around the corner somewhere.

But then Moreau stopped at the door to their compartment and paused for a moment with her hand on the door handle. "It is a very different train," she agreed as she flung the door open. "Every compartment is first class, minimum. But ours is a little something extra."

Ritchie had no idea what that could even mean. How could first class be the minimum? What could possibly be *beyond* first class?

But then she followed Moreau inside, into a vast space that extended up and down the entire length of the train car. The exterior wall was floor to ceiling windows, currently offering views of the passengers and other people milling on the platform, the sun setting low over the ocean beyond. Ritchie tried to drink up every pink, rose and golden hue of that sky, as if she could save it all up for when she was back at the academy, back in a world full of whites and grays.

Moreau dumped her bag unceremoniously on one of the chairs set around a long dining room table under a free-floating chandelier, currently unlit, then threw herself down on one end of a horseshoe-shaped leather sofa built around a low table, perfect for sitting with a dozen friends and watching the sunset outside.

"Can they see us?" Ritchie asked. But no one seemed to be looking in at them.

"No, and I'm telling you now we're going to be setting it to opaque before we jump," Moreau said sternly. But then she lightened up. "You have your own cabin down the hall there, also with full windows, if you really want to drive yourself crazy looking out at the abyss."

"My own...?" Ritchie said, but couldn't finish that thought. It was too much. "How much are you paying for this?"

"Not a thing," she said with a shrug.

"How much are *your parents* paying for this?" Ritchie pressed.

"They won't even notice," Moreau said. "Honestly, I'm so much easier on their bank accounts now that I'm at the academy. I used to party like we've been doing the last few weeks all the time. It was very expensive to maintain my lifestyle, but they never said a peep. Not about that, anyway. So don't worry. And don't ruin it for me. It's my little treat for you."

"I really didn't need another thing," Ritchie said. "These last two weeks have been..."

She couldn't think of words big enough to contain everything she was feeling. It wasn't just that being planetside on an actually pleasant planet for the first time in years had been like a balm to her soul. Although it had.

And it wasn't just the magic of living a life of complete luxury on board a yacht that hovered smoothly over the waves, that was linked to satellites that could literally divert weather patterns to give them endless sunny days and gentle rains in the early hours of the morning, the better for sleeping to the soft musical patter of droplets on the decks.

It had taken Ritchie a few days to accept that it really was true. She could replicate anything she wanted any time she wanted, and no one cared. She and Moreau had replicated entire outfits for every time of day, recycling them back when they were done before replicating something new.

And the food! Not just replicated, but fresh, sold by local farmers and fishermen on every beach where they stopped in the evenings to feast around a roaring bonfire. She had eaten too many fantastic things for her to ever remember the names of them all.

But none of those things had been what she really wanted to thank Moreau for. No, the biggest thing was something very different, and something that didn't really come directly from her family's money.

Moreau had given her two weeks among a group of kids their age who were fun and interesting, and not a one of them attended a foreign service academy or had any interest in politics or diplomacy or union affairs or anything remotely related to those things. She had loved hanging out with them all even before she had found herself loving hanging out with just one of them in particular.

Ritchie realized she was still standing there, hands grasping the air as if she could somehow find the words there, but Moreau just grinned at her.

"I know, buddy. You don't have to say it. I know."

"I needed it," Ritchie said at last.

"I know that too," Moreau said. "I don't know what you needed the break from more: Fitz and his games or that thing you do where you get too deep and dark inside your own head."

Ritchie wanted to object to the second thing, but her own mind betrayed her by getting hung up on the first. She wanted to argue about that word. Games. It didn't feel like Fitz was playing games with her.

But since he wasn't really talking to her, she had no idea what he *was* doing. Which was frustrating.

That wall she had sensed between them at the beginning of the last semester had grown twice as tall and twice as thick and had acquired a moat. Or at least that's how it felt to Ritchie.

Her mind wanted to run over that last real conversation they'd had on the shuttle when they had landed after their trip to the Julius Henry

Observational Center to see Keller and Weld. Had she said something wrong? Should she not have hugged him so tight?

But she fought the urge to relive that moment again. It never provided her any insight, anyway. All she knew was that he was closed off to her now. He spoke to her in class about class things, and he spoke to her at their task force meetings with Colonel Hansen and the others about task force things. But that was it. And that had no warmth.

Plus, he never looked her in the eye anymore.

Still, she wasn't angry with him. Confused and a little heartbroken, sure. She missed their friendship, and she didn't know why he had cut her off without an explanation. But there was no anger in her over it.

But she *did* worry. If he wasn't talking to her, he needed to be talking to someone. He couldn't isolate himself from absolutely everyone.

At least he had taken Wyss with him on his own trip to see his parents.

"I wonder how he's doing?" she found herself saying wistfully. "Fitz, I mean. I sent a dozen messages to Wyss, but he only responded once and had absolutely nothing useful to say."

Moreau turned around to look at her over the back of the sofa, fixing her with a mock-stern glare. "Vacation time is *not* over," she said. "You promised we wouldn't talk about him, remember?"

"You're the one who said his name," Ritchie said.

"But apparently you're the one who sent Wyss a dozen messages... what, asking how Fitz was doing?"

Ritchie felt her cheeks flush hotly. She had deliberately not let Moreau know she was trying to check up on Fitz, because she knew she would take it just this way. All the anger Ritchie hadn't been feeling towards Fitz, Moreau had been feeling in spades on her behalf. Ritchie just knew that she would start with the eye-rolling again in another few seconds.

"I think it's good he took Wyss with him for the midyear break," Ritchie said. "If he doesn't want to be my friend anymore or yours, at least he has Wyss."

"He's not—" Moreau started to say with a dark glower, but stopped abruptly. There was a sneaky sort of smile on her face as she sank back down into her seat, turning away from Ritchie to face the window once more.

"Moreau?" Ritchie said, but then heard a soft knock on the open door behind her and turned to see Guy Travert standing in the doorway. He looked like he'd just come down off the deck of his yacht, his long, thick brown hair in wind-tousled waves, his tan several degrees darker than her own, his eyes almost the exact shade of blue as the shallows of the seas of Epsilon 20.

And all thoughts of Fitz were gone from Ritchie's mind, just like that.

"Hey. Can I come in?" he asked.

"Of course you can, Mr. Travert," Moreau called back over her shoulder. "Our girl is getting maudlin already. Can I get your help with that?"

"Maudlin?" Guy said as he stepped into the cabin and closed the door behind him. "Already?"

"She exaggerates," Ritchie said. But she couldn't deny she felt better just seeing him again. Even if it had only been a few minutes since she'd seen him last.

That feeling she had like she had caught the warmth of the sun inside her skin? His skin had that tenfold. When he put his arms around her, she could smell the salt from the sea and the smoke from the nightly bonfires all around her, and she could feel the warmth of the sand below and the cloudless sky above radiating out from him.

The last nine days spending every waking minute with Guy had been like living an entirely different life. She pushed down the thought that it was all about to be over soon and rose up on tiptoe to give him a quick kiss.

"Ugh. I can hear you," Moreau said loudly from the sofa the moment their lips met.

"I suppose it is a bit rude," Guy said, a mischievous smile in his eyes.

"She's the one who insisted I'm still on vacation," Ritchie said, and tugged him down to kiss him again.

"*We* are still on vacation," Moreau said. "You and me." But then she sat up to peer over the top of the sofa at the two of them, and her expression was nowhere near as grumpy as she sounded. "Not that you're not welcome, Guy."

"Pretty sure I'm always welcome," Guy said, then took Ritchie by the hand. They settled onto the leather sofa a respectable distance away from Moreau, but not from each other.

"Of course you are," Moreau said. "Although why you'd want to spend who knows how many days riding with us to Oymyakon is beyond me."

"Is it?" Guy asked absently. He still had Ritchie's hand resting on his palm and was tracing up and down the lengths of her fingers with his other hand.

"You guys are crazy," Moreau said with a little laugh, then got up to head to the replicator. "One last round of that local fruit cocktail thing before we leave the sun behind?"

"Please," Guy said, his focus still on Ritchie's hand.

"Me too," Ritchie said, resting her head on Guy's shoulder. But then she picked it up and looked at him until he finally felt her gaze and lifted his eyes to hers. "She's not wrong," Ritchie said softly. "I've known you for exactly nine days."

"Fourteen," he said. "I *did* talk to you at that first party. I talked to you the first time I saw you. I made a point of it."

"All right," Ritchie said, although she still remembered that first party very differently. "It's not like five days more changes my point at all."

"I know," Guy sighed. "We talked about this already. You have another year at the academy—"

"Year and a half," Ritchie corrected.

"And four years at the university after that," Guy went on.

"Maybe longer if I apply for one of the extended training programs," Ritchie said.

"Then, after that, a career that could take you anywhere inside or even outside of the Union of Free Worlds. And you could be moved around randomly, without warning, at a whim," he said. But that smile was still in his eyes.

"I don't think you've even heard me," Ritchie said.

"I've heard you," he said. "I have a lot of friends who went the foreign service route. I'm not unfamiliar with what's required of you. But I don't think *you*'ve heard *me*."

"Heard you say what?" Ritchie asked.

"See? You didn't listen," he said. "And now you're making me brag all over again."

"Like you've ever had trouble with that," Moreau said as she brought two brightly colored drinks in tall frosted glasses to set on the table between them and the window.

"It's one of my skills. I'm quite good at it, you know. Maybe the best," he said.

"No one beats you at bragging," Moreau agreed.

Ritchie just grinned at them both. This felt so different from it had when she had first met Moreau, when she had felt left out by the commonalities Moreau and Fitz had shared and that she had decidedly not. The long years of parties and functions they had both attended together. Well, had been thrown together at by their parents, really, for most of those years.

But she didn't feel left out of the conversation this time. Maybe it was just that she knew Moreau better now and knew how lightly she took all of that society stuff. She genuinely envied Ritchie not having to deal with any of it.

Or maybe it was just that Guy was a total open book. He had a feeling, he spoke that feeling. He had a thought, he spoke that thought. No secrets, ever.

It was such a refreshing change, knowing with absolute certainty where she stood.

"You were about to brag," Moreau reminded Guy as she settled back down onto the sofa with her own drink and took a tentative sip.

"Right," Guy said, turning back to Ritchie. Even through the depths of his tan, she could see his cheeks coloring. He was going to brag, sure, but he was also a bit embarrassed about bragging to her. And she realized too late to stop him what he was about to say. She *did* remember having this conversation. "Murdina Ritchie," he said with all seriousness, "I'm wealthy. Beyond wealthy. I could live a thousand profligate lifetimes and not spend half of what my ancestors have accumulated. Not that I intend to do that!" he said, raising a finger as if in warning.

"Perish the thought," Moreau said and took another sip of her fruit cocktail.

"Yes, I have aspirations of my own," he said, as if it was Ritchie who had spoken and not Moreau. "I have an academic career of my own to pursue, and beyond that, a business to run. I have no intention of living a profligate life even though I have the means to do so."

"Guy," Ritchie started to say, but he placed a finger on her lips to silence her.

"Now she remembers we talked about this before," he said to the room at large.

"Of course she does," Moreau said.

"Guy," Ritchie said again, pulling his hand away from her mouth.

"I was almost finished," he said.

"We've already said all this," Ritchie said.

"Please?" he said.

She gave in with a nod.

"I'm not throwing all that away to chase you around the universe. Which seems to be what you keep hearing, because I can see the panic in your eyes. I'm not going to smother you with attention or stalk you or anything like that. I'm just saying, if I'm a day late or two to the start of the semester, it's okay. Because I can buy the college if I need to." His eyes were twinkling, so she knew he was joking about that last bit.

Except he was only half joking.

And he wasn't wrong about the panic. Not that she was afraid of what he might do. No, she was afraid of what *she* might do. Because ditching her whole future to spend more time with him now didn't feel like such a terrible idea.

"It's just one train ride," he said, speaking softly. Moreau, for her part, pretended as if stirring the ice in her beverage were the most engrossing activity in the world.

"And after that?" Ritchie whispered back.

"I hope you'll message me when you can," he said. "And don't freak out if I message you every day. I know academy life can be overwhelming and you can't respond to everything and I don't expect you to."

"Especially not at first," Ritchie said, almost desperately.

"I know, Murdina," he said. "You'll be up a mountain for days and days."

"Extreme environment tactical training," Ritchie said.

"Like I'm saying all those words," he said.

"At least she didn't hit you with just EETT," Moreau said. She was still looking down into her glass, acting as if those words hadn't just come out of her mouth.

"When the semester is done, we'll figure out what comes next," Guy said. "I would like us to spend more time together. Not the entire break, obviously. I know you have family to see and, knowing you, studying to do."

Moreau snorted.

"I *do* have to see my family," Ritchie admitted.

"See? And I get that," Guy said. "But surely I can be on the train that comes to pick you up. And we can get off at the first depot we reach and take a proper shuttle the rest of the way. You know, my family's personal shuttle. Well, one of them. We have a fleet." That twinkle was back in his eyes.

"Is your shuttle anything like your yacht?" Ritchie asked.

"You know, I'm actually afraid to answer that question," Guy said.

"Wait until she sees your homeworld," Moreau said.

Ritchie started to laugh at the picture that conjured: her *way* outside of her social comfort zone.

Then she realized that Moreau hadn't stressed the first syllable, home. She had stressed the second, world.

"Guy, does your family own a *world*?" she asked.

"Moreau, you're trouble," Guy said.

"Just looking out for my buddy," Moreau said. "It's more than my job. It's my calling."

A tone sounded throughout the train and then they were lifting off from the ground, spiraling up into the sky.

It was like they were chasing the last of the sunset, making it last if only a moment longer.

"Let's just enjoy the train ride," Guy said close to her ear, and she snuggled closer to his side. The blackness of space was descending down on them from above, or rather they were rising up into it. Either way, it was like Ritchie could feel the coldness of it seeping into her, settling into her very bones.

"For as long as it lasts," Ritchie said, and buried her nose against the warmth of his neck, inhaling the last bit of ocean smell she'd have for quite some time.

2

SHACKLETON FITZ IV poked at the contents of his beef and broccoli noodle bowl with his fork, not quite eating. He had his chin resting on his hand, but wasn't quite looking at either Kristof Wyss sitting across from him eating his own noodle bowl with gusto, nor out the open shuttle window at the total blackness of jump space that pressed in all around them.

He toyed with the thought of turning on some music, but wasn't quite in the mood for that either.

The spicy, salty smell of his food was reminding him that it was just the sort of thing he absolutely needed to indulge in now, before he returned to the Oymyakon Foreign Service Academy and its wide array of far blander meal options, but he just wasn't hungry. Or rather, he didn't have any appetite. For anything. He pushed the bowl away.

"Sorry. Do you want me to close it?" Wyss asked, gesturing towards the blind for the window.

"No, it's fine," Fitz said.

"Is it? You just made a noise like you were bothered," Wyss said.

"I don't think I did," Fitz said. Wyss shrugged and turned his attention back to his food. Then Fitz found himself saying, "you know who likes to look out into jump space? Ritchie."

"Ah," Wyss said, as if that simple statement had been some massive revelation.

"What?" Fitz asked.

"That's what's bothering you," Wyss said.

"Nothing is bothering me. I'm just saying, most people don't like to even glimpse at jump space. But you're drinking it in like it's endlessly fascinating. And that reminds me of Ritchie. That's all," Fitz said, and really wished he could make himself stop talking.

Wyss nodded, then stood up to pull the blind down over the window. "I don't think it's jump space that has you thinking about Ritchie. Did you want to talk about what happened last night?" he asked, making a fuss over the window blind and carefully not looking at Fitz as he asked.

"No," Fitz said.

Wyss nodded again before sitting back down and shoving another forkful of noodles into his mouth. "You were right, by the way. This is really good," he said before he'd quite finished chewing.

"Yeah," Fitz said, glancing down at his own untouched bowl cooling on the table before him. He sighed and realized that was exactly the sound he had made before that had started Wyss talking in the first place.

He hated himself a little bit for indulging in dramatic sighs, even unconsciously. But Wyss wasn't wrong about last night being the trigger. He was an expert at suppressing his own thoughts and emotions while projecting a devil-may-care attitude to the rest of the world.

But last night had just been so very confusing. It was hard to process. It had been like being trapped in a movie where he had followed the plot just fine, but on reflection afterwards realized he had missed all the subtext.

There had been so much subtext.

"Thanks again for bringing me with you to the capital world," Wyss said. "And for letting me drag you to every museum and library in the area."

"Well, like I said, you were really doing me a favor," Fitz said. "You were an adept buffer between my parents and me."

"Your mom is great," Wyss said.

"She is," Fitz agreed. When Wyss and Fitz first arrived at the apartment that was his parents' temporary home, she had taken one quick glance at Wyss' list of places he wanted to visit. By the next morning, she had arranged private tours in all of them with friends and friends of friends who could get them into all the basements and archives and private galleries the general public never saw.

Wyss had been in heaven. Fitz's mother had thoroughly enjoyed his delight. And Fitz had just been happy that she was happy and that his father was, as usual, too busy to spend more than a fleeting few minutes with them all at dinner, when he was home at all.

Up until last night, anyway, when he had decided to throw a dinner party.

"What do you suppose Cicey Travert was giggling about all night?" Fitz asked.

"So you *do* want to talk about last night," Wyss said.

"Not really," Fitz said. He knew Wyss was just trying to be helpful, and all he needed was a clue from Fitz what helpful looked like. But honestly, Fitz didn't know what he needed either. He hadn't sorted out his own thoughts yet.

"You just don't want to talk about Feena," Wyss guessed, scraping at the last bits of noodle on the bottom of his bowl.

"No sane person ever wants to talk about either of the Berwegers," Fitz said.

"We probably shouldn't have joined a task force dedicated to keeping track of their doings, then," Wyss said. Fitz marveled at how he could say it without the slightest hint of irony. But then again, Wyss didn't have a sarcastic bone in his body.

"That's not why she was there," Fitz said.

"She was there the same reason Cicey Travert was there," Wyss said. "They couldn't get out of being dragged there by their elders. An invitation to a Fitz family dinner party is too rare an opportunity to pass up."

"Yeah, that's what they *said*, but I couldn't help but notice that neither of their brothers were there," Fitz said.

Wyss gave him a sharp look, as if trying to determine if Fitz was messing with him or not.

"What?" Fitz asked.

"Isn't it obvious?" Wyss asked.

"Clearly not," Fitz said.

"Either one or both of your parents was trying to match-make you up with one of them," Wyss said. "That was the whole point of the dinner. It couldn't have been more clear if they had hung banners with it all spelled out."

"That's—" Fitz started to say, but then broke off and really thought it through. "That's exactly what was going on, wasn't it?" He buried his face in his hands.

"Well, in your defense, after what happened after dinner and all the work we did to clear your father's name from that meddling woman's lame attempt at a blackmail scheme, any attempt at a matchmaking sort of fell by the wayside," Wyss said.

"Did it, though?" Fitz asked.

"If you're saying Feena maneuvered things to remove the only other player from the board and get you all to yourself, I wouldn't disagree," Wyss said. "On the other hand, she wasn't wrong. Cicey isn't a foreign service academy student. She didn't swear an oath like we did to serve the Union of Free Worlds with loyalty and integrity. But on the *other* other hand, using the truth sparingly when it serves her own aims is a very Berweger thing to do. Given enough time, we could probably parse that all out between the two of us and reach some sort of conclusion. But of course that would involve talking about Feena."

"You're right, that's unavoidable," Fitz said.

"Not as unavoidable as she's going to make herself once we get back to school," Wyss said. "Face it. She's locked her targeting mechanism on you. She was fawning over you from afar all last semester, despite how close we came to sending her parents to jail and getting her and her brother expelled. Now she's stalking you over the break. Just wait until we start classes again. I'm sure she's found ways to get closer to you anyway she can. She's not going to let you get away."

"She's just trying to make trouble," Fitz said.

"I know she's probably evil on a cellular level," Wyss said, again not remotely sarcastically. "She was created in a lab to achieve bad ends.

No argument there. But it's not inconceivable that all of that could be true, but also the fact that she just really likes you."

"Do you actually think that?" Fitz asked, a sick feeling in his stomach.

Wyss shrugged. "She seemed sincerely thrilled to be working with us to solve a crime. She dug in and did the work, no question about it. We wouldn't have found the culprit without her."

"That's debatable," Fitz said grumpily. "We would've been fine on our own. It just might've taken a little longer to put the pieces together."

"I never interact with that level of society, and you deliberately have blinders to it," Wyss said. "She made connections we never would have on our own."

"So now you're on her side?" Fitz demanded.

"Facts are facts," Wyss said. "Look, she clearly wants to be your new Ritchie. She as much as said so."

"I don't need a new Ritchie," Fitz glowered.

Wyss bit at his lip, his hands touching the tabletop as if he longed to grab a tablet and start studying something. But Fitz had made him leave all his tablets in his cabin.

"What?" Fitz asked.

Wyss didn't say anything for several long minutes. Fitz watched his face as he considered then discarded several responses. But he bit his own tongue, refusing to speak again until Wyss said out loud what he was thinking.

"I was just wondering myself about what Cicey Travert meant last night," he said at last.

Fitz was dead certain that had not been among the first twelve thoughts that Wyss had run through just then, but he let it go. "She's a sister of an acquaintance," he said. "She's also a known troublemaker, if not on a Berweger scale. I'm not sure she meant anything at all."

"Here's the thing," Wyss said, all but squirming in his seat as his fingertips rubbed over the tabletop, still in that nervous pantomime. "I've been exchanging messages with Ritchie during the semester break."

"School-related?" Fitz asked.

"Of course not," Wyss said, still with that total lack of irony. "She's worried about you."

"I'm fine, obviously. Until Feena turned up last night, I couldn't even remotely be considered in any kind of danger," Fitz said.

"Worried is maybe not the right word," Wyss said. "Look, I'm not really good at this. But she was hoping I would take the time to talk to you while we were away from the academy."

"And you waited until now to bring it up?" Fitz asked.

"This sort of thing is not really in my skill set," Wyss said, squirming again. "But it's not like you were ever going to invite Moreau or anything."

Fitz sighed, really wishing he could avoid asking the question. But he needed to hear the answer. "What did Ritchie want you to talk to me about?"

"Well, it's not exactly a secret that you've stopped talking to *her*," Wyss said almost defensively.

"Nonsense. I talk to her every day," Fitz said. "Maybe not over the break, but at the academy, I do. Every single day."

"Come on," Wyss said. "You know exactly what I mean. After you two came back from the Julius Henry Observational Center, you've not said a word more to her than you had to. Moreau even joked that she and I should wear parkas to the task force meetings. Because we were getting secondhand frostbite from the freeze out you were doing on Ritchie."

"Totally Moreau's words," Fitz guessed.

"But she's not wrong," Wyss said.

"I wasn't freezing Ritchie out," Fitz said. "I've just been busy and distracted and... whatever. It's not even a thing."

"Ugh, this is not my skill set," Wyss lamented to the shuttle ceiling before turning his gaze back on Fitz. "Look, I'm just going to say one last thing and then we'll drop it."

"Fine, but I swear nothing is going on. Ritchie is just—"

"Don't you dare say Ritchie is just being too sensitive," Wyss said with real anger in his voice. Fitz sat back and blinked. He had never heard that tone in Wyss's voice, not even when Wyss's own best friend had betrayed him.

"No, that would never be a thing that would describe Ritchie," Fitz agreed. "But—"

"Just, stop it," Wyss said, holding up a hand as if that could hold back whatever Fitz had been about to say.

"Fine. Say your one last thing," Fitz said resignedly.

"It's clear to all of us that you're keeping secrets from us," Wyss said. "We three have discussed it amongst ourselves, and we all agree that feels like what's happening. But none of us has any idea what you're not sharing with us. Us, your best friends. It's no exaggeration to say we've all saved each other's lives. We share bonds stronger than mere friendship. But you put up a wall between you and Ritchie, all of a sudden with no warning, and it simply doesn't make any sense."

Fitz said nothing, but neither did Wyss. The silence stretched out between them. But Fitz knew he would lose this game. Wyss could wait forever to speak again, but Fitz just had to fill the space between them with noise somehow.

"You've spent nearly fourteen days in my home with my family," he said. "I'm sure the entire time you've spent in my father's company could be best measured in minutes, but he makes a big impression." He looked up at Wyss for confirmation.

"He does," Wyss agreed. "And it was clear even in that time that he really doesn't like Ritchie. Like I said, that little dinner party last night wasn't a work thing for him. It was an attempt to use either Feena or Cicey as a wedge between you and Ritchie. But that doesn't make any sense. Because you've already been apart in any way that matters for months now."

"I know," Fitz said. Wyss saying it out loud was making him feel it in a way that just living through it hadn't.

He missed his best friend.

"But if he's the whole reason, then why doesn't he know?" Wyss asked. Then, before Fitz could speak, he added, "is it all a game between you? You can't let him know when he's winning? Then what's even the point?"

"It's complicated," Fitz said. "But I promise you, I swear to you, it isn't a game."

Wyss met his eyes steadily. The shuttle around them lurched ever so slightly. They were out of jump space. They'd be landing on Oymyakon soon.

"I believe you," Wyss said at last.

"Thanks," Fitz said. Then, realizing that he had the opposite thing to Wyss, a tendency for too much sarcasm, he tried again. "No, seriously, thank you. Thank you for believing me."

"If you say you have a good reason for keeping a secret, then of course you do," Wyss said. "But Fitz, is it worth what it's costing you?"

"Yes," Fitz said firmly. On that score, he had no doubts at all. He had spent little time with his father over the break, and none of that had been the two of them alone, but he could tell his father's wishes had not changed. And neither had his feelings about Ritchie.

"I'm not so sure of that," Wyss said, but he didn't press the point.

"It can take an hour or a day to land, depending on the weather," Fitz said. "But just in case it's an hour, we should maybe get into uniform and pack the last of our stuff."

"Sure," Wyss said, and got up to take his bowl and fork to the replicator for recycling.

Fitz got up with his own still-full bowl in hand. He set it into the machine next to Wyss's bowl, but caught Wyss before he could leave for his cabin.

"Say, you said you knew what Cicey found so amusing last night," he said.

"No, I said I was wondering," Wyss said.

Fitz nodded impatiently. "Yeah, yeah, but with you, that usually means you already have a theory. And your theories have a really good track record."

Wyss sighed. "Look, I don't know for sure what she meant."

"But?" Fitz prompted.

"But, like I said, I was exchanging messages with Ritchie over the break," Wyss said.

"Because she wanted you to talk to me," Fitz said.

"Yeah, and I didn't message back because I hadn't talked to you yet and it was awkward to keep telling her I'd get to it when I was clearly not getting to it."

"And?"

"Well, after four or five days, she stopped messaging me," Wyss said.

"Because you weren't answering," Fitz guessed.

"I thought so at the time," Wyss admitted.

"Come on, man. This is like pulling teeth here," Fitz said.

Wyss heaved another sigh. "Do you even know where she was going?" he asked.

"Somewhere with Moreau," Fitz said.

"They were on Epsilon 20," Wyss said.

"The aquatic world," Fitz said, nodding. "I've been there, actually. A few years back, I spent a whole summer there. Nothing but waves, sun and sand. Deep sea diving and fishing by day, parties by night. I hated almost every minute of it."

"It sounds like paradise," Wyss said, and Fitz remembered that Wyss had grown up on a space station. Anything on a planet was paradise compared to that, even a hellhole like Oymyakon.

"Oh, the planet is great, highly recommend," Fitz said, giving him two thumbs up. "The only problem is it's almost entirely the playground of the insanely rich. The seas are rough, and only the hover yachts are safe enough for travel..."

Wyss lifted his eyebrows after Fitz trailed off, as if waiting for him to make the connection.

The connection he absolutely didn't want to make. But once he did, the images wouldn't stop blossoming in his mind. Waves, sun, and sand. And Ritchie.

"Ritchie was on some rich guy's yacht with Moreau, possibly the worst chaperone ever," Fitz guessed.

"Is that fair?" Wyss asked.

"I've been to parties with Moreau before," Fitz said dismissively.

"Before she and Ritchie became buddies," Wyss said.

"Fine, Moreau is looking out for her," Fitz gave in with, he knew, very bad grace. "So you're saying Ritchie stopped messaging you because she was having such a good time? Does that sound like Ritchie to you?"

Wyss shrugged. "I'm just saying, Cicey clearly saw her at parties, and was mentioning her to you to get a rise out of you."

Fitz barked out a humorless laugh. "Must've been so frustrating when I didn't react since I had no idea what she was talking about."

"I suppose that's the upside," Wyss agreed.

"Still, aside from why she would even care, how did Cicey even know that Ritchie and I knew each other?" Fitz wondered.

"Well, if I had to guess, it's because Ritchie mentioned you," Wyss said. "And then she stopped mentioning you. Because something else was going on."

Fitz glared at him for a minute, then a thought struck him and his glower deepened. "Are you saying she *met* someone? *Ritchie*? At a party like they have on Epsilon 20?"

Wyss shrugged again. "Cicey was certainly implying it."

"That's ridiculous," Fitz said. "More likely, she got caught up in studying in advance for our classes this semester and got all distracted. She forgot about the other party kids, because of course she would. They aren't her type of people, are they? And she forgot about messaging you, so by extension she forgot about me. I'd prefer that wasn't because of homework, but what are you going to do? It's Ritchie, right? Always be over-prepared; that's her motto."

"Sure, I'm sure that's it," Wyss said, and beat a hasty retreat to his cabin before Fitz could detain him again.

But it had to be all in Fitz's imagination, given Wyss had no capacity for irony, that it sounded like there had been just a hint of sarcasm in Wyss's voice.

No, Wyss knew Ritchie nearly as well as Fitz did. He had definitely imagined that sarcasm.

But the unsettled feeling in his stomach didn't dissipate as he went to his cabin to get into his uniform.

3

RITCHIE WOKE to a haze of gray outside the window next to her bed. They were no longer in space; they were in the stormy atmosphere of Oymyakon. She felt a stab of panic that her time left with Guy would be all too short.

But then she checked the screen built into the wall over the head of her bed and saw the train had descended to a point as far from the Oymyakon Foreign Service Academy as it was possible to go without just going down over the second, smaller continent. She had slept through several hours of uneventful travel, but there was still a long way to go. Not only that, but the snaky line that showed the planned route was filled with the flashing lights of other stops on the way. She had thought the train was mostly filled with her fellow cadets, but clearly she had been wrong.

She got up and dressed in civilian clothes. The schedule had them set to arrive at the academy just around dinnertime, but that was likely to be delayed by the weather, and there was no reason to get into uniform until the very last minute, anyway.

Then she headed out to the sitting room to find Moreau already awake and dressed in her usual vacation loungewear. She was sitting at the dining table under the soft glow of the free-floating chandelier and sipping at a cup of coffee the size of a soup bowl, quietly gazing out the window at the dark gray clouds and blackish mountainsides passing by.

"Did I oversleep?" Ritchie asked, glancing at her implant's chronometer.

"No, you just slept through the bumpy entry a few hours ago. I did not," Moreau said, then covered her mouth before yawning.

"It looks intense out there," Ritchie said, pressing her face close to the glass. She was used to stormy skies. They were, after all, the reason that travel to any point on Oymyakon was done by the intergalactic train and not by chartered shuttles. Private vehicles like the one Fitz's parents owned could handle all but the worst of the weather, but the larger vehicles built to handle public transport were treacherous in this tempestuous and thoroughly unreliable atmosphere. The train pierced through a narrow break in the storm anywhere over the continent, then once it was under the worst of the winds, it wended its way around just over the surface, avoiding the wildest storms.

But Ritchie could feel the train under her feet lurching in the winds, something she had never felt before. And the sky was the darkest she'd ever seen, aside from the constant electric blue flashes of lightning striking the mountaintops.

"We're pretty close to the equator still," Moreau said, holding her bowl of coffee in her hands without drinking it, as if she just needed to be touching something warm. "Closer to the school, this is going to be more snow and ice. Although apparently still with the lightning."

"Snow and lightning?" Ritchie asked. That actually sounded pretty exciting, but she was certain Moreau wouldn't think so. "How do you know that?"

"I went for a walk earlier and was chatting with some of the other cadets," Moreau said with a shrug. "So many rumors."

"About the weather?" Ritchie said, disbelievingly. But then she thought it over as she sat down across from Moreau at the table. "Actually, that makes sense, since half of us are going up the mountain tomorrow."

"I've been trying to forget," Moreau said and took a long drink from her cup. "Fourteen days of sea and sun, but that was only a momentary distraction. Now we get to freeze our tails off for days and days. In low oxygen. In climbing gear. And sleeping in tents." She shivered so violently she had to set her cup down to keep from spilling it. "Ugh, Ritchie. *Camping*."

"We'll make it through all right," Ritchie promised her. By a supreme effort, she managed to disguise the fact that she had been looking forward to this particular class since she'd arrived at the Oymyakon Foreign Service Academy.

It was the most extreme, most challenging, most test-of-her-true-mettle moment she was likely to have before moving on to university. Everything they'd been learning about survival training and pulling together as a team was about to be tested in the harshest way possible.

Far from school, at an altitude so high they would be carrying their own oxygen, climbing all day for days on end until they reached the summit.

And then there would be combat drills. Battle simulations. All on top of a peak that wasn't accessible by shuttle ninety percent of the time because the weather on that particular mountain was always harsh, the wind always variable.

Ritchie knew that Moreau had been dreading this adventure. But the look on her face now was beyond dread.

"Oh," Ritchie said, finally putting it together. "This weather is going to last for a bit, I take it?"

"It is unseasonable," Moreau said, "but the systems predict it will hold for weeks. So no waiting a few days for it to blow over. It's going to be a long, hard winter. And we'll spend it far from the comforts of our damp, cold home away from home."

Ritchie nodded and tried to look grave, but inside her emotions were a twisting maelstrom as excitement and fear whirled around in nearly equal measures.

"I was going to eat," Ritchie said, and got up to head towards the replicator. But then there was a soft knock on the door and she changed course, opening the door to let Guy in.

"I hope I'm not too early," he said after kissing her hello.

"No, we've been up for a bit," Ritchie said. "I was just going to sort out breakfast. Are you hungry?"

"Starved," Guy said.

"I think we should eat in the dining car," Moreau said suddenly.

"Oh? Sure," Guy said, but looked to Ritchie for confirmation.

"Not here?" Ritchie asked.

"Well, I told you I heard rumors, but I didn't tell you all of it," Moreau said. "I was only in the corridor for a minute, but the weather isn't the real topic of the day."

"What is?" Ritchie asked.

Moreau bit her lip as if struggling to find the words. Which wasn't like her at all.

"Moreau? What is it?" Ritchie asked again. She traded a nervous look with Guy.

"People are saying something is going on with Colonel Hansen," Moreau said. "But what I heard was pretty garbled. I don't want to repeat anything, especially not from the sources I was hearing it from, but I think we should figure out what's going on."

"A bunch of cadets spinning yarns is what's going on," Ritchie said, her voice harsher than she intended. But then she added, "wait, you don't think it's anything to do with us on the task force, do you?"

"What's this task force?" Guy asked with eager interest, but Ritchie ignored him.

"It doesn't seem so," Moreau said. "I'm sorry. The weather had me in a bit of a funk, and I was focused on the wrong things." Then she blanched and rushed to add, "I didn't mean anything backhanded by that, I swear!"

"Okay," Ritchie said, trying to work out what Moreau was apologizing for. Then she remembered Guy still standing behind her and listening to them talk, and she felt her cheeks heat. "You're right. We need to focus on this. Tell me what's going on."

"You know, I really want to find someone a little more trustworthy to get the real story from first," Moreau said.

"I suppose we should eat with the others, then," Ritchie said, but it was easier to hide her enthusiasm for their upcoming extreme environment tactical training drills than it was to pretend enthusiasm for sitting with the other cadets, even just for breakfast.

She wasn't ready to be back in that world yet.

"I tell you what," Moreau said as she pushed up from the table to carry her empty coffee cup back to the replicator. "Why don't I go? You guys can stay here and dial up your own breakfast from the replicator."

"Are you sure?" Ritchie asked.

"Yeah. Now that I think about it, it's probably faster if I talk to everyone on my own," Moreau said.

"If we split up, we can get to everyone twice as fast," Ritchie said.

"Maybe," Moreau said, but Ritchie could tell she was only pretending to consider that plan before she shook her head. "No. There's really only a few people who would know anything remotely likely to be true. I'll hit them all up and head back after. Do I need a special knock when I get back, or..." she trailed off.

"Stop it," Ritchie said, grabbing her by the shoulders and guiding her towards the door. Moreau stepped out into the corridor, but Ritchie caught her arm before she could quite leave. "Moreau."

"Yes?" Moreau turned back to ask.

"If you need me, come back and get me," Ritchie said. "I don't need to tell you I'd do anything to help Hansen if he's in trouble. Or go after the rumormongers if it's all lies."

"I know. I feel the same," Moreau said. "I'll tell you what I know when I get back."

"Right," Ritchie said, then leaned out through the doorway to whisper a quick, "thanks."

"I'm going to be thorough," Moreau said as she walked away, backwards down the corridor. "Very thorough. I might have to double check some things before I get back. Are you sure no special knock?"

But she had reached the door between their sleeper car and the next and didn't linger for Ritchie to come up with a response. With a soft hiss of air, she was gone.

"Task force?" Guy asked the minute Ritchie had turned back around.

"Never mind about that," Ritchie said mock sternly. "What are you hungry for?"

"Well, I've pretty much dialed up a whole buffet here while I was not listening to whatever you and Moreau were whispering about in the corridor," Guy said. Then he opened the door on the front of the replicator and the smell of cheesy scrambled eggs, peanut butter waffles, and warm maple syrup filled the whole train car.

"I guess you did," Ritchie said with a grin.

To his credit, Guy didn't bring up either Hansen or the task force again, although Ritchie knew he was curious about all of it. Instead, they chatted and laughed about random nonsensical things as they ate. For a few minutes, it was really nice. Ritchie had a warm feeling all inside of her, and it was only partly on account of the mountain of food she was putting away.

But then the last of the syrup had been mopped up, and the coffee pot was empty, and she suddenly realized their merry conversation had died when she hadn't quite been paying attention. Now Guy was just sitting back in his chair watching the patterns of lightning dancing over the mountaintops. What little of it that could be seen through the sheet of thick rain that washed over the window in a continuous sheet that was always being whisked away by the speed of the flying train.

"You know, you said this planet was bleak. I confess I thought you were exaggerating," he said. "Now I see that in fact you are the master of the understatement."

"It's not usually this bad," Ritchie assured him.

"Isn't it?" he asked. He sounded far away, like he was lost in deep thoughts. Dark thoughts.

"There is an upside," she leaned in to whisper to him.

"No droughts?" he guessed.

She laughed, but then got up from the table, catching his hand to draw him after her towards the seating nook by the window. "I meant, because the weather is so bad now, it's going to take all day for us to get to the school. We have one last day together."

"That *is* an upside," Guy agreed, but his smile faded even before they'd quite settled onto the couch together. "Seriously, Murdina, why do this? Why live another minute on this miserable excuse of a world?"

"Because the academy is here?" she reminded him.

"I know," he sighed. "How I wish you'd run away with me. You'd be much happier at my school. You wouldn't even have to study business or intergalactic commerce like I do. They have all sorts of programs you'd excel at."

"I'm sure that's true," she told him.

"But it's not what you want," he finished for her.

"Exactly," Ritchie said. Although, in truth, that was only the tip of the iceberg.

There was no way she was going to start a conversation about her lack of finances. It would only lead to Guy offering to pay for everything, and then when she refused, things would get really awkward.

Also, she couldn't abandon Moreau. They were buddies. In the foreign service academy, that meant something.

And she couldn't abandon Fitz, even if with the way he'd been acting lately he would totally deserve it.

She really couldn't talk to Guy about that.

They spent several long hours there, just cuddling on the couch and watching the storm. The occasional stop along the way provided a few glimpses of non-academy life on the planet, but even that was grayish and bleak. The architecture was as brutally harsh and unfriendly to the eyes as the landscape. There was simply nothing on Oymyakon to recommend it.

They had eaten so much for breakfast that it was well past the lunch hour before Ritchie started to feel hungry again. She and Guy replicated sandwiches and tea, but still there was no sign of Moreau.

"Did you want to go look for her?" Guy asked between bites.

"If she were in trouble, she would've called for me," Ritchie said. "And if she had any kind of lead that was more than a rumor, she would've called me."

"Do you get this a lot at your school? Unfounded but upsetting rumors?"

Ritchie was about to say no, but then shut her mouth with a frown. "We didn't use to," she said instead.

"What changed?" he asked.

"The Berwegers arrived," Ritchie said.

"Ah. No need to explain," Guy said. "Their parents are close to my parents, or maybe it's more accurate to say that the other way around. Either way, I've had my fill. And I'm so sorry for you."

"It's made life interesting," Ritchie said, but the words were bitter on her tongue.

Suddenly, the door banged open, and Moreau was back. She looked pale and deeply distracted, almost surprised to see Ritchie and Guy there at the dining table.

"What did you hear?" Ritchie asked.

Moreau looked at her steadily for a long moment, but then just shook her head.

"Nothing?" Ritchie asked.

"Nothing... that needs to be said just now," Moreau said, and her eyes darted towards then quickly away from Guy.

Right. Ritchie knew what she really meant.

"I can step out if you need to—" Guy started to say, but Moreau turned to him and gave him her most radiant smile. She didn't usually gift anyone with its presence, and Guy seemed momentarily stunned by its light.

"It's fine," she assured him. "We're nearly at our station. In fact, Ritchie and I should probably get into our uniforms about now, so we're ready to jump off into that torrential downpour when the train stops." Then she turned to Ritchie. "It'll keep until we get to the barracks."

Her words said there was no emergency, but her tone was all grave again. Ritchie's stomach was in knots, but she just nodded at Moreau's words.

All too soon, they were in uniform, complete with parkas under calf-length rain ponchos. Because as much as it was still rain and not yet snow, Ritchie didn't need to step off the train first to know that the air this high up the mountainside would be frigid all the same.

"Wow," Guy said as she came out of her cabin, tugging a fleece-lined hat low over her eyebrows. It had flaps that covered her ears, but she left the strap unfastened for now. Guy stepped up to her and gave her hat an entirely unnecessary adjustment, unable to fight the urge to touch those fleece-lined ear flaps. "Last chance," he said to her.

The train was already decelerating. She could feel it under her feet.

"We're going up the mountain tomorrow," Ritchie told him.

"I know," he said. "You've already told me. So many times."

"Sorry," Ritchie said.

Guy leaned down until his nose was touching hers. She took in a deep breath, her last breath of the sun and sand and salty warm sea that lingered on his skin and in his hair. It was only the faintest of aromas now, but just the hint of it was enough to make her feel like she wanted to cry.

Oymyakon really was a miserable hole of a world.

"It's time for me to go," she told him.

"I'm going with you," he said.

"What? You can't!"

He laughed at her panic. "Not forever, silly. Just long enough to say one last goodbye."

"Which of us is being silly here? You're going to be soaked through inside of a second. And unlike me, you're not remotely dressed for it."

"I'll change when I get back to my cabin," he told her. "My cold, lonely cabin."

"Let's go," Moreau said, brushing past the two of them with her pack over her shoulder. The train was barely at a crawl now, and Ritchie knew it was only moving that slowly because the hover disks were having trouble finding secure locations in the runoff from the storm rushing down the side of the mountain.

Guy's hand gripped hers strongly, his flesh almost too warm. She tried to focus on that, but it was like she kept losing time. It was all happening too fast, and the seconds were winking out of existence before she could even experience them. Time was jumping and skipping away from her.

It was like she didn't even walk down the corridor through the first-class sleeper cars to the airlock doorway on the side of the dining car where the other cadets were gathered. She just blinked, and she was already there.

Another blink, and all the other cadets were gone, and she was stepping outside into the storm that instantly slapped her in the face with stinging, freezing rain.

But the hand holding hers was still warm and dry. Then Guy gave her a tug, and she was in his arms. He bent to tuck his face inside the voluminous hood of her poncho. He brushed back the flap of her hat to say something close to her ear, but the pounding of the rain on her hood drowned out his words.

Perhaps he had realized this. Either way, the last kiss he gave her said everything his words hadn't.

Now time ticked by in slow motion, every second an hour.

But all too suddenly, he stepped back from her. She was alone inside her hood, the rain once more free to pelt her reddening cheeks.

Guy smiled at her one last time, still radiating warmth despite being soaked through with streams running off the ends of his long locks of hair. He started to take a step back, then he looked up in surprise at something on the train platform just behind her. She was just wondering why seeing Moreau standing there with them should elicit that response when he said, "Hey! Shack! Haven't seen you in ages! I had no idea you were serving time here too!" But the train behind him was already moving away, and he swung up into the airlock before turning back to wave goodbye to Ritchie.

She watched until the train was out of sight in the storm, which didn't take any time at all. She was just turning to ask Moreau what that last bit had meant when she saw Fitz standing behind her, his face a stony mask.

Oh. Right. *Shack*. Everyone she knew except his mother only called him Fitz and had for as long as she had known him. But of course with a full name like Shackleton Fitz IV, someone who didn't know him well might think that Shack was something he would respond to.

Somehow, she didn't think the nickname was why he was glowering at her just now.

She felt a warmth spreading throughout her chest, a warmth that kept burning hotter and hotter. With stupid slowness, she realized that she was feeling anger. Who cared why Fitz was there or what he was thinking or feeling? He certainly wasn't going to make her feel bad just by glaring at her without speaking to her. Not anymore.

Ritchie hitched her bag a little higher up on her shoulder under her poncho, then turned to Moreau. "Let's go," she said.

"Sure thing," Moreau said. Ritchie guessed her anger was pretty apparent on her face, because Moreau looked quietly delighted as she fell into step beside her. "I like Guy. He brings out the best in you," she whispered to Ritchie as they hiked up the mountainside.

Ritchie didn't answer. She reminded herself it had only been nine days. And it would be nearly two hundred days before she'd see him again. And no matter what, that was going to be weird.

But if she inhaled slowly enough, she could still smell the last vestiges of his scent inside the hood of her poncho. She would carry that with her as long as she could.

4

IT WAS no weather to be outdoors in, there was no question about that.

It hadn't been when Fitz had let Sokolov and Wyss convince him that they just had to go down to meet the train at the station. It had been even less so during the walk down the mountainside. At least the stony prominences around the academy buildings provided some break from the shear winds, protection the path down to the platform itself had none of.

And now, out on the platform, the train long gone, the wind like a thousand knives as the rain turned to pellets of ice that were, if anything, even sharper? Definitely not weather to be standing around in.

Fitz knew the other two were thinking it. But since this whole debacle of an exercise had been their idea in the first place, neither of them could exactly say it out loud. Or anything else to get Fitz unfrozen from the spot he had suddenly found himself rooted to on the platform.

Finally he looked up at Wyss, finding his eyes in the depths of his poncho hood. "Was that Guy Travert?" he asked.

"I don't know. I've never met him," Wyss said, shifting his weight from foot to foot. "I guess he looked like a taller, older, more masculine Cicey. So, yes?"

"That was Guy Travert," Fitz said to himself, nodding.

"He seemed to know you," Sokolov said. She almost winced at her own words, as if they had come out lamer than she had thought.

"Yeah," Fitz said, finally turning to look in the direction the train had long since disappeared into. "I mean, not well. No one who knows me well calls me Shack."

"I thought that sounded weird," Sokolov said with a relieved smile.

"We should get back," Wyss said, holding a gloved palm up towards the sky. "This is going to be snow soon."

"Snow would be an improvement," Sokolov said.

Fitz just nodded, and the three of them started the long walk back to the library building. He could feel them both looking over at him constantly, but refused to let them off the hook.

"I'm really sorry, Fitz," Sokolov said, and she sounded so miserable that all the anger just rushed out of him.

"For what? You guys wanted to walk down to the train platform, so we walked down to the train platform," Fitz said with too much forcefulness. "Mission accomplished."

"Right," Sokolov murmured, then fell silent.

The sound of rain pelting on his poncho hood grew softer, less hard chunks of ice and more wet clumps of something that was not exactly snow, but soon would be.

Of course, it was nothing like the snow that fell on the slopes of the mountains where the really good resort villages were, on planets far, far away from this one. The snow there was a crystalline marvel, delicately shaped snowflakes that glistened in the bright sun like diamonds. Snow that covered the mountainsides in perfectly skiable drifts and blanketed the roofs of the chalets like mounds of icing.

No, Oymyakon snow was nothing like that at all. It was slush, or it was ice. There was no perfect in-between.

At the moment, it suited Fitz just fine.

But then he realized he was thinking of resort villages nestled among ski slopes because the last time he had seen Guy Travert was at Guy's parents' chalet, and his mood soured even further.

Most of the cadets had jogged up the path as quickly as possible. Wyss and Sokolov might have wanted to run as well, but they silently let Fitz set a slower but steadier pace. Another pair of cadets in billowing ponchos were walking just ahead of them, occasionally lost to view when a gust of wind clouded the air between them but mostly visible as dark smudges against the grayer background of the mountainside.

When the three of them reached the airlock into the library building, this pair was still trying to fight their way inside. The gusts of wind were alternately trying to slam the doors shut or carry them away all together. The five of them finally managed to get inside with the doors closed behind them, and everything was suddenly mercifully silent, the sounds of their labored breaths almost inaudible after the roar of the storm outside.

Then the dryers kicked on and they all shook the moisture off their ponchos. Once the ponchos were dry, they pulled them off over their heads. The dryers continued blasting them with air, their boots and hair still wet and their whole bodies cold down to the bone.

Wyss' fine blonde hair dried the quickest, and the continuing blasts of hot, dry air soon had every follicle standing up and out like a staticky hedgehog. Fitz' hair was thicker, and he ran his hands through it to keep it from drying in funny clumps. Sokolov's dark brown hair was, as always, in a thick crown braid that had stayed dry despite the blowing rain and was now staying neatly arranged despite the blasts of air.

But it was only when the dryers kicked off again that Fitz realized it was Ritchie and Moreau standing in the airlock with them. Moreau's blonde hair was having nearly as tough a time as Wyss's, but she had come prepared. The minute the fans stopped, she took a tube of something out of her pocket and squeezed a bit into her hands. She stroked it over her hair and was instantly back to her usual flawless state.

Ritchie, on the other hand, didn't look like her usual self at all. Her space station dweller's pale skin was a deep golden brown, like it had been throughout their childhood together on Buennagel. And her honey-blonde hair was lighter, almost golden at the ends, and far curlier than he could ever remember seeing it.

She was also glowing with a happiness that he was certain had nothing to do with her past few days in the sun.

Ritchie saw him looking at her and gave him a nervous smile, but quickly dropped her eyes when he didn't return it.

Moreau was glaring daggers at him, but Fitz ignored her entirely. She had been doing that to him for months.

But why weren't the doors opening to let them inside? They were totally dry. They weren't about to drip onto the fine library floors. What was the holdup?

Ritchie looked up at him again, her lips parted. She was about to say something to him.

"I didn't know you knew Guy Travert," he blurted out. She blinked in surprise, and he realized his tone had been far nastier than he had intended. "Not that it's any business of mine," he added.

For some reason, it was that second statement that made her flinch.

But she recovered quickly, turning to Moreau to say, "you were going to tell me something?"

"I suppose this is the appropriate time," Moreau said. "The gang is, after all, all here."

"What's going on?" Sokolov asked, a tad too eagerly.

"I've been compiling rumors I heard on the train," Moreau told them. "Rumors about Colonel Hansen. Ridiculous things. They couldn't possibly be true."

"Oh, I'm afraid some of them are," Sokolov said, but before any of them could respond, the doors finally opened. The sound of cadet voices filled the library, nearly as brutally overwhelming as the wind outside. The five of them bustled quickly through the library to the study room in the back corner that was, if unofficially, their private place.

Fitz was the last one in. He made sure the door was closed, and the walls set to opaque. Then he turned to face the others, arms crossed over his chest as he leaned back against the wall. "Who goes first?"

"Sokolov, if what she knows is true," Moreau said, taking a seat at the table. Wyss headed to his bank of computers in the corner. They sensed his approach and fired up before he even settled into his chair.

"I know the colonel has been suspended," she said.

"Suspended?" Ritchie and Fitz exclaimed at once. Ritchie flushed red and dropped into the chair next to Moreau, but Fitz remained standing. He looked Sokolov in the eye. "Suspended?" he said again, more calmly this time.

"I don't have all the details. I've only been back a day myself," she said, all but squirming in her chair.

"I've heard two things," Moreau said. "Both wildly implausible."

"Two things?" Sokolov asked.

"I heard a female cadet accused him of something," Moreau said. "But nobody knew who the accuser was or what exactly she accused him of doing. But the theories tend to the salacious."

"Of course they do," Ritchie said, her eyes still fixed on the table. Not looking at Fitz.

"No, that's not remotely it," Sokolov said. "I mean, the accuser is a female cadet, but the rest of it? No way."

"So what was the second thing?" Fitz asked Moreau.

"It's even more unlikely given what we know about Hansen," she said, pausing for dramatic effect before finally saying, "treason."

"*Is* that implausible?" Wyss piped up from his corner.

"This is Hansen we're talking about," Fitz said. "So, yeah."

"Only it isn't," Sokolov said. "He's been accused of being some sort of spy. He's been confined to quarters since before I got here. I wasn't even allowed to see him. But I don't think anyone in charge really thinks he's guilty or else he'd be arrested and gone from here already, right?"

"Why do *you* think it isn't implausible?" Ritchie asked Wyss.

"Well, it depends on a lot of things," Wyss said. "Treason is a politics-infused offense. I mean, one person's treason is another person's patriotism."

"Are you saying the Berwegers accused him of this?" Ritchie asked, her face flushing in anger. "Feena Berweger. She's a female cadet."

"It wasn't her," Fitz said.

"Oh, you know her so well?" Ritchie demanded, her chin going up in challenge.

"It couldn't have been her," Wyss said. "She wasn't here during the break."

"You know this for a fact?" Ritchie asked.

"She was at my parents' house the last night of the break," Fitz said. "We can probably assume if she was here to accuse the colonel of treason, as a witness she wouldn't be back at the capital before the end of break."

"I wouldn't assume anything of the sort," Moreau said. "Money buys a lot of privileges. Berweger money in particular."

"My extra task force permissions will let me into a lot of the systems," Wyss said. "I can figure out exactly what he's accused of."

"That wouldn't be in the school system, surely," Ritchie said. "It would be a foreign service matter of the highest order. Top secret. Sealed files."

"Okay, I might have to break into a few things," Wyss admitted with a wry grin.

"Not yet," Ritchie said. "We should do the groundwork that doesn't involve breaking the rules first."

"I can get a list of which cadets were here over the break," Wyss said.

"We can divide them up and question everybody," Moreau said. "How many were there, do you think?"

"It was dozens," Sokolov said. "I don't remember any of the names, I just remembered it was a longish list when I took my own name off of it to spend the break with my mother."

"That doesn't leave us much time," Ritchie said with a frown.

"Time before what?" Sokolov asked.

"Oh, that's right, you two aren't going," Ritchie said, then flushed a deep scarlet. "Sorry, that sounded so cliquey."

"What are you talking about?" Sokolov asked.

"The upper two classes are going up the mountain tomorrow for extreme environment tactical training," Ritchie said. "Fitz, Moreau and I are all going."

"But surely that's been canceled?" Wyss said with a frown.

"Why would that...?" Ritchie started to say, but then ended with an inarticulate groan.

"Won't they give us a sub?" Moreau asked. "Someone must've run that class before Hansen arrived here. It's one of the only reasons anyone ever chooses to come out to this school. Best extreme environment tactical training in the foreign service academies."

"Maybe not this year," Wyss said.

"But we have to!" Ritchie all but wailed.

"Liar!" Moreau said, and it took a moment for Fitz to realize she was joking. With Moreau, it was often hard to tell. But Sokolov was also gaping at her, so Moreau added, "she's been pretending like she's dreading it as much as me, and I knew she wasn't. I knew it!"

"I wasn't dreading it," Ritchie admitted. "But that doesn't mean I enjoyed our vacation any less."

"I heard the weather on Epsilon 20 was perfection," Sokolov said without a trace of envy.

"Of course it was. They program it to be that way," Fitz said.

"I've heard the deep sea diving is quite a sight to see," Wyss said, glowing with something like his bottomless museum energy. "The coral cities sound particularly spectacular. Tell me you checked them out, and it wasn't all parties."

"I didn't," Ritchie said, her cheeks flushing once more, but now it was *her* exact mood that Fitz couldn't pinpoint. Was she embarrassed? Happy? What? "But Moreau did," she said.

"You opted for parties?" Sokolov asked. *Her* Fitz could read easily enough. She was surprised that studious Ritchie would've chosen parties over an enrichment activity, but also happy shading into proud that she had leaned into the more frivolous choice for a change.

"I... yeah," Ritchie said, staring at the table once more.

"Let me bail you out," Moreau stage-whispered to her, then sat back in her chair to announce to the rest of them, "Ritchie doesn't like enclosed spaces. Like the inside of diving suits."

"Oh. Right," Wyss said with a sympathetic nod.

"It wasn't the suit. I don't freak out in a spacesuit," Ritchie insisted.

"It was the water," Fitz said before he could stop himself.

"Yeah. It was too much like being... never mind," she said, and shrank down in her seat as if she wished she could disappear.

Underground, Fitz finished for her, but only inside his own head.

"Well, that's weird," Wyss said suddenly, but an instant later Fitz knew what he meant. They had all just received a summons for their first task force meeting immediately after dinner.

"There's no way we're getting a sub for this," Moreau said.

"No, it's definitely from Colonel Hansen himself," Wyss said. "Check the metadata."

"Well, I guess all the rumors were a big stir over nothing," Moreau said. But no one responded, and from the look on her face, not even she really believed it.

"We'll know everything soon enough, straight from the source," Fitz said, and turned to open the door. The sound of a hundred conversations washed over him like a wave. Yes, they were definitely back in school.

He held the door for the others. Sokolov and Wyss went out first, talking together about their schedules. Sokolov was expecting a lot of extra free time over the next few days while Colonel Hansen was away leading the extreme environment tactical training. Wyss, between his full course load and his independent studies on top of their task force responsibilities, had almost no free time. Just the way he liked it.

Moreau and Ritchie still had their packs with them. Moreau hoisted hers up easily, which was impressive given that it was nearly half her size. She gave Fitz a look as she brushed past him. He felt like telling her she could stop with that since he never understood what she was trying to nonverbally tell him, but he bit his tongue and let her pass.

He knew when his bad mood was about to become a problem. He wasn't totally clueless. He quickly tamped it back down.

Then he realized that Ritchie was standing beside him, both hands holding the straps of the pack that was slung over his shoulder. She was looking up at him anxiously, like she was afraid he was about to bite her head off.

Could he blame her? Given how he had treated her since Finn Berweger had called him out?

No, he could not.

But neither could he stop pushing her away. From somewhere out in that library, he felt Finn's eyes on him even now. It wasn't safe for either of them to be close. Not anymore.

"What is it?" he asked her, rubbing at his forehead tiredly.

"Nothing," she said. But she didn't move either, just stood there twisting the straps in her hands. They were already bloodless from the weight of her pack. She was going to have to set that down soon or put it on properly. One or the other.

Finally, she took a step, but that only brought her closer to him before she stopped again. "Feena Berweger was at your house?"

"My parents' house," he corrected her.

"But, it was, like, a party?" she asked.

"Not as much a party as what happens nonstop on Guy Travert's yacht," he said.

Then he decided to stop holding that door if she wasn't going to move through it, pushing it open before walking away, but not far enough. He heard it catch her on her pack-laden shoulder and knock her off balance. Her sharp inhale of pain was like a knife to his heart.

But Finn's eyes were still on him. He didn't stop walking away from her.

5

AFTER DAYS OF FANTASTIC FOOD, a dizzying array of fruits and fish pulled fresh from the ocean just before being cooked, the glop that the Oymyakon Foreign Service Academy called dinner was even less appetizing than usual. Grayish ground meat molded into balls and drowned in lumpy gravy, with a side of greens cooked down to a sludge that might still have been edible if any real butter had been available. But the yellow stuff that sat in bowls next to the bread baskets was not even pretending to be butter. It was a bit of a mystery, just what it really was. But not a mystery Ritchie felt any need to crack.

Ritchie chided herself for this new disdain towards the school's food. She had gotten awfully spoiled in just a handful of days. She reminded herself how lucky she was to even be here. And if she had never come here, she never would've met Moreau and, by extension, Guy. That was worth a few bad meals.

But this one felt drabber than usual.

Not that Moreau and Sokolov seemed to mind. They chatted together, mostly about Epsilon 20 and its many natural wonders. Ritchie tuned them both out, trying not to look over at the door too frequently. But when Wyss finally came in to join them, he was alone.

And Ritchie wasn't the only one to notice. Feena actually got up from her table to catch Wyss by the arm. They exchanged a few words before parting. He headed towards the food line with no particular expression on his face, but Feena went back to her table with an exaggerated pout of disappointment, and her brother gave her a reassuring hug. Then he started to look up towards Ritchie but just as quickly looked away, refocusing on the cadet at his table, still telling him some long-winded story he clearly wasn't listening to.

Ritchie frowned. As much as most of her worrying had been fixed on the sudden, inexplicable change in Fitz since returning from their first task force mission, this wasn't the first time that she had felt something weird coming from Finn as well.

It wasn't fear or respect or anything like that, even though she and Fitz had gotten very close to taking him and his sister and their parents down. No, this was different. He was definitely avoiding her, but something in her bones was telling her that it didn't have anything actually to do with her.

Which made no sense.

She wondered what Fitz would think about it. He knew the Berwegers better than she did. He might have a good theory.

But he wasn't there to ask. As usual.

Her implant notified her of a new message in her inbox. From Guy Travert.

"I have to take care of something before the meeting," she said, picking up her tray of mostly uneaten food.

"What could be more important than our meeting?" Sokolov asked.

"It's not more important, but it'll just take a minute," Ritchie said.

"Let her go. It *is* important," Moreau said to Sokolov.

Ritchie shoved her tray into the open slot of the return station for the cadets on kitchen duty to recycle the leftovers and wash the dishes. She headed for the doorway just as Wyss passed by on his way to the table. He gave her a questioning look, but didn't detain her. She all but ran down the hall to the barracks.

Her and Moreau's roommates, Frei and Grof, were still eating, so Ritchie had a rare moment alone in their barracks room. She flopped down on her bunk and pulled out her tablet.

"Hello, Murdina!" Guy said warmly. She knew it was just a recording, but it felt like he could really see her. She could tell by the background of the image that he was still in his cabin on the intergalactic train, even still on Oymyakon, to judge from the stormy skies through the window behind him.

"Miss you already," he said. "I was surprised to see Shack there. I guess I knew he was a cadet, but I thought he'd washed out of every academy in the Union of Free Worlds. But maybe he had one or two left, right? Not to slag on your choice of schools. Or to imply you had a choice, as I'm remembering now that you didn't, actually."

He seemed to feel like he'd gotten off track and heaved a sigh. "Never mind. I know the reputation of your school has doubtless gone up since you started there. You keep unearthing major conspiracies that affect all of us, despite your remote location. Imagine what you could do from *my* school, at the center of all things. But never mind. In a year and a half, we'll at least both be on the same planet, if not the same continent. But that's the future. Right now, you just focus on conquering that mountain with extreme tactics, or whatever it is you cadets will be doing."

Then his face softened, and he sat back in his chair a little bit as if gathering his thoughts. "Stay warm. And safe. It's not my place to worry about you, but I think I'm going to be doing it, anyway. Sorry. No, not sorry."

Then he laughed suddenly. "Say, I was talking to my sister—you remember Cicey?—and she was at a dinner party the other night at Shack's house. Sorry, she informs me that he hates it when I call him that. I had no idea. Anyway, Shackleton Fitz IV. Although technically it was the Third throwing the party? But apparently it was *insane*. His dad put everyone under house arrest and they were interrogated one by one because somebody had touched something in his office? I admit, it doesn't make a lot of sense. But then again I'm getting this from Cicey, who is, shall we say, *not* a reliable narrator. If you get the details, you *have* to share. When you have the time, of course. I'm only half dying to know. I'm sure once I get to my own school I'll have distractions enough to fill my time. But I'll still want to hear it all from you. Or anything at all from you."

His eyes darted to one side, and he winced just a little. "I promised to keep this short. I know it's your first night back and you're crazy busy. But I miss you already. Wait, I already said that. Well, it's true. I count the days. But not in an obsessive way, of course. I have many other interests. Well, two other interests. Okay, I'm signing off now. See you, Murdina Ritchie."

Ritchie gaped at the now-blank screen of her tablet for far too long. She had intended to message him back straight away, even if she could only do it this once when classes hadn't started yet and she wasn't buried in classwork.

But now she had to know what all of that was about first. What exactly had happened at Fitz's house? Not that he would tell her, but maybe she could corner Wyss.

Wyss, who was probably finishing off the last of his dinner before heading to Colonel Hansen's classroom for the task force meeting.

Okay, so meeting first, find out exactly what this was about a dinner party at the Fitz house next, and then message Guy back.

Ritchie shoved her tablet into her bag, then jogged back up to the main hallway. Colonel Hansen's classroom was so far from the front area of the school that it had windows that looked over the farside of the mountain. But she wasn't late yet. She didn't have to break into a full run to get there on time.

As she fast-walked, she cast back in her mind for the few memories she had of Fitz's parents from when they had been kids, before she had left the planet Buennagel for good.

She could remember his mother Luana pretty well. She had been the most beautiful woman Ritchie had ever seen. In all fairness, she probably still was. She had been a professional dancer before she had married into a very different kind of lifestyle, that of the wife of a military officer who was constantly changing stations. She had managed to keep a home in one place, on Buennagel, from the time Fitz turned five until he had started his time at his first foreign service academy. Ritchie doubted she had managed more than a few months in the same home since. Ritchie knew she still worked with other dancers, but remotely, from wherever her husband was currently posted.

As a little girl, Ritchie had always been in awe of her, like she was a fragile work of art that Ritchie knew she wasn't supposed to touch. But for her part, his mother had always been warm and kind, never minding being interrupted by her only son and his closest friend. If they needed something for some game they were playing, or wanted more of a treat they didn't know how to replicate themselves, she was always there to help.

Not that *that* had ever come up much. Fitz had always been a very independent kid. The two of them had generally been capable of fending for themselves, whether they were romping through the wilds around their Buennagel homes or roaming the endless corridors of his family's palatial estate.

But Fitz's father? Ritchie barely had any memories of him at all. Fitz and his mother had remained on Buennagel for several undisturbed years, but his career had carried on. His time on Buennagel had been little more than breaks between postings.

But even in his physical absence, Fitz's father had loomed large and cast a long, dark shadow. Ritchie's father had been a diplomat, one of the top researchers in alien language systems in the Union of Free Worlds. But his rank had always been more of an honorary one. He had never been in charge of others.

But from a very young age, Ritchie had understood that Fitz's father was a very important man, not a guardian or a diplomat but a high-ranking military official with thousands of lives under his command. She couldn't remember ever hearing him yell or tower over them or threaten in any way.

And yet she remembered clearly just how very afraid of him she'd always been.

She had a hard time imagining her memory of him morphing into the sort of man that threw dinner parties. Certainly nothing Fitz had ever said about him had changed her picture of him.

All she could guess was that it must've been a work thing. Or Cicey was wrong, and it was Fitz's mother who had hosted the party.

"Hey, there you are," Moreau said as Ritchie turned down the last corridor towards the open door to Colonel Hansen's classroom.

"I'm not late," Ritchie said, but checked her chronometer to be sure.

"Of course you're not," Moreau said. "How's Guy?"

"Are we going in or standing out here all night?" Fitz asked from behind her before she could reply. She had, in fact, not even stopped walking, so his accusation of standing around was a bit unfair.

Had he been walking silently behind her the entire time? Like some kind of cat stalking its prey?

"Which do you think?" Moreau asked him, unbothered by his grouchy attitude. Which seemed worse than before he had left for break. Because of that party?

She was getting more curious about just what had happened by the minute.

"Hansen's not here yet," Sokolov told them as they stepped into the classroom. She was sitting behind the desk at the front of the room, shutting down the screens that were still showing diagrams and illustrations from the last class he had taught before the break. As if he had sprinted out of here and never come back.

Except the only way those accusations made sense were if he had been here the entire time, like he had over the same mid-semester break the year before.

"He's coming," Wyss said as he scurried into the room. Sokolov shut down the last screen, then fled from behind the desk. They all stood at attention by their usual seats at the front of the room.

"At ease. Take your seats," Hansen said as he came in, a tablet in one hand and a steaming mug in the other. Ritchie got just enough of a hint of the aroma to remember the taste of his favorite tea, some reddish-brown smoky blend he drank staggeringly strong and with way too much sugar.

She had tasted it once. Once had been enough.

His jet black hair looked recently cut, the angles sharp and the length precise. As short as it was, it was far too thick for any of his scalp to peek through. But her attention, as always, was drawn to the filigree of scars that deepened into furrows dangerously close to his eye. They stood out a pale silvery gray against the olive of his skin. She wondered for the thousandth time why he had never had the surgery to cover them up.

He wore them proudly, but he never told anyone where he had gotten them. She had uncovered other secrets about his past, but some mysteries still remained.

"I'll start with what I'm sure is on all your minds," he said as he set the tablet and tea down on his desk, then turned to face them all. He leaned back against the desktop, arms crossed, and fixed them all with his gaze one by one. "I don't know exactly what you might've heard, but I can assure you it isn't true. Unfortunately, since it is still considered an open investigation, I won't be answering any questions about it. Absolutely none. And believe me, I do know how hard that will be for some of you."

Now his gaze was fixed just on Ritchie.

"What about the weather, sir?" Moreau asked. "The last I checked, the storm was still expected to worsen over the alpine training range. Are we still on for EETT?"

Colonel Hansen gave her a wry smile. "We are indeed still on. Don't worry on that score, cadet. The skies themselves could fall, and we would still be on for EETT. The more extreme the environment, the better the training."

Moreau said nothing, but Sokolov shot her a look of deep sympathy. Even Wyss looked a little relieved that he wasn't due for EETT until next year.

"The Berwegers didn't transfer," Fitz said, and the smile vanished from Hansen's face.

"No, but that hope was always a longshot," Hansen said.

"Are they behind your current troubles?" Ritchie asked.

"Cadet, I'm not answering questions on that matter," he admonished her as he turned to pick up his tea. Then over the rim of the mug he added, "but no."

"They haven't sent out any messages about another meetup like last semester either," Wyss said. "Tracking what messages they have been sending, I would say they are staying focused on building more one-on-one relationships. But to what aim, I can't say."

"Any pattern in who they are targeting?" Hansen asked.

"I think they are targeting specific cadets to build some sort of network," Wyss said. "And it's not just cadets here. They were both very busy making connections with other cadets from other academies over the break. The one message I keep seeing repeat is just a generic 'see you when we're at university' type of thing."

"They want to hit the colleges already connected with other cadets," Ritchie said. "If they try to have a meetup there, they'll already know people. Lots of different people."

"They're vetting people, then," Fitz said. "The next time they send out invites, they'll already be sure that no one is going to be there who isn't sympathetic to their cause."

"And we won't be there yet," Moreau said. "They won't have to worry about us crashing their gatherings."

"Will we even still be a task force next year when they're gone?" Sokolov asked almost wistfully.

"We aren't here specifically to target the Berwegers. We are trying to root out a conspiracy among all the cadets. They didn't create it, and it will still be here when they leave. Our work won't be done," Hansen told her.

"And we still don't know how anything connects with Keller and Weld," Ritchie added. Hansen gave her a considered look, but said nothing.

"Is there anything you want Wyss and I to work on while the rest of you are up the mountain?" Sokolov asked. Ritchie could see she desperately wanted to ask about the treason charges again, but she bit down hard on her lip to hold it in.

"Wyss is already hunting for patterns in the messages among the cadets," Hansen said. "That's a good start. But until we have a lead, that's as far as I want to dig."

"I've anonymized all the data," Wyss said. Then at Hansen's icy stare he added, "as much as I could."

"Spying on people is creepy," Ritchie said with a shiver.

"And yet, it's been made necessary," Hansen said.

They all fell silent for a minute, the only sound the tinkling patter of freezing rain against the windows and the howl of the wind.

"The shuttles can fly in this?" Moreau asked.

Hansen gave her a look that was suddenly, surprisingly kind. "We'll all be okay, cadet," he told her. "In fact, you should probably get back to your barracks to finish packing. Task force business can wait until we're back down off the mountain."

"There is one other thing, sir," Wyss said. His cheeks were a blazing red, but it wasn't until she saw his eyes darting away from meeting Fitz's gaze that Ritchie could guess why.

"It isn't relevant," Fitz said sharply.

"Well, now I'm really curious," Hansen said, setting his tea aside again. "Spill, Wyss."

"Feena Berweger was at Fitz's house the last night of break," Wyss said, still avoiding Fitz's eyes. "By invitation..." he broke off suddenly, and Ritchie had the urge to kick Fitz in the shin so he would stop glaring and just let Wyss talk. But then Wyss said, "I guess she was there with her uncle and aunt, who had been invited to a dinner party. But her brother wasn't there."

"Did something happen at this party? Did she do anything suspicious?" Hansen asked.

"She was pushy, like she always is," Fitz said, and Wyss looked almost relieved not to be the center of attention anymore.

"Does she get invited to your house a lot?" Hansen asked.

"I usually avoid visiting my parents when they are at the capital planet townhouse," Fitz said stiffly. "Specifically because I hate the parties. I mean, my mother's parties are at least tolerable, but this was one of my father's affairs. They are a lot of work."

Hansen took another sip of his tea as he considered Fitz's words. "Your father arranges social gatherings for the purpose of throwing you together with certain people, I take it?"

"Precisely," Fitz said. "They used to be about steering me towards the military, but when I insisted on pursuing foreign service as a career instead, then it's been all about networking me with the top guardians in the Union of Free Worlds. Which was hardly necessary when I was twelve."

Fitz looked like he had a lot more thoughts to express, but Hansen gave him a chastising look, and Fitz stopped complaining about his father at once. He nearly slumped back in his seat in a huff, but leaned forward instead, keeping his back as straight as a cadet's was always supposed to be.

"So was this little party another networking thing?" Hansen asked.

"No," Fitz said, but Wyss was nodding emphatically. Now Fitz did throw himself back into a slouch.

"Wyss," Hansen said.

"Well, it seems to me that Fitz's father has given up trying to drive his career aspirations," Wyss said. "He seemed very accepting the few times I heard him speak about it."

He glanced nervously at Fitz, who just shrugged in a very agitated manner.

"So this wasn't so much networking as matchmaking?" Hansen asked.

Ritchie couldn't stay out of this, no matter how much she wanted to. She spun in her seat to look right at Fitz. "Did your father choose her because of her family connections, or did she manipulate your father into it?"

"I don't think the two of them had ever met," Wyss said.

But Fitz was glaring at Ritchie now. "In a way, this is all your fault."

"My fault?" Ritchie repeated. Her shock morphed to anger pretty quick.

"Makes sense," Hansen said, as calm as ever. "As I understand it, the general does not approve of the two of you being friends."

"That's not *my* fault," Ritchie said. Then she realized that she too was slouched low in her desk and forced herself to straighten up.

"I don't think she could've manipulated the general," Wyss said. "She said she hadn't been there in years. And she seemed very pleased to see us there when she arrived. Like she hadn't expected us to be there. Or rather, pleased to see Fitz, anyway."

"So she *is* targeting you," Hansen said to Fitz.

"That's how Wyss sees it," Fitz said.

"Interesting," Hansen said, stroking his bottom lip as he thought. "Does she think you'll tell her what we're up to?"

"She's not that stupid," Fitz said.

"She might think she can get you to reveal something unknowing-ly," Hansen said. "She's not wrong to think she can get people to reveal things they'd rather conceal."

"She was designed to do just that," Wyss said.

"Well, not me," Fitz said crossly.

"No, of course not," Hansen said. Ritchie couldn't tell if he was serious or if he was teasing. Then he said, "maybe we can work with this."

"No," Fitz said, holding up his hands desperately.

"It wouldn't be hard for you to tell her things we want her to know. She could be a useful tool to us," Hansen said.

"No way. I don't want to mess with any of that. No," Fitz said.

"Sir, I think she is looking to use Fitz for her family's ends. But I also think she genuinely likes him," Wyss said.

"How can you tell?" Ritchie asked, a bit too sharply.

Wyss took a deep breath while he considered his response. "All the things she does to get a guy's attention? She dials it back with Fitz. I mean, I'd have to bring equipment to check, but I don't think she's trying to sway him with her pheromones or anything."

"She knows it doesn't work with me," Fitz said.

"Sure, but also, I think part of her doesn't want it to," Wyss said. Then he shrugged. "It's just a sense I get."

"What about the rest of you?" Hansen asked, looking to Ritchie, Sokolov and Moreau.

"To tell the truth, I haven't been paying attention," Moreau said, and Sokolov nodded her agreement to that.

"We can watch now," Ritchie said. "I think we'll end up agreeing with Wyss, but we can test it to be sure."

"Perfect," Hansen said, and pushed away from his desk.

"Wait, what did we just agree was happening?" Fitz demanded.

"Nothing dangerous, cadet," Hansen told him as he gathered up his empty tea mug and tablet. "We just need you to talk to a girl, maybe even flirt a little."

"I'm not going to be a honeypot," he said, his ears red to their very tips.

"At this point, we're just sounding Feena Berweger out."

"But we'll be doing EETT for days now," Fitz said.

"I'm sure you'll have lots of opportunities for conversation on our way up the mountain," Hansen said and slapped him on the back before heading out the door.

Ritchie lingered over leaving her desk, carefully untwisting the strap to her bag as she fought the urge to step closer to Fitz.

Just a few months ago, this would've been the most natural thing in the world. She knew how he felt about Feena. She knew how upsetting this new plan was for him. She hated seeing how much this was disturbing him. She wanted to stay in that room and talk to Fitz about it until he was calmer.

But his feelings about Ritchie had changed. That was no longer possible now.

And for all she knew, his feelings for Feena had changed as well.

"Ritchie? You coming?" Moreau called from the doorway. Fitz looked up from the desk where he was sitting, glaring down at his own hands. He seemed startled to see her still standing there. Then his brows furrowed down into that now all too familiar glower.

"Coming," Ritchie said. She had only managed to twist her bag strap more tightly and somehow gotten it into a knot, so she just hugged it close to her chest as she swiftly left the room.

She would send Guy a message, but she wouldn't mention anything about Fitz or his sister. She hoped he'd take the hint, but if he didn't, it would be weeks before she could message him again. Surely by then she'd have enough else to share that the topic of that matchmaking party would be forgotten.

By him, anyway. She doubted the ache in her stomach was going to fade anytime soon. Feena Berweger was trouble in human form, and as annoyed as she was with Fitz, as hurt and as abandoned by him as she felt, she wouldn't wish Feena Berweger onto her worst enemy.

6

FITZ FELT like he'd only just managed to fall asleep before his roommate Stucki was shaking him awake again. The room was almost completely dark, and all he could see was the outline of Stucki's head beside his bunk. He had a vague sense that Stucki had a finger pressed to his lips. Like Fitz was going to open his eyes and immediately start shouting or something.

Great. He was waking up grumpy. Well, only an hour or two of sleep would do that to anyone. Still, it was getting exhausting, always being in a bad mood. His head ached from it.

Fitz rolled soundlessly out of his top bunk and dressed in the dark. Which took forever. Their alpine tactical uniforms had many layers, each with far too many closures to fumble with in the low light. Then, over all of it, he had to strap his safety harness. If that wasn't done correctly, he just might die up on that mountain. Or so the briefings had told them all, over and over again.

Not that keeping quiet mattered much. He could see Wyss was awake in the bottom bunk, sitting up and yawning.

"You've got a few hours yet," Fitz whispered to him as he fastened the cuffs of his parka snugly over his woolen wrist gauntlets.

"I know. I wanted to give you something I was tinkering on last night," Wyss said, and got up with a yawn to fetch something from their shared desk.

"You were up late," Fitz said.

"Yeah, but I wanted to make sure we didn't lose contact when you guys were up on the mountain," Wyss said. Then he turned to hand Fitz what felt like a bulky tablet. Fitz ran his fingers over it and felt a seam running around it. So it opened up like a clamshell. Only the hinge of the clamshell had a thick cylindrical object adhered to it.

"What is this? A stylus?" Fitz asked, trying to get a better look at it in the dark.

"It's a signal booster," Wyss said. "Like an antenna. Communications up there are notoriously spotty. I think that's deliberate, part of the training. Your implant won't connect to anything unless you're in one of the base camps, and even then it's a local intranet type of thing. You three should be able to contact each other, but it will be tricky to contact Sokolov and I. This will boost your signal."

"Do I want to know how?" Fitz asked.

"It's piggybacking on some satellites it's not supposed to," Wyss admitted. "Keep it hidden, and don't use it around others unless you trust them not to tattle. But it might come in handy."

"You and Sokolov are already planning to dig into the charges against Colonel Hansen, aren't you?" he guessed.

"Wouldn't you if you were staying behind?" Wyss said.

"Fair enough," Fitz agreed, and stuffed the bulky tablet in his already very heavy pack. "If you learn anything, let me know. And I'll be watching Hansen, of course."

"You and Ritchie and Moreau," Wyss said.

"Sure," Fitz said. He was in too much of a hurry to argue. Stucki and Imhof had already left the barracks for the rendezvous point out on the athletic fields.

Because why leave from the warm, dry hangars when you can muster the cadets in the freezing rain?

"Good luck," Wyss said as he headed back to his bunk.

Fitz jogged to catch up with the other cadets on their way out of the school building. He was surprised to find the storm had relented, the wind dying down to nothing and the rain a mere misting fog. But it was a dense fog, one that distorted the sounds around him. He could hear voices and laughter, but he never seemed to be drawing any nearer to them until he nearly tripped over the heavy-duty landing gear of one of the shuttles.

"Fitz, join us," a voice called. He didn't need to look up to know that it was Feena Berweger. He wondered if her enhanced eyes could see heat signatures through the cold fog or if she just sensed his presence like some kind of radar.

He looked up to see her snuggled back into one of the padded seats in the back of the shuttle. She hadn't put on either her skull cap or her fleece-lined hat yet, and her long blonde hair was dancing wild and loose in the cross breeze between the two open doors. Because the normal uniform rules didn't apply to the Berwegers, apparently.

She was smiling at him warmly, and part of him had to admit that empirically, she was attractive. It was just that there was something otherworldly about her beauty, something alien that was unsettling.

And yet, so few people seemed to see it.

Ritchie saw it. Moreau and Wyss noticed it when they focused on it, which mostly happened only when the Berwegers were at a distance. But most of their fellow cadets were completely under the Berwegers' spell.

And now he was supposed to pretend to be in her thrall as well? Just how was he going to pull that off? Even being this near to her made him slightly queazy. Didn't Hansen realize that?

Suddenly, a hand tapped his shoulder. He looked away from Feena to see Finn leaning out the open door, one hand gripping the safety strap near the doorway, the other extended as he waited to help Fitz up.

"We're about to take off. They say it'll only be a brief break in the weather, so we have to hurry," Finn said, and shook his hand around as if Fitz had missed seeing it.

Fitz took his hand with a sigh and hoisted himself up into the shuttle. Finn settled into a seat next to his sister, who was busy plaiting her hair before takeoff. Fitz took off his pack and stowed it in the floor compartment with the others, carefully fastening the bungees that held it in place before taking the closest empty seat.

Besides himself and the Berwegers, there were two other occupants of the shuttle. He recognized cadet captain Milla Wyder from the dark brown of her skin, the only part of her he could see under the layers of her alpine gear. He respected her as a cadet captain, although he didn't know her personally. She met his eyes and gave him a distracted smile. He was sure she had a hundred things on her mind, given that she and Blaser would be largely in charge of the cadets up on the mountain. The only instructor in attendance would be Colonel Hansen himself.

The last cadet was vaguely familiar. Her face certainly fit in with the others in his memory, and he was sure they all ate together and probably studied together as well. He was fairly certain she was also a last year cadet, but he had to read her name tag to see that her name was Joosten. Then he remembered her from the Berwegers' eating group. She was the squat blonde that looked like she could wrestle bears.

She didn't smile at him. He promptly looked away from her.

"Aren't you excited?" Feena asked him. She already had her shoulder restraints locked down and was holding the padded bars like a kid wearing a backpack, eager for their first day of school.

"Not particularly," Fitz said, remembering too late that he was supposed to be befriending her or whatever.

"I don't know. It could be fun," Finn said. Fitz looked at him closely. Was his sister rubbing off on him? Because he sounded all friendly and not remotely arch and sarcastic like Fitz was used to.

He was too tired to be sure. He pulled his own restraints into place and let his head roll back so he could close his eyes.

The darkness outside and the steady hum of the engine were soporific, but before he had quite drifted off, he felt a lurch and they were up in the air.

What seemed calm and still on the ground was anything but up in the air. He was familiar with the strange pockets of different air temperatures that formed around the academy's mountaintop abode. He had flown through his share of them during glider training. But under his guidance, the glider would coast through them with only the smallest of bumps. In the shuttle, it was a constant hard jostling that made him very grateful for the excessive tightness of the restraints.

They lifted up high over the peaks that ringed the academy grounds, then hovered for a moment as if waiting for the rest of the shuttles to gather together. Then they all flew in a tight formation due north to the tallest peak on Oymyakon.

Fitz and the other cadets often used that mountain as a landmark when flying the gliders, since it sat right on a cardinal point from the vicinity of the school and was impossible to miss. Its dark purplish bulk was always a thick smear on the horizon. As far as he could recall, he had never seen its peak. Not even at that first moment when the momentum from the glider launcher died away, just before gravity took over. That point was so high up it was nearly at the edge of space. But even from there, the peak of that mountain was always hidden from view.

It was like it owned the clouds around it. Like it wore them like a cloak, never letting strangers see its true face.

And that was just where they were heading. Up through that persistent cloud cover, to the highest elevation on an already mountainous planet.

As they approached that mountain, the air grew choppier, and the rain returned with a vengeance. There was a brief moment where the sound of it hitting the outside of the shuttle was the ping of ice, but then it was suddenly a white-out blur of snow. The featureless whiteness was pressing against every window like they had just crashed into a drift.

Only they were definitely still in motion.

"All right?" Wyder called out to the rest of them.

Finn and Feena both yelled back, "great!" at once. Joosten looked greenish, but managed a nod. Fitz gave Wyder a thumbs-up, then turned his attention back to the white nothingness outside the window.

The shuttle banked, bumped over air pockets, then banked more steeply. They were spiralling down towards their landing zone.

"Restraints on until we get the command," Wyder reminded them. "Then we hustle out. The shuttles have a very narrow break in the weather to get back to the school."

Fitz gripped the bars of his shoulder restraints, watching the red light over the doorway. He could see out the window through his peripheral vision as the whiteness disappeared for an instant to give a glimpse of gray clouds in the distance. Then it was snow again, then gray clouds.

The minute the actual rocky mountainside came into view, he could feel the landing gear touching down. He unlatched and lifted his restraint as the light switched from red to green, the same instant as Wyder gave the command. He tore the bungees off his pack and jumped out the door before it had even finished opening.

Finn hit the ground beside him, both of them crunching through the icy top layer into the wet snow below. They jogged clear to make room for the other three to follow. Less than five heartbeats passed before Wyder was slapping the panel to close the shuttle door. The pilot lifted off the ground before the door had even come halfway closed. Then it was gone.

Fitz hoisted his pack up onto his back and adjusted the straps so that it rested as comfortably as possible, flush against his body. He wasn't loving how heavy it felt, and the tablet he had added at the last minute was sitting funny, digging into his ribs, but he was sure he'd get used to it.

"Do you see Blaser?" Wyder asked him as she rose up on tiptoe to scan the clusters of cadets scattered across the snow-covered meadow around them. Everyone was in full winter gear, bulky coats and hats and hoods. It was impossible to know who anyone was without getting close enough to see their face inside their hoods.

"There," Finn said, pointing to a group on the far side of the meadow. Fitz was about to wonder again at whether the twins had superhuman long-range vision on top of their other enhancements when he realized that Blaser, like Wyder, had a horizontal gold stripe around his parka. He was also waving in their direction. Wyder waved back, swinging her entire arm from the shoulder.

"Okay, we head up," she said. "Blaser will bring up the rear. You guys can walk vanguard with me."

Joosten fell into step beside Wyder, and Fitz belatedly remembered that the two of them were buddies. Finn walked a few paces behind them, hands in his pockets like he was just taking a stroll through the aggravatingly deep and thoroughly uncooperative snow.

Which left Feena alone at Fitz's side.

"I feel like I should thank you again for a lovely dinner party. I can't remember the last time I had so much fun," she said to him, her voice a throaty coo. But there didn't seem to be any extra oomph to it. He wasn't totally immune, after all. Usually, he had to take a second to tune out her pheromones.

Maybe Wyss was right.

Or maybe the extra layers of clothing were working in his favor.

"No need to thank me. My parents invited you. Or my father invited your aunt and uncle, anyway," Fitz said.

"Sure, but it wouldn't have been so much fun if you and your little friend hadn't let me play detective with you," she said.

"His name is Wyss," Fitz said.

"Right. Wyss," she said gamely. Then added, "Kristof. See? I remember."

"And we didn't let you do anything. You just refused to leave," Fitz said.

"Oh, I know. I'm terrible," Feena said, grabbing his arm and hugging it.

He reminded himself he was supposed to be getting friendly with her as he fought the urge to pull away.

"I know I'm not your first choice in partners," she said to him conspiratorially. "She wasn't there that night because she was partying on Guy Travert's yacht, right?"

"I guess that's where she was," Fitz said. "But again, it wasn't my party. I didn't send out any invitations."

"I know," Feena said, hugging tighter on his arm. "Do you know what else I know?"

Fitz's blood ran cold. His mouth was suddenly dry, and he had to try three times before he managed to croak out, "what?"

"I know your daddy doesn't really like her," Feena whispered up to him. Then she let his arm go. The path was getting steeper, and Fitz could see the first of the climbing segments up ahead of them. They'd be attached to safety lines there, definitely not clinging to each other.

But Feena wasn't done talking. "Which I admit I don't get. Ritchie is perfectly lovely. And such a good influence. I would think she would be any parent's dream. I know I could never replace her."

Fitz said nothing.

"But I can't help but notice she's not here with you now either," Feena said with what really, truly sounded like genuine concern.

Damn, she was good. He almost believed she was worried about Ritchie, or at least that Fitz might be feeling blue because of something Ritchie had said or done.

She might not be using her pheromones on him, he couldn't tell for sure one way or another, but she was projecting hard just how willing she was to be a shoulder to cry on.

"She's back behind us somewhere, probably with Moreau and Frei and Grof," Fitz guessed. He didn't bother looking back to check.

"Oh, sure," Feena said. "She's just not here with you, is she?"

"No, she's with her buddy," Fitz said. "Don't you have a buddy?"

"Sure, she's right here with us," Feena said with a laugh.

Fitz turned to see another cadet following close on their heels. She was nearly as short as Moreau and even slighter of frame, but the way she walked reminded him acutely of his mother. Impossibly graceful given all the layers of their alpine weather gear. She fairly danced over the top of the snow.

As if she felt his eyes on her, she lifted her hooded head and looked up at him. He saw wisps of black hair at her temples, pale skin and very dark eyes.

But he would swear he'd never seen her before in his life.

The name tag on the breast of her parka said her name was Heim, and the notches in the tag's border indicated that she, like Feena and the others he had shared a shuttle with, was in her last year.

"Is she new?" Fitz whispered to Feena when he'd turned his attention back to the path ahead of them.

"Oh, goodness, no. She's been here for the full four years," Feena said. "She's a little quiet."

"I guess," Fitz said, almost amused. It was a strange quality for a cadet to have in a foreign service academy, where standing out was such a huge part of advancing in one's career.

The first stretch of climbing wasn't too tough. It was more like a walk up a steep slope that only occasionally needed hands as well as feet. The main object seemed to be getting used to having your safety harness tethered to the guide rope. But Fitz saw Colonel Hansen standing at the top of the cliff-side looking down at all of them, and he knew this segment was easy on purpose, to let Hansen know who would need to be watched more carefully or even sent back. A few cadets were indeed having trouble keeping their safety lines from getting tangled.

At least while following the guide rope, they had to walk in single file. It made for a nice break in his conversation with Feena.

The weather was still holding off, although when he reached the higher meadow at the top of the cliff, he turned to look back to the south and could see the dark mass of clouds smothering everything for kilometers around the school.

"Is that storm heading this way?" he asked aloud.

Colonel Hansen, still standing lookout at the very edge of the cliff, glanced back at him. "Soon enough," he said. "Grab a quick lunch here. We press on as soon as the last cadet is up. Pass the word."

"Yes, sir," Fitz said.

Luckily, Wyder had overheard and took over the word-passing duty. Fitz left his pack on his back and unzipped the pouch on the strap that crossed at his waist. He took out a protein bar, then used his teeth to pull off his climbing gloves so he could unwrap it.

Everyone coming over the side of the cliff was looking at him standing so close, and sooner or later it would be Ritchie. He moved away from Hansen, chewing as he walked, no real aim in sight except to enjoy a quiet moment alone, away from the others.

He missed Wyss. That thought kind of surprised him. He had been without a buddy for so long, he thought that was his more natural state. But actually, he kind of hated being alone. Looking back, he could see now he always had.

It was a weird feeling.

"All good?" Wyder asked, suddenly at his elbow.

"Yeah. Fine," he said.

"You should stay closer to the others. White-out conditions can blow up out of nowhere in an instant. It's best not to be alone," she said.

"You were up here last year, right? Was it bad?" he asked.

She shrugged, and he realized she looked even more tired and withdrawn than he felt.

"Is everything okay with you?" he asked.

She looked surprised at the question. "Sure. I just need you to stay close to the others."

"Roger that, cadet captain," Fitz said. She narrowed her eyes at him as if trying to decide if he was being sarcastic or not. But he wasn't, or wasn't intending to be, anyway. In the end, she just nodded, then headed further along the cliff to where two other cadets were standing a little too close to the edge.

"Cadets! Step back from there!" she called as she scrunched over the snow.

Fitz stayed where he was as he put the last of the protein bar into his mouth. As he chewed, he laboriously pulled his gloves back on over his already-freezing hands. He tugged the cuffs of the gloves up over his gauntlets, making sure he had left not even the smallest patch of exposed skin. He had a second, warmer pair of gloves in his pack, but they lacked the nanofabric that these thinner gloves had. The nanofabric adhered to anything he pressed his hand into. He could dangle from his fingertips without slipping, if he had to.

Not that he wanted to test it. He had visions of his hands sliding out, of himself plummeting to his death while his gloves fluttered in the wind above him, still adhering to the icy glacier. He wasn't exactly a climbing novice, but ice and rock were two different things, and he much preferred climbing rock.

Especially if that rock was somewhere warmer than this.

He was feeling a little sleepy, or more like dreamy, like he wasn't really there on the mountain doing any of this. He wondered if he was feeling the altitude already. He didn't think so. They weren't going to need supplemental oxygen until they were past the third base camp, he remembered. That was two days of climbing away yet.

No, clearly he was just tired. He stopped fussing with the wrist closures on his gloves and was about to join the others when he saw that the two cadets were still standing at the edge of the meadow, half a step away from a very nasty fall. They had taken a step or two inland when Wyder had told them to, but apparently they had just gravitated back towards danger immediately after.

The two had their faces close together as they spoke to each other, and the taller of the two was gripping the arm of the shorter one. Despite the layers of padding, he could tell that the shorter of the two had a very meaty arm. Still, the shorter one flinched at this, then tried to pull their arm away. The tall one wasn't letting go, but the shorter one was putting more muscle into it. If they kept pulling at each other like that, they were both going to go over the side.

"Hey!" Fitz called, and started walking towards them.

The shorter one was facing him, but he couldn't see her face until she darted it around the taller one's shoulder. It was Joosten. This time, when she wrenched at her arm, the other cadet let her go. She stumbled, then ran back towards the rest of the cadets already gathering on the far side of the meadow.

Then the taller cadet turned around, and Fitz saw it was Finn.

"What's going on?" Fitz asked.

"Nothing at all, buddy," Finn assured him. "Just a little conversation. No deep, dark secrets here. I'll leave that to you and your friends, yeah?"

He slipped his hands back into his pockets and strolled across the meadow. Finn stood uncertainly at the edge of the cliff, then looked down over the side. Was there some reason they had been arguing here, at the very end of the meadow?

He squinted against the reflected light from the snow, but there was nothing to be seen there. Had he really expected there to be? Whatever they had been discussing so intensely must have been a personal matter.

But what could possibly be personal between suave, debonair Finn Berweger and the decidedly plain Joosten? Joosten, who had no social connections that Fitz knew of, no skills that would make her of interest to the likes of the Berwegers.

At least for her part, Joosten seemed to have lost the fawning adoration of the twins he had witnessed on far too many occasions in the dining hall. From the look she had given him before stomping away, she just might loathe Finn as much as Fitz himself did.

So what exactly was up?

Fitz didn't want to venture a guess. But he was keeping an eye on Hansen for Wyss and on the Berwegers for Hansen and the rest of the task force. He might as well add Joosten into that mix.

He went to join the others, suddenly eager to get to the first base camp and call it a day.

$$7$$

FOR RITCHIE, the climb before lunch had been a piece of cake. She didn't have as much climbing experience as most of the other cadets, but she had spent a lot of time familiarizing herself with the equipment. The gloves felt strange when they adhered to surfaces, but she soon got a hang of just the right movement to disengage the nanofabric so she could reach for the next handhold without jerking her whole arm. And unlike many of the others, she never once got tangled in her safety line.

But it was a good thing she didn't let herself feel too smug about how she had tackled the first slope, because the four climbing segments they tackled between lunch and dinner grew successively harder. And each time, the walking segments between that offered something like a moment's rest were shorter.

It was fully dark before they even reached the bottom of the ropes of the last cliff-side they had to scale before reaching the first base camp.

And then it started to snow in earnest.

There had been a few meandering flakes all afternoon, drifting down out of what for Oymyakon passed for a cloudless sky. But Ritchie had noted how dark the storm locked over the school to the south was, and how imposing the roiling clouds between them and the peak still north of them were becoming. She hadn't taken those flakes for granted. Wherever they had come from, they presaged more to follow. She had known worse was coming.

But she could've wished it hadn't come all at once out of nowhere when she was testing one foothold before stepping up to find the next.

She could hear Moreau cry out from somewhere behind and below her, but the wind tore her shouted words of comfort away. There was nothing to be done but grip the rock-face with her gloved fingertips for dear life and wait for the smallest break in the white-out to take the next step.

She really didn't want to test how the safety line attached to her climbing harness worked. At least, not on the first day. She knew the rope was made of nano-materials, just like the gloves. It might look like a mere silk cord, but it would hold any cadet with the strength of a steel line. Even so, it was meant to be a last resort.

She gripped with her fingers and toes and slowly, methodically, crawled up the rock-face.

Finally, she reached the top and scrambled over the edge, but stayed where she was sitting in the snow until Moreau was up beside her. Then the two of them walked shoulder to shoulder so they didn't lose sight of each other, straight towards where the blur of grayish snow was a bit lighter.

The light led them to the base camp's only permanent structure. She already knew what was inside: communication and rescue equipment, camping supplies, and stacks of rations. But it was off limits to cadets save for the two captains.

Cadet Captain Wyder was standing directly under the flood light with an all-weather tablet in her hands. There was a stack of sleek, square objects nearly the size of their packs beside her, rapidly disappearing under the accumulating snow.

She peered up at Ritchie's and then Moreau's faces through the tunnels of their hoods, then pointed to something behind them. She leaned in to yell over the wind, "you're bunking with Frei and Grof. They got up first, so they're already setting up your tent. The third tent along spoke two. Follow the red cord until you find them."

Ritchie saw she was pointing to where a stake had been driving deep into the bedrock. An array of colored cords were extending out from the ring at the top of the stake. They radiated out, indeed like the spokes of a wheel, and Ritchie chose the one heading in the direction Wyder had been pointing. She and Moreau followed it past an already assembled tent, then past three cadets huddled over one of the squarish packages, apparently arguing over what exactly to do with it. A little further and they reached Frei and Grof, who had just finished erecting the tent.

"Great, you're here!" Grof said. "I was hoping not to have to open the door twice in this weather. Let's get inside!"

Ritchie nodded. Frei had already run her hand down the seam of the tent door to open it, and the two ends were flapping wildly in the growing wind. The four of them rushed inside. Ritchie helped Grof catch the flaps and hold them close until Frei could seal them shut again.

For a brief moment, Ritchie was afraid they were going to spend the night just like that, all cramped together with no room to even lie down in. But then she realized that like the library back at the school, the tents had double entryways to keep the elements out of the indoor spaces. They helped each other brush the snow off their parkas, then stomp it off their boots. Then Moreau found the seam for the inner door and they all tumbled inside.

"I have the light box," Frei said, setting a squarish object about the size of a nightstand against the central pole of the tent. She touched a few panels, and the box began to glow with a warm reddish light. It provided little light, despite its name, but it was slowly warming up the air around them.

Which was great, since Ritchie could feel the snow crunching down under her feet. There was a thin layer of plastic between them and it, but when they spread out their sleeping bags, they were going to feel it beneath them for sure.

Moreau must have realized the same, to judge from the horrified look on her face. Ritchie gave her an encouraging smile. "Just think what your mother would say if she could see you now," she said.

"I've just decided, I totally want to be a diplomat," Moreau said.

Frei laughed. "Hey, most guardians never go through this sort of thing again after training."

"This is full-on soldier stuff," Grof agreed. "Still, it'll be nice to say we've done it."

"Sure. After we've actually done it," Moreau grumbled.

They each picked a corner of the space that was about half the size of their dorm back at the school and set their packs down. Frei and Grof sprawled out on the cold ground and chatted together about the day so far. Ritchie could see that Moreau wasn't in a hurry to sit on the plastic-covered snow just yet, as much as she looked dead on her feet.

"Doing okay?" Ritchie asked as she set her own pack flat on the ground, then perched awkwardly on top of it. It wasn't comfortable, and she was too tired to bother figuring out what exactly was poking into her butt, but at least it was warmer than the ground.

"Yeah," Moreau said, but absently, as if she hadn't quite heard. Then she saw Ritchie sitting on her pack and set her own flat on the ground. But before she sat down, she suddenly seemed to come fully awake. "Wait, I saw Wyss last night."

"Okay," Ritchie said, not sure why that was such a declaration. Then a thought struck her. "Did he tell you something about that dinner party at Fitz's place?"

"What? No," Moreau said as she dropped to one knee, then started digging through her pack. "He gave me something he thought would be able to reach from here down to the school."

"In this weather?" Ritchie asked as the wind rippled over the roof of their tent. "And it looked even worse down at the school."

"He thought so," she said. Ritchie saw she had something in her hand, but she froze before drawing it out. "He said not to—" But she broke off mid-sentence to look up at Frei and Grof, who were standing over her.

"Wyder is distributing food rations now," Grof told them. "A soup packet for each tent, plus a bread and butter allowance. But no sense in us all going back out into that. If Frei and Grof fetch it tonight, you two can grab it tomorrow night?"

"Absolutely! Thanks!" Moreau said.

"Sure thing," Grof said, then she and Frei went out through the tent door.

"He said not to let anyone see it, I'm guessing," Ritchie said, crawling closer to Moreau's side.

"Right," Moreau said, taking out what looked like an industrial tablet, the kind workers used in the higher risk areas of the space station where Ritchie had grown up. Did weather-proofing look like vacuum- and radiation-proofing?

Moreau opened it up, extended the telescoping antenna at the back until it brushed the top of the tent overhead, then touched the keys to bring the screen to life.

"Why would we need to talk to Wyss, anyway?" Ritchie asked as the tablet searched for a signal. "Wait, is that thing commandeering foreign service satellites?"

"Wyss said not to worry about that," Moreau told her with a wry grin.

Then Wyss himself was there on the screen, if blurry, the image of him washed out of color. "Hey," he said as he looked out at them. "We only have maybe a minute before the signal drops. Any news on your end?"

"None," Moreau said. "I've been watching Hansen all day. He's watching us, but just because it's his job. No one is getting more or less of his attention that I can see. Honestly, if I had to guess, I'd say whoever accused him isn't even here."

"How can we know that?" Ritchie asked.

"Why would you think it's someone in the lower two classes?" Wyss asked.

"Do you think the administration would have let Hansen up here basically alone with his accuser?" Moreau said to them both.

"You have a point," Wyss said. "But Sokolov and I will keep hunting down the names of who was here over break. With a charge like treason, Hansen might not even know who his accuser is, you know."

"Great. But you're right," Ritchie said. "There's all sorts of ways this is going to be tougher than solving a murder. So you're still searching the names. No other leads?"

"Not so far," Wyss said. Then added, "how's Fitz doing?"

"No idea," Ritchie said, far too breezily. Moreau glanced over at her but said nothing.

Fitz had spent the entire day chatting with Feena. Chatting with, walking arm and arm with, just generally hanging out with Feena. Ritchie had even seen him talking to Finn once.

"He seems to have new friends now," she said bitterly.

"Hey," Wyss objected.

"He's only doing what Hansen asked him to do," Moreau said.

"Exactly," Wyss said. "Look, I'm about to cut out here. I can't risk leaving the signal up in case anyone notices what I'm doing. Not until it really is a call that you have evidence that's going to uncover a conspiracy to commit treason. But call again tomorrow night, even if there's no news. Just to check in, in case we have something down here."

"Got it. Say hi to Sokolov from us," Ritchie said.

"Will do," Wyss said, and disappeared from the screen.

Moreau had just closed the tablet up and stowed it away in her pack when they heard the sound of Frei and Grof entering the outside door. Ritchie got up to meet them at the inner door and help carry whatever they had inside.

The soup packet turned out to be just that: another sleek, squarish object with no outward features she could see. Frei set it on top of the light box. As if it detected what was wanted, a small corner of the light box glowed a more intense, darker red. Frei took out her utility knife to slice open the top of the packet, and the smell of potato and leek soup with generous cubes of ham filled the tent. She set a metal container of water on another corner of the surface and it, too, began to bubble almost at once.

"How hot is that?" Ritchie asked.

"More like how high up are we already," Frei said. "By the next base camp, we'll need to put the pressure sealing lid on the water pot or it will boil away before it's remotely warm enough for tea. The soup too, I'm sure. Unless we're on an all hard tack diet by then."

"The upper classes tell stories," Grof said with a grin. She divided the soup into four metal mugs, then handed them around.

The bread was a dark, whole grain roll that felt too hard in Ritchie's hand when she took hers, but once she had her own share of the soup to dunk it in, she realized it was perfect that way. Of course, she had to use her utility knife to slice it open so she could smear the butter packet across its interior.

"Is it just me, or does this taste better than the food we get at the cafeteria?" Moreau asked.

"It's better," Ritchie said.

"I don't know. Hunger is the best sauce, they say, and all that climbing has made me well and truly hungry," Grof said.

"No, it's definitely better," Ritchie insisted. "This here is real butter. Look at how it melts when you dunk it into the soup. That's no cheap vegetable oil."

"Well, we earned it," Moreau said as she scraped the last of her soup together to make one final spoonful.

"Imagine what we'll get tomorrow," Frei said with an eager grin.

Moreau seemed less enthused, but said nothing. For Ritchie's part, she just hoped the snow let up again the next day. Climbing and walking through a white-out was stressful, but also visually uninteresting. She wanted to see everything around them again like they had that morning.

Oymyakon may be a planet with very little to recommend it, but this particular upthrusting of its tallest mountain chain was definitely the highlight for her. Seeing actual mountains spread out below her was just awe-inspiring.

It was almost enough to make her forget treason and conspiracies and betrayal.

Almost.

8

SURE, he was up before dawn for the second day in a row, but at least this time Fitz had gotten a full night's sleep. He had crashed hard immediately after dinner, waking only briefly when Stucki and Imhof were telling someone at the door to bug off before drifting off again.

Now that he was awake with a belly full of warm breakfast, fully dressed and helping the other two stow the tent and return it to the supply building, he found himself wondering who had wanted to come in. It was just the three of them in the tent, since his buddy Wyss wasn't in a high enough class for the trip. If whoever it was had been looking for Stucki or Imhof, those two would've just let them in or gone out themselves.

It must've been someone looking for Fitz. But who?

Wrack his brain as he might, he couldn't recall a thing about the murmuring voice coming from outside the door. Male or female? Even that detail eluded him.

He was about to ask, but before he could, Colonel Hansen was whistling sharply for everyone to join him at the far end of the base camp.

At least it had stopped snowing. The temperature had plummeted to truly uncomfortable levels of cold, but the air was clear and the sun was bright. He hoped it lasted. That climb the night before in the whiteout snow had been unpleasant.

"Listen up, cadets!" Hansen snapped, and all the chatter around Fitz stopped. "You are all familiar with the route for today. As you've probably noticed, there are only two climbing segments on today's path. Two *very long* climbing segments. The first will be more challenging than yesterday, but nothing you haven't handled on the climbing walls down at the school."

He stopped to make eye contact with a few choice cadets. Alas, with everyone in parkas with their hoods up, Fitz had no clue who he was singling out.

At last he looked up at the group as a whole and said, "the second climbing segment is the shorter of the two, but it will be all ice. Up the side of the southern glacier! Don't worry, the base camp is on rocky ground when you get to it. We'll leave camping on ice until two nights from now, eh?"

This brought another wave of murmuring over the crowd. Hoods dipped together as cadets whispered nervous laments or words of encouragement to each other.

Fitz looked around. Stucki and Imhof had moved closer to the front of the group. Fitz was at the back, all by himself. He couldn't even see where Moreau and Ritchie were. He thought he spotted Moreau in a gap of the crowd ahead of him, but when she turned to look back towards the supply building, Fitz realized it was just Feena's quiet buddy. What was her name?

Heim. That was it.

Fitz realized he had missed Hansen saying something else, but apparently it was just dismissing them all as the group began to break up and move in clumps towards the cliff-side at the far end of the meadow.

Fitz turned back to look to the south, but the dense cloud mass was still settled firmly over the location of the school. It was like that tempest was trapped there among the lower mountain peaks, spinning and spinning but unable to blow clear.

He looked up towards the mountain peak above them. Those

clouds were even less friendly. They weren't going to get anywhere close to that point even by the end of the day today, but in a few days, they'd be up in that. It looked damp and miserable. It was also going to be cold and very nearly airless.

In a perverse way, he couldn't wait to get there.

The bottom of the climbing trail was around an outcropping of rock. Fitz could see cadets already making their way up the cliff. There were ropes for tying off their safety lines like before, but this time, they might actually be necessary. This was no steep but walkable slope. It was all handholds and footholds from here.

Fitz dug out his climbing gloves as he walked around the rock outcropping. The second glove didn't want to come out of his pocket and he had to look down to tug it free.

He looked up again just in time to draw up short, not quite outright colliding with Finn and Joosten in the middle of another intense conversation. Joosten shot him a look of pure hate, and he almost wanted to apologize for continually interrupting them.

Only this trip was no time for whatever sort of shenanigans the two of them were up to, or fighting over, or whatever. Plus, why should he have to apologize? All he was doing was walking around.

Joosten let out a growl of frustration, then left Fitz and Finn standing there, heading towards the bottom of the ropes at something close to a run, or at least a really fast waddle. The snow had gotten deeper and more cumbersome in the night.

"Aren't you going to interrogate me, Fitz?" Finn asked him.

"Wasn't intending to," Fitz said, pulling on his gloves. Finn watched him do it before pulling out his own climbing gloves.

"Pity. You've been avoiding me for ages. I've missed our little tête-à-têtes," Finn said. He tugged on his gloves, then looked up as if noticing for the first time that it was only Fitz there with him. "Where's your girlfriend?"

"Everyone but us is higher up the slope, Berweger," Fitz said.

"I was really hoping you'd ask who I meant," Finn said as they started walking towards the bottom of the cliff-side.

"I figured as much," Fitz said.

"Well?" Finn said.

"I'm not here to entertain you," Fitz said.

"It's a lot of climbing, but there's no reason we can't all make a bit of a holiday of it," Finn said as he attached his harness to the safety line, then considered his first options for handholds. Fitz did the same at the other line.

Fitz was an excellent climber. He should be able to pull ahead of Finn and leave him too far behind to carry on this conversation.

He started climbing, picking out the best holds almost by instinct, falling quickly into a rapid but steady pace. It felt pretty good, actually. The exercise warmed his body, and even the pack on his back didn't seem like such an encumbrance.

"All this place needs is chalets with warm fireplaces instead of the crappy tents," Finn said, and Fitz realized that not only was Finn right there at his elbow, he was keeping pace with Fitz with an ease that said he could be going much, much faster if he wished to.

But he didn't. No, clearly, he preferred hanging close to Fitz, making sure he stayed miserable.

"My sister was hoping you'd chat with her after dinner last night," Finn said.

Fitz let out what he hoped was a suitably vague grunt. But at least that was one mystery solved. It wasn't hard to guess why Imhof had chased her off. He was surprised that Stucki hadn't tried to get her to come inside, but maybe he had. Maybe that was why that conversation had lasted more than a few words.

"I know you don't trust her. But you of all people know that neither my sister nor I were ever found complicit in any wrongdoing. And haven't we been such good cadets since then? Doesn't it seem like you and your friends showed us the error of our ways?"

Fitz grunted again. He looked up past the next handhold to see he still had an infinitely long way to go. He didn't want to slow down, even though he knew he wasn't presenting Finn with anything like a challenge. But he couldn't keep up the pace he was at and talk both at once.

"Well, at the very least, don't you believe in keeping your friends close but your enemies closer?" Finn asked.

Fitz kept his attention on his climbing and studiously said nothing.

He slowed his pace a bit, but Finn slowed down as well to stay by his side.

"She really does just find you fascinating," Finn went on. "Not that I get it. I don't see the appeal at all. No offense. Sure, your father is militarily connected, but our family has no need of more military connections. She says she just likes you, but even she can't say why. So I don't get it, but I believe her. She is clearly smitten. Well done, you."

Fitz said nothing, and Finn finally fell silent, too. Which would've been more of a relief if Finn hadn't been radiating a certain smugness. Like he thought they were such good friends, they could enjoy a companionable silence together. But on top of that, certain knowledge that Fitz couldn't summon the breath to set him straight on that score.

It was a lot of smugness. A lot of layers.

The two of them caught up with the other cadets near the top of the cliff, having to hang onto the rock face and wait for slower cadet after slower cadet to get their bodies over the edge and out of the way. Finn hoisted himself up and over like an accomplished swimmer after an easy set of laps in a pool. Fitz was not quite so graceful, but he ended up on his feet, not flopped on his back, gasping for breath like far too many of his fellow cadets.

"Is it always this bad?" Fitz asked Hansen, who was standing nearby. Hansen looked back down the cliff-side before realizing that Fitz had been gesturing to the winded cadets. He seemed distracted, and for a moment Fitz didn't think he was even going to answer.

"Some of them are feeling the altitude already," Hansen told him at last. "The food has pharmaceuticals in it that will help, but if it's this bad tomorrow, some of you will be starting supplemental oxygen earlier than others. Good of you to bring up the rear, Fitz. I know you're one of my strongest climbers."

Fitz flushed red, not wanting to take the compliment for something that had happened quite by accident. Then he realized that compliment hadn't included Finn because Finn was no longer standing near him.

Well, that was a relief. Perhaps the afternoon would be more pleasant, ice climb or not.

"Wyder!" Hansen yelled so loudly that Fitz flinched. But Hansen just marched away across the meadow to meet Wyder and Blaser and give them a bevy of orders. They both nodded, and he turned away from the entire group to march out of sight around a bend in the mountain trail they'd all be following soon enough.

Fitz took out another protein bar and once more ate it while standing apart from the group. They were still largely anonymous to his eyes, but when he saw a tall one and a short one once more having close words at the other end of the meadow, he knew with certainty he was looking at Finn and Joosten again.

He took a quick swig of water then, before he had quite thought through whether this was a good idea or a bad idea, started off to find Ritchie.

Something was going on. As much as Finn had said that Fitz had been avoiding him, he knew it was just as true that Finn had been avoiding Fitz as well. So why the sudden need for conversation? Had he just been bored, or had he been trying to distract Fitz from thinking about what was going on with Joosten?

He didn't know. But maybe Ritchie or even Moreau knew something he didn't.

But before he'd taken two steps, Wyder was calling the group back onto their feet to carry on to the next climb. Everyone got up and moved forward at once, eager to get this second more challenging day over with and dig into some more of that first-rate food.

Fitz felt that motivation, too. But it dimmed next to his urge to find Ritchie. The cadets were already packed shoulder to shoulder, and the ledge only got narrower as the path went on. There was no way to push his way forward through that crowd.

He likely wouldn't stand a chance of finding Ritchie until that night, when they were once more in camp.

In camp, where there would be eyes and ears everywhere. And no one was allowed to wander off alone, not even in a pair. Until the morning call to muster, no one was allowed to leave the tents.

Well, if they had to huddle from the wind against the back of the tent, that's what he'd do.

It chilled him, the idea of talking with her, really talking with her. But it especially chilled him that he wanted to talk to her about Finn.

Well, Finn and Joosten, but still.

He had to admit to himself that he had a very real fear that Finn would hear his own name if it were mentioned. Like some sort of vindictive mythological spirit. It was a crazy thought, but he just couldn't shake it.

The glacier climb was shorter than the first climb, but far more challenging. Fitz glanced up more than once from his own climb to see yet another fellow cadet slipping away to snap and dangle from the end of their safety line. It was more than a little disconcerting, given that he was climbing just below them. If they hadn't tied off their safety line correctly, they could have come down right on top of his head.

That was a really unpleasant image.

The next time he stopped for a quick breather, he opted to look side to side rather than up ahead of him. Once again, he was climbing near the back of the pack, but this time, there were others around him. He looked down to be sure no stragglers were being left behind, but the few who were lower than him were still climbing at a steady, if slower, pace.

Perhaps he should wait for them to pass him by before continuing on. He kept three point contact, not relying on his safety line to hold him as he took another sip of water. His eyes still scanned the whites and blues of the ice around him as he put his water bottle away.

Then he saw Ritchie. Ritchie, all alone, fussing over her gloves or something in her hands. Her safety line? He doubted she was in any kind of trouble, but it was odd that Moreau wasn't right there with her.

He took the grappling gun off the side of his pack, then fired it to a point higher than them both, but about midway between them. Then he cut his safety line and kicked away from the ice, swinging out over nothingness, then back towards the face of the glacier.

He stuck a perfect landing on the narrow ice ledge where Ritchie had stopped and even reattached his safety line below her own on the guide rope she was using.

Even mid-swing, he had heard the way she was swearing up a storm at him, and he could tell she was currently resisting the temptation to strike him. Only her worry that he would fall was keeping her hand fluttering around him without quite touching him.

"What?" he asked.

"That was really, really dangerous, Fitz!" she snapped at him. But he wasn't actually listening to her words, because he could see that her hands were trembling. Was she already feeling the effects of altitude sickness? Or maybe hypothermia?

"You're shaking. Are you okay?" he asked.

"Of course I'm okay! I'm shaking because you just scared the life out of me!" she all but shrieked.

"Fear. Right. No anger there," Fitz said with his most charming smile.

The corner of her mouth twitched, but she didn't smile back.

Finally, she took a deep breath and said, "Fitz. What did you do that for? We're nearly at the top. Couldn't you have spoken to me there?"

"Maybe, but this is better," he said.

"How is this better?" she asked.

"We're alone here," he said.

She seemed to realize that was true only after he said it. Then her face started to color again, and he braced himself for another outburst of raw anger.

Only she wasn't looking at him. She was looking up.

"What is it?" he asked, following her sight line. He could see boots far overhead. Someone was nearing the top. Beyond them, he could see Colonel Hansen leaning over the edge, extending a hand as if to help.

But something was wrong.

"It's Wyder," Ritchie said. "She's sliding."

Wyder was indeed sliding. It was hard to tell from directly below her, but it looked like her gloves were failing to grip on the ice properly, and so were the toes of her boots.

"Her safety line will catch her," Fitz said.

But some instinct had him reaching down to cut his line and Ritchie's off the main rope.

Ritchie didn't notice. She was transfixed by the sight above them. "Fitz! She's falling! She's—"

But before she could say another word, Fitz snaked an arm around her, pulling her close to him even as he kicked away from the side of the glacier. They swung out into open air, Ritchie screeching the entire time in a shrill mixture of startled anger and fear.

Then Wyder fell past them, almost close enough to brush them on the way down. Ritchie clung tight to Fitz to tuck her body away from Wyder's. Her face was pressed against his neck, and she didn't move from that spot.

So only Fitz saw Wyder as she fell past them, a useless length of rope still clutched tightly in one of her hands. Her other hand was thrust out, fingers spread wide, grasping desperately at the air.

It felt to Fitz like he started into Wyder's eyes for an eternity, forced to be witness to every one of her emotions as fear became acceptance of her rapidly approaching fate. Much as he had done with Cadet Captain Jeger the year before.

But he couldn't have been looking into her eyes the entire time, because as his booted feet slammed back down against the wall of the glacier, he knew for sure he had seen something else.

Both ends of that rope had been burned through. Not cut, not rubbed apart against sharp ice, but burned a charry black.

And so had the palm of her outstretched glove.

"Safety line," Fitz said to Ritchie. His arm was still around her, his other hand wrapped around the rope that extended from his grappling hook. She quickly dug in with the toes of her boots until she was securely anchored back on the narrow ice ledge. Then she bent to tie her line back onto the guide rope and then his as well.

He had no worries about the quality of her knot work, so he didn't bother to double-check, no matter what the climbing protocols said.

He never heard the thump of a body hitting anything behind and below him. But perhaps that was a mercy.

He did hear the cries of shock, then confusion, and finally dismay as the other cadets realized what had just happened.

But Ritchie beside him didn't cry out, even though she was still shaking like a leaf. She just quietly gasped, but there was the most profound level of shock in that little intake of air. This wasn't about Wyder. This was about something new.

Fitz looked up, once more following her sight line to see Colonel

Hansen's face above them. He was already on top of the glacier, looking down.

And in his hands he was reeling in the last of a foreshortened length of rope. He saw the two of them looking up at them, but his face revealed nothing when he met their gaze.

Then he disappeared from view, taking the rope with him.

9

RITCHIE WANTED TO LOOK DOWN, to see if there was any sign of Wyder below them, but she was afraid trying to do so would give her vertigo. Her hands were already shaking so badly it was hard to keep a hold on the guide rope. But the ice ledge she was standing on was only wide enough for the very tips of her toes. The micro-spikes on the bottom of her climbing boots were wedged in deep enough to hold her weight, being of the same nano-materials as her gloves, but if she started to tumble backward...

"We probably shouldn't rely on that," Fitz said to her. She realized he meant the guide rope and grabbed at an outcropping of the ice itself. Her gloves might be designed to cling to the ice, but it still felt far from secure.

"It's not the same rope she was holding," Ritchie said.

"I don't think we should trust any of the ropes just now," he said. She had never seen his face so grim. He clung to the ice with one hand and both booted toes, using the other hand to tug at the guide rope. It held fast, but his expression didn't change.

"What did we just see?" Ritchie asked. "Hansen was trying to help her, right?"

"I don't know," Fitz said.

"He must've been trying to help her. He was reaching out to her," Ritchie said.

"I don't know," Fitz said again. "He might've been reaching down to cut the rope."

"He would never—" Ritchie said firmly.

"Well, it looked like he was pulling that rope back up to hide the evidence," Fitz said. His eyes were sweeping the glacier over them, but she had no idea what he was looking for. "I saw the rope in Wyder's hands when she fell past us. It looked like it had been burned."

"Burned? How?" Ritchie asked.

"I don't know. But we need to focus on finishing this climb. The wind is picking up again," he said.

"How are we going to make it the rest of the way up without trusting the guide ropes?" Ritchie asked. "I really don't want to try it with just the gloves and boots. I'm not that practiced with ice climbing."

"Are you kidding me? I've seen you climb before." It might have been a compliment, but not when said in such an impatient, irritated voice.

"I'm not ready to do this without a safety line," she said firmly.

"Fine," he said. At first she thought he was just resuming the thing where he just didn't talk to her. But then she realized he was looking around, chewing his lip, and thinking something through. She waited. "My grapple line is secure," he said at last. "We can use that most of the way up. You have your grapple gun on your pack?"

Ritchie nodded, but made no move to reach for it. She was still shaking, although that was becoming less from the shock of seeing Wyder fall and more from the dropping temperature. Fitz was right; they needed to finish the climb. She needed to get moving. But she had to get her body under control first. She closed her eyes, took a deep breath, and willed the shaking to stop.

"Are you all right?" Fitz asked. She nodded again, eyes still closed as she focused on her breathing. "You looked like you were having trouble with something before I swung over here."

"That's why you did that?" she opened her eyes to ask.

"No, I wanted to talk to you about something," he said. "Never mind. We'll discuss it when we're both standing on solid ground. Are you ready to do this?"

"Lead the way," she said.

"Switch the safety lines to this rope, then we'll walk it out until we're under the hook," he said. He reached a hand behind her to hold her by the top of her safety harness so she could use both her hands to tie the ropes. It was part of their training, but there was also something comforting about that gesture.

He wasn't going to let her fall.

Ritchie's hands made quick work of the knots. She had a sudden memory of Guy back on Epsilon 20. He had seen her practicing a few basic knots in preparation for this training and had shown her dozens more, knots he had learned as a kid after he had read that sailing ships used to use them way back before the dawn of spaceflight. His own yacht had no sails, of course, but he just loved ocean-going ships, ancient as well as modern.

She finished, then looked up to give Fitz a nod. He was giving her a strange look, and she realized she had been smiling to herself while she worked. There was no way he could guess what she was really thinking about. He probably thought she was just geeked to tie knots or something. "Ready?" she prompted him.

"Let's go," he said, and waited for her to secure her gloved hands on the ice outcropping again before letting her go. Then he started climbing up the face of the ice, not really relying on the rope for anything other than a failsafe. Ritchie watched where he planted his gloves and the toes of his boots, then followed behind him.

He never looked back down at her, but he must have known she was mimicking his moves because he picked his way up with a deliberate slowness, making sure she saw everything he touched. Ritchie focused only on his hands and feet and then hers, but a part of her mind was aware that the sounds of other cadets around her had faded away. Nearly everyone had been in front of her even before she had stopped to adjust her gloves. She was pretty sure they were the only two still climbing.

Fitz reached the point where the hook he had fired from his grapple was buried deep in the ice and hung there one-handed, only one boot anchored on the ice, turning to look back down at her.

"I'm okay," she assured him.

"I need your gun. Come up another half-step and I'll grab it off your pack. Tell me when you're ready," he said.

She reached up for another handhold, then moved her opposite foot up another step. She made sure she had firm contact with the ice with all four points, then said, "ready."

She barely felt him draw her gun out of his harness, but she definitely heard him fire it. The hook hit the ice with a loud crack.

"Not far to go," he said as he put her gun back on her pack.

"Should I switch the safety lines?" she asked, not savoring the idea of trying that without the benefit of a ledge to stand on.

"No, it's not far to the top. The other line will be safe enough," he said.

She realized as she looked up again to watch him climb that the cutting wind was filled with snow now, and the sky was getting darker. It was late afternoon, but not so late for the sun to be down yet. This darkness was from a storm blowing in.

Fitz glanced down at her only once, as he reached the edge of the top of the glacier. Then he pulled himself up and over. He disappeared from view, but only for a single second. Then his head poked out back over the side, watching her climb the rest of the way. He grasped the back of her harness again to help her get over the top. She didn't sprawl out on her back to catch her breath. The ice beneath them was far too cold for that. But she did stay where she was sitting close to the ledge, and he sat quietly beside her.

It felt like old times. He was so close, she could just lean up against him. Put her head on his shoulder, like she'd done so many times before.

"Get up," Colonel Hansen said, and she looked up to see him towering over the two of them. "You're the last, and everyone is waiting for you. Get up."

They scrambled to their feet, but in the deepening snowstorm, there was no sign of the other cadets.

"Cadet Wyder—" Ritchie started to say.

"There's nothing to be done about that now," the colonel interrupted her. "We need to get to shelter. Everything else can wait."

She would think it was a convenient excuse not to be questioned, if not for the fact that the cold, darkness and deepening snow made it clear he wasn't exaggerating. The snow blowing over the top of the glacier was dancing around hypnotically at her feet, sweeping around in eddies, then shooting away when the wind picked up to a straight-line blast.

Then they were off the ice and on a rocky path that cut between two large prominences, giving them a welcome shelter from the wind. The other cadets were waiting for them here, huddled together in groups for warmth. No one was talking. Blaser in his gold-striped parka stood at the head of the group, and when he saw them draw near, he gave the colonel a wave. The colonel returned it, and Blaser started yelling for the others to resume the march.

It wasn't far to the base camp, which was configured exactly like the first base camp. Blaser gathered everyone around the central building until Hansen arrived to open it up so he could start distributing the tents.

The cadets weren't supposed to go inside the shelter, but Fitz walked right in through the open door. Ritchie didn't even hesitate to follow him.

"Sir," Fitz said.

"Save it, cadet," Colonel Hansen said. He shoved the hover pallet stacked high with tents back out the door towards Blaser, then turned his attention to the communication until built into the wall.

"Sir, what happened with Cadet Captain Wyder?" Ritchie asked.

"I'm dealing with it, cadets," the colonel.

So they were just cadets now in his eyes. She could take the hint. This wasn't a task force matter. Their input meant no more than any other cadet's. He was pushing them away, keeping them at a distance.

She didn't like it. But he was the colonel. She couldn't argue with him.

She watched as he attempted to get a signal to connect with the school through the storm. From what she could see of the panel, he wasn't going to have much luck. The surrounding storm was blocking everything, both direct to the school and via overhead satellites.

Ritchie wondered if she would have better luck trying to reach Wyss with that tablet. But that was still in Moreau's pack, and she wasn't sure where Moreau was exactly. Somewhere in the crowd of cadets outside. She had been climbing with Frei and Grof, making much better time than Ritchie had. The ice had made her far more nervous than she had expected.

She thought about mentioning the tablet Wyss had given her, but quickly opted not to. It might come in handy, having a means of communication that Hansen didn't know about.

He was always brusque, and she knew he wasn't lying about having things to do that weren't any of her business. The first of which would be reporting what had happened to the academy administration.

But she couldn't shake the feeling that he was acting guilty. Like he was fussing over the communications panel, not because he thought trying more would get a signal through, but because he didn't want to turn around and make eye contact with the two of them.

"Sir?" she said.

"Cadets, get to your tents," he said. "Your only responsibility right now is to set up camp. I will take care of the rest."

Ritchie wanted to stay and argue, but Fitz put his hand on her arm and guided her back out into the storm. The pallet sat empty in the snow, all the other cadets lost to view in the blowing snow and darkness. They walked to the stake in the ground, and Ritchie found the colored cable that would lead her to her group's tent.

"You're red?" Fitz said.

"Yes. Third tent out from center," she said.

"I'm black, second tent," he said. "I still need to talk to you."

"About Hansen?" she asked.

"More than that, but yes," he said. "There are a couple of things going on I want to get to the bottom of."

"Sure," she said. But she couldn't summon any enthusiasm to go with that answer.

"Ritchie," he said, and stepped up closer, close enough for their two hoods to form a dark bubble of warmth apart from the storm, a quiet place out of the wind. "We need to work together on this. Something is going on, and I'm not sure we can trust Hansen. Or even all the cadets up here with us."

"But we can trust each other," she said with a sigh. She wasn't sure if that was even still true. He was talking to her now, but there was barely more warmth in his manner towards her than there'd been during the long months of his freeze-out.

But he didn't seem to hear any doubt in her voice. He just nodded and said, "we can trust each other. I'm going to find my tent and dump my pack. Can we meet in your tent?"

"Yeah, but it's not just Moreau and me, you know," she said. "I trust Frei and Grof, but you don't sound like you want to trust anybody."

"Not if I don't have to," he said. "But if you say they're trustworthy, I won't argue."

He looked like he was going to say something more, but in the end, he just nodded and stepped away. Then the wind and the snow were back, lashing at the skin of her face like icy knives and coating her lashes in heavy chunks.

She pulled her hood down low and followed the cable to her tent.

10

FITZ TOOK a moment between the two sets of tent flaps to shake as much snow off of his parka and pack as he could and stomp it off his boots. It was bad enough that for the second day running, he hadn't been there to help set up the tent. He didn't need to bring in any more of the cold than he had to.

Then he stepped into the main compartment of the tent already saying, "sorry I'm late. I wasn't ditching you guys."

"We know," Stucki said, his usually buoyant personality tamped down to something downright serious.

"We figured you were working the case," Imhof said.

"The case?" Fitz repeated.

"Wyder. Was it an accident or what?" Imhof asked.

"I don't know," he said, sliding his pack off his back to set it on the ground. He rolled his shoulders. Exercise and body-numbing cold were two things he definitely didn't like to experience together. "Did you two see what happened?"

"Not really," Stucki said.

"We were in the first group that made it topside," Imhof said. He was fussing with the controls on the light box, even though they'd all learned the night before there was no way to get it to heat up the space any faster than it was already doing it.

"Was Hansen already up there?" Fitz asked. He had been wracking his brain for some time now, trying to remember where he'd seen Hansen before and during the climb. But he had been so focused on Finn and Joosten that he just couldn't place the colonel anywhere with any certainty.

"Yeah," Stucki said as if surprised by the question. "He was supervising from the edge, watching everyone like a hawk. A scary but protective daddy hawk. You know how he is."

"He was worried about the weather," Imhof said. "It was about to shift. I mean, it didn't look like anything was going on to me, but my implant wasn't telling me anything. No signal, no weather updates. Anyway, I guess he was right."

"He's been up here before," Stucki said.

"He told you guys this?" Fitz asked.

Stucki shrugged, but Imhof shot him a look of annoyance. "Not to us. He was telling Cadet Captain Blaser to keep all the cadets together when they got topside. He was watching the climbers still on their way up, but there was a danger of getting caught in a whiteout up on top of the glacier where we were. We were in more danger in a way, not having our safety lines attached to anything. Someone might panic and walk right off the glacier or something."

"He didn't say that," Stucki said.

"He didn't say much, but I could tell he was thinking it from the way he watched us," Imhof said.

"So he wasn't acting odd at all?" Fitz asked as he opened his pack and dug out Wyss's tablet. His desire to keep it secret fell second to checking in with Wyss before he saw Ritchie again, just in case he and Sokolov had learned anything.

"Just normal Colonel Hansen stuff," Stucki said. "Why? You don't think he's responsible, do you? That's crazy."

"I don't want to think it," Fitz said, and left the rest of the thought unspoken. He sat down on the cold ground and opened the tablet on his knees. He extended the antenna, and both Stucki and Imhof's eyebrows shot up, but neither said a word.

He had no more luck than Hansen getting a signal through. But Wyss's tablet gave him better feedback as to what was going on. He could reach the satellites, no problem. But the satellites couldn't reach the school.

"If it's any consolation, the weather down at the academy is even worse than it is up here," he said as he shut the tablet and stowed it back in his bag.

"At least they aren't sleeping in tents," Stucki said.

"Come on. This isn't so bad," Imhof said. Stucki just raised his still-gloved hands. It was going to be awhile before it was warm enough to shed any layers.

"I have to go find Ritchie," Fitz said. "If Hansen or Blaser stop by, cover for me?"

"Don't even worry about it," Stucki said.

Fitz almost changed his mind when he opened the outer flaps of the tent. The wind had become a constant sound that his mind just tuned out while inside the tent, but now it was a bone-chilling reality that was shellacking him with icy wet globs of snow. But his implant wasn't reaching anyone but Stucki and Imhof behind him, so if he wanted to talk to anyone besides his roommates, he'd have to brave the weather.

He followed the cord back to the storage building. Luckily, when he had been out there before, he had counted the cables between his and Ritchie's because perceiving color was impossible at this point. The light that glowed over the storage building's door was completely failing to penetrate through the falling snow.

He couldn't see any of the tents until he was practically touching them, and the snow that was plastered on his face was starting to freeze in some horrible parody of a mask before he finally reached the door to her tent. He slipped inside, then once more set about shaking all the snow and ice off of his clothes. He had to press his gloved hands to his face and melt that ice away before it would let go of his face. He didn't need a mirror to know his face was already frostbitten. He could feel it, but the burning pain was welcome. Dead numbness was what he dreaded.

"It's me," he said before parting the inner set of flaps. Frei and Grof both jumped to their feet, but Ritchie and Moreau just looked up from where they were sitting on the floor, a tablet identical to the one Wyss had given him balanced on a pack between them.

Wyss could've told him he'd made two. And at what point had he given one to the girls? When had he had the opportunity?

And wasn't it supposed to be a secret?

Well, he couldn't exactly chastise them for letting their roommates see it when he'd just done the same thing. "Any luck?" he asked.

"No. The weather is too bad. We were almost reaching the school at first, but the longer we try, the more satellites are dropping out of contact. It's getting worse up here too," Ritchie said.

Fitz nodded. He didn't realize how normal this felt, just discussing things with her, until he saw Moreau glaring up at him with a warning in her eyes. He raised his eyebrows questioningly, but she just furrowed her brow further.

Fitz wondered if she even realized how little he gathered from these nonverbal communications of hers. He doubted it. She had the air of someone who just knows they were understood.

"Were any of you near to Hansen when Wyder fell?" he asked, opting to look at Frei and Grof instead of Moreau and Ritchie.

"Not really?" Grof said, exchanging a glance with her buddy.

"We were in the middle of the pack, not really anywhere near the edge when it happened," Frei said.

"Was he ordering you away from the edge?" Fitz asked.

"Yes, but not the way you're making it sound," Grof said with a frown. "The weather was about to change, and he was anxious not to lose anybody."

"But he didn't want you near him," Fitz said.

"He didn't want us near the edge," she countered. "He needed to be there to watch the others. But those of us who were already topside were supposed to cluster around Blaser, well away from the sides of the glacier. We were awaiting orders when we heard... her scream, I guess."

"What kind of orders?" Ritchie asked.

"Blaser said we'd either be scrambling back to help the others finish the climb, or we'd be following Blaser ahead to the safety of that canyon. It ended up being the second, but only after Wyder fell," Moreau said.

"Interesting," Fitz said.

"It doesn't necessarily mean anything," Ritchie said to him.

"I don't understand," Grof said. "Are you thinking that Hansen was negligent? Surely you don't think this was deliberate?"

"I'm not thinking anything until I have more to go on," Fitz said.

"Because we all know that Hansen is in some kind of trouble down there, and there's been a lot of grumbling up here that we shouldn't be alone under his command," Grof said.

"I haven't heard that," Ritchie said.

"I have," Moreau said to her. "A lot of people aren't happy."

"But these charges are surely nonsense," Ritchie said.

"Just because you don't want to believe it doesn't mean it isn't true," Fitz said. She gave him a look of deep hurt, and he felt compelled to add. "Not that I want to believe it myself. I don't. I almost can't."

Now Moreau was shooting him dagger-eyes again. For months she was pissed at him for not talking to Ritchie, and now she's pissed because he was? He couldn't win with her.

"You think this is about that treason charge?" Grof asked. She was whispering, even though with the storm raging outside, it was impossible for anyone to overhear them.

"You know about that?" Ritchie asked. "Like, details?"

"I don't have the same level of access I had when I still worked for Colonel Devereux," she said. "But I do hear things. I know he really was charged."

"Do you know who accused him?" Ritchie asked.

"No, that I don't know," Grof said.

"We know it was a female cadet," Fitz said.

"And it had to have been someone who was here over the semester break to witness... whatever they witnessed," Ritchie said. "Do you know of anyone who fits that bill?"

"Wyder, maybe?" Fitz asked.

"I don't know. We weren't here," Grof said, looking at Frei, who also just shook her head. "We can ask around, though."

"There's another thing," Fitz said. "Three times I've seen Finn and

Joosten arguing passionately about something. They always stop before I can catch any words, but it looks serious."

"There's no way they're fraternizing," Frei said with a dry chuckle. "Finn and *Joosten*? No way. Finn might be open to anything with anyone, but Joosten just hates everybody."

"Seriously?" Fitz asked.

"Well, I don't know her well," Frei admitted. "She certainly seems to hate everybody."

He looked to Grof, who pondered, but then nodded her agreement with her buddy's assessment.

"No rumors about the two of them, then?" he said with a sigh.

"We can ask around," Grof told him.

"We'll be discrete," Frei promised. "If any of you three ask, everyone is going to know something's up. We can be like your inside gals."

Fitz wasn't sure he wanted to shift pretty much the whole investigation over to someone else, but Ritchie leaned closer to him so say, "it's a good idea."

"Really?" he asked, surprised she was so willing to let someone else take over.

"I mean, it frees us up to focus on—"

But whatever she had been about to say was left unspoken as they heard the sound of someone coming in through the outer flaps of the tent. They had a bare moment while the visitor fastened the outside door and shook off the snow. Moreau shoved the tablet into her pack, and Ritchie stepped between Fitz and the doorway.

As if she were remotely big enough to hide him.

But he found himself taking a step back, away from the light box, further into the shadows. Just in case.

"Cadets," Colonel Hansen said as he stepped through the inner flaps of the tent. He had their evening rations in his hands.

"Delivery, sir?" Grof asked as she took the block of soup from his hands and set it on the light box.

"Dinner and a head count," Hansen said. "No one is to leave their tent for any reason until you're given the command to muster. This storm is not something to mess around with. Am I understood?"

"But, sir, Cadet Captain Wyder," Ritchie said. "Her body is still out there."

"It will have to remain where it lies, cadet. I won't lose more lives retrieving a corpse."

Ritchie flinched. Only slightly, but both Fitz and the colonel saw it.

"She isn't the first casualty of this training, as you all well knew from the pre-mission briefing," he said, with not a hint of empathy. "If her body can be retrieved, it will be. But not now, and not by you cadets. When the weather breaks, you will be pressing on to the next base camp. This training has not yet even begun. Do you understand me?"

"Yes, sir," they all said together.

"Good. Eat, rest, and be ready in the morning. Those are your orders," he said and turned to go. But just before disappearing through the flaps, he looked back over his shoulder and added, "and Fitz, get back to your tent."

"Yes, sir," Fitz said.

It was a long, awkward moment before he realized that Hansen was going to stand there holding the tent flaps open until he came out.

"Talk in the morning," he whispered to Ritchie.

He watched as Hansen carefully sealed the tent's inner flaps. He had to say something, but what?

Hansen spun on his heel and glared down at him as if Fitz had spoken that flailing thought out loud and was waiting to hear what he planned to follow it up with.

But then his face softened. Not a lot, and that web of scars stood out all the darker against his cold-reddened skin, but he looked almost approachable.

"Look out for each other," Hansen said.

"Yes, sir," Fitz said, confused. Did the colonel mean he and Ritchie each other, or every cadet in the camp each other?

But the colonel just pushed out into the blowing snow and disappeared so quickly it was like the alpine storm just swallowed him up whole.

11

RITCHIE WAS PRETTY sure she'd never once woken up panicked about how well rested she felt.

But panic wasn't an overreaction. Not only did she live a highly structured life in the academy, even during her breaks from school, she kept her implant alarm set to wake her early in the morning. Opening her eyes to a feeling of blessed restfulness, like she had taken a long lie-in on the sort of holiday she never gave herself? That wasn't normal. Not at all.

And the only explanation for that abnormality was someone was messing with her implant. Again.

"Relax. It's all of us," Moreau said. Ritchie couldn't even see the top of Moreau's head, she was so deeply buried inside her puffy sleeping bag, but she must be at least partly awake to hear Ritchie sit up with a gasp like that.

"We *were* given orders to rest," Grof said. "The colonel can override alarms on our implants. Although doing it without telling us is obviously not cool."

"Why would he do it, though?" Ritchie asked, climbing out of the warmth of her bag and reaching for her boots. Grof just shrugged and yawned. She was poking at another meal ration package that was just starting to send up curls of steam from on top of the light box. "You went out already?"

"No, this was sitting inside the door," she said. "I guess we're still under orders to stay inside the tents."

Ritchie finished fastening her boots and walked over to see some sort of thick savory porridge, bits of egg and bacon mixed into a creamy oatmeal that smelled of a variety of herbs. Climbing all day in freezing weather was almost worth it just for the improvement in the food.

"Will he lock down my implant if I break that order?" Ritchie asked, but she was only half-joking. Until she had come to the Oymyakon Foreign Service Academy, the piece of hardware that lurked within her brain wasn't something she had ever had cause to worry about. But since then she had realized just how vulnerable it was to manipulation.

Implants were supposed to be unhackable. It required someone both skilled and driven to even attempt to mess with it. But since leaving home for the Oymyakon Foreign Service Academy, Ritchie had kept running afoul of skilled and driven people who really wanted to mess with her.

Now even a minor thing, like snoozing her alarm, made her both fearful and angry at once.

She stepped into the tent doorway and opened the outer flaps to look outside. The wind had stopped at some point during the night—she had a vague memory of the howling dying away and herself drifting into a deeper sleep afterwards—but snow was still falling heavily. The tents around theirs were mere suggestions of lumps under thick blankets of snow.

And no one was out there. There weren't even any tracks leading up to the door. A lot of snow had fallen since their breakfast had been delivered.

"Moreau, Frei, get up and let's eat," Grof said as she moved the porridge off the light box. The smell of bacon was strong enough to lure Ritchie away from the open door. She ducked back inside, but before she had quite fastened the inner flaps, there was a rustle from where she had just been standing.

"Knock-knock?" someone called, and then a head popped into view.

Feena Berweger. Ritchie didn't know what she had been expecting, but it definitely hadn't been that. Feena smiled at her and then thrust a large metal thermos through the flap, holding it out to her. "We brought coffee. Not the school stuff, either. This is my own personal stash I'm willing to share with you guys. Can we come in?"

"We?" Ritchie said, suddenly terrified that Finn Berweger was going to be the next face to pop through that door.

But the sight of Joosten's face wasn't exactly a step up.

"We brought our own food. We just didn't want to eat alone," Feena said as she stepped inside. She thrust the coffee into Ritchie's hands, then turned to wave for someone else to follow her and Joosten into the space between the tent doors.

The last cadet was buried deep inside her parka, and only after the door was firmly sealed did she push back her hood enough for Ritchie to see it was Cadet Heim. She looked anxious, like she very much wished to be anywhere else but here, imposing on another tentful of cadets while her own roommates carried on breaking rules.

"Come on in," Ritchie said to her with a smile. "We certainly have room enough." Feena was already inside, and Joosten didn't spare Ritchie a glance as she brushed past her. But Heim was still hovering uncertainly near the door. "It's not like you left the camp or anything. We're still together in a group, out of the weather. I'm sure it's okay."

"You're right," Heim said, but couldn't quite get the twitching in her lips to form a smile. Her eyes had the dry, glassy look of someone who had needed to cry hours ago but hadn't had a moment alone to do it. Ritchie suddenly felt guilty for her long, deep night's worth of sleep.

"I'm sorry, I have no idea, but was Wyder your buddy?" she asked.

"Me? No, Joosten was Wyder's buddy," Heim said.

"Oh, that's right," Ritchie agreed, although she wasn't sure she had ever known that. "Wait, that means you and—" she couldn't finish the thought, but Heim just nodded sorrowfully. "Wow. You have my sympathies."

That got the smallest of smiles out of her.

"Ritchie? You eating?" Grof called.

"Yep!" Ritchie said, then gestured for Heim to precede her into the main room.

Moreau was sitting up but still inside her sleeping bag, her hair twisted into knots all around her head. She poked out a single arm to take the bowl that Frei was holding out to her, but then had to bring the other arm out to grasp the spoon.

"It's been such a long night, especially for Thecla," Feena was all but cooing. Ritchie guessed that Thecla was Joosten's first name, although nothing on Joosten's face showed any awareness that Feena was talking about her. She just carried on eating her porridge as if none of them were there at all.

Was she in shock?

Ritchie wasn't sure. If she had to guess, she'd say that Heim was more distraught over Wyder's accident than Joosten was, but not everyone processed emotions the same way. She could see that Heim had been holding her own feelings in. Who was she to say that Joosten wasn't doing the same, only with far more success at hiding the effort?

"Were any of you there when she fell?" Ritchie asked.

"What kind of question is that?" Joosten asked. Her words were weirdly inflected, not displaying any outrage or dismay or anything, really. But it was very aggressive wording.

"Ritchie was there," Moreau said, trying and failing to push the tangles of hair out of her face. "She was right under Wyder when it happened. If Fitz hadn't been there, she might've been hit."

"Well, of course Fitz was there," Feena said with a sly smile, her eyes bright.

"What's that supposed to mean?" Moreau asked, not seeing Ritchie's hand gesture for her to drop it. She didn't need to listen to Feena's thoughts about her and Fitz. She wasn't even curious.

"Only he likes to be heroic, doesn't he?" Feena said. "In fact, he's rather good at it."

"If he had been feeling heroic, he could've saved the actual cadet in danger," Joosten said. Again, the aggressive words paired up with the voice like an automaton. It was actually kind of irritating, and Ritchie had to remind herself that this was a person who probably needed a little sympathy, even if she wasn't showing it.

"We didn't see her slipping until it was too late," Ritchie said. But then she couldn't help adding, "where were you? You're her buddy, right?"

Joosten's face went a livid shade of purple. Feena set her own bowl of porridge aside to put her arm around Joosten. Ritchie remembered what Moreau had said, about the hypnotic power of Feena's touch. She had never felt it herself. Certainly, Joosten looked unmoved. But Feena kept up the friendly embrace, looking fondly at Joosten as she said, "Wyder told us to go on ahead. All three of us, right, Heim?"

Heim jumped, as if startled to hear her own name. But she quickly recovered and said, "Cadet Captain Wyder ordered us to fall in with Cadet Captain Blaser. He was on point, and we'd be moving forward at his command. Wyder was falling back to check on the end of the column of climbers."

"So she got to the top then came back down?" Ritchie asked. Heim nodded. Ritchie made a mental note of that fact, but she wasn't sure if it meant anything at all.

"I know I should've been with her," Joosten said in her robotic voice. "I regret I wasn't there. I regret what happened to her. Not that I even know what *did* happen to her."

"It's different when your buddy is a cadet captain," Feena assured her, patting her on the back in a gesture that Ritchie was sure Joosten was only tolerating.

"Have you guys known each other long?" Ritchie asked. "I mean you and your brother and Joosten here."

"Why do you ask?" Feena asked without so much as a trace of suspicion in her tone.

"You seem... close," Ritchie said. She could sense Moreau covering up a smirk, but didn't dare make eye contact with her.

"We met last year," Joosten said. "We've been friends since."

"Good friends," Feena assured her, brushing a loose strand of hair back from Joosten's eyelashes.

"And Finn?" Ritchie asked.

"Why, Cadet Ritchie, is this a sudden interest in my brother I'm sensing?" Feena asked. She was cooing again.

But through it all, she didn't seem to be using her real powers. Was that a deliberate choice? Looking back, Ritchie couldn't think of a time when she'd seen Feena try to put the whammy on someone all on her own. She did it with her brother, and not necessarily at his command or anything. And she thought maybe she had seen Finn do it alone on occasion. But never just Feena.

Of course, she wasn't a guy. And neither was Joosten. Maybe it was different when Feena was alone with a guy.

Maybe it was different when she was alone with Fitz.

All of them in the tent gasped in one breath as their implants suddenly started receiving an influx of messages. Most were the usual school announcements, plus messages from friends and family and the like. But all together, it meant that the communications equipment in the supply building had connected with the school again.

But before they could touch any of it, they received the command to muster immediately.

"It's from Blaser, not Hansen," Moreau whispered to Ritchie as they hurried into their parkas and other outerwear.

"I know," Ritchie said. "What do you think it means?"

"No idea," Moreau said.

The seven of them headed outside to see the last of the snow had finally stopped falling. But the ground was covered in a new blanket of thick, white sludge that made the hike towards the center of the camp slow, awkward going.

They were among the last to gather, but even so, no one seemed to know what was going on. There was a lot of fidgeting and shuffling about and an indistinct murmur of whispers. Ritchie turned her attention to her inbox.

Twelve messages from Guy. More than the one a day he had promised. And no hope of a private moment to view any of them until she got back to school.

But the time stamps ended abruptly several hours before.

"I think we only got a partial download," she said to Moreau, who was still trying to get wayward strands of her long blonde hair tucked up inside her hat. Her gloved hands weren't exactly helping.

"You're right," she said. "I even have a corrupted download. The signal dropped before it had finished. He must've gotten the communications up, but only for a moment."

"But who's *he*?" Ritchie wondered. "Hansen or Blaser?"

"Attention, cadets!" Blaser called. He stepped up onto a box so they could all see him, and they pressed in closer, both to hear him better and for warmth. Even without the wind, the air was far below freezing.

"I suppose you've noticed I managed a short link to the academy, but it went down again almost at once, so we're still on our own up here."

"Are we going on to the next base camp?" someone asked.

"Good question. Yes, we are, but it's too late to start out today. As my fellow last-years will tell you, this leg is the easiest hike, but the longest day. And the end bit is very tricky, a narrow ledge with death on either side. We won't be attempting that in the dark. But we will be heading out first thing tomorrow morning."

"Where's Hansen?" Fitz asked. He was suddenly standing so close to Ritchie she nearly jumped when he spoke. A few others in the crowd repeated the question, followed up with several more questions, and Blaser had to hold up both of his gloved hands to signal them to quiet down.

"That's why I gathered you all here," he said. "Has anyone seen the colonel since dinner last night?"

Murmurs rippled through the crowd, but all the heads were shaking no.

"Did you deliver breakfast?" Fitz asked.

"I did not," Blaser said. "Does anyone know what time that happened?"

Another frustrating round of head shaking. No one had been awake to see it. But the packages had been left just inside the outer doors of each of the tents. That was starting to feel deliberate. Maybe even sneaky.

"Right, so it sounds like the colonel is missing," Blaser said. "The colonel is missing, and we're down one cadet captain."

"But did he leave us, or was he taken away?" Fitz whispered to Ritchie.

"I don't know which is the more upsetting possibility," Ritchie whispered back.

"Last-years, I'm going to divide you up into search parties," Blaser was saying, but Fitz took Ritchie by the elbow and pulled her further out of the crowd of cadets.

"I don't know either," he said. "But let's start finding out."

"How?"

"Let's check his tent."

Ritchie couldn't believe that Blaser wouldn't have done that already, but she just nodded. If only the last-years were going out on the search parties, there was nothing more they could do where they were. And she had to be doing something.

12

THE TWO OF them were outside the perimeter of the camp before Fitz found the flaw in his plan.

He had no idea which tent was Hansen's.

"Where are we going?" Ritchie asked when they had left the last of the tents behind. He spun on his heel to look back at the camp.

Like he was going to admit that the main thing he had wanted was to get away from all the others. But their presence was like an increasing pressure on his mind. It was nearly impossible to know who was who until you were practically nose to nose with them, except for Blaser with his gold stripe.

Finn was the tallest, but Fitz couldn't shake the feeling that Finn could make himself seem smaller if he wanted to blend in.

"I wanted to ask you something," Ritchie said. He looked over at her and her cheeks were flushed, not from the cold. "Never mind," she said and even took a step back from him.

"What is it?" he asked. It's not like he knew where to go from here, anyway.

"Well, before Blaser called the muster, Feena, Joosten and Heim were in our tent," she said.

"Learn anything from Joosten?" he asked.

"Not really. She's... strange."

"Yeah, I can't get a read on her either," Fitz sighed. Then added, "go on."

"Yes, well, it's just... that thing the Berwegers do? She wasn't doing it."

"Okay," Fitz said, not really following her at all.

"You know what I mean. She does it to girls as much as guys. She can spin Moreau up if she focuses on it, and I know she's done it to Joosten before, too. I've seen it in the cafeteria back at the academy."

"When she wants something," Fitz said. "Did she want something?"

"No, that's not what I'm wondering," Ritchie said. She seemed to be feeling frustrated, not able to find her words. But he was getting a little frustrated, too.

"Are you afraid she's going to turn her attention on you?" he asked. A touch more aggressively than he had intended to. "Is she threatening you?"

"No," Ritchie said. "No threats, and I'm not afraid of her, even if she did try to threaten me. Not that I want to be left alone with her to test how I'd hold up to her focused attention or anything. But that leads back to my question. Is this something she only does when her brother is there?"

"No," Fitz said, but then had to think about it. "I don't think so?"

"You're not sure?" She sounded decidedly nervous by his answer.

"You know they don't get to me the same way they get to other people, right?" he said.

"But how is that possible?" she asked.

"Not a clue. It's just something I've noticed," he said.

"No technique to share with the rest of us?" she said, too earnestly to really be joking.

"Sorry," he said. "But I can tell when they're trying to put the whammy on me. I mean, I feel *something*. It's just not overwhelming for me."

"And?" she prompted.

"I'd have to really think about it some more, but off the top of my head, I'd say they definitely do it more when the two of them are together. Like they feed off each other. But Finn will try it on his own too."

"And Feena? Does she try it on her own?" She sounded weird, like she was trying too hard to sound casual. Like she desperately wanted this to seem like a mere question of general scientific interest. Nothing personal at stake for either of them at all.

"Wyss doesn't think she's been trying it on me," he said.

"What's that supposed to mean?" Ritchie demanded, suddenly inexplicably angry. "I wasn't asking what Wyss thought."

"Well, I don't think so either, but it seems like the input of an impartial observer might mean something here," he shot back.

"Right. You're right. I'm sorry," she said.

"I hate this with the Berwegers, you know. I hate that I have to tangle up with them at all," he said.

"I know. I only wondered."

"If Feena has been trying to put the whammy on me?" he asked, then held out his arms. "Behold her lack of success."

Ritchie flushed again. "Actually, I was wondering if she's only doing it because her brother wants her to. Like if he wasn't there, she'd be a different person."

"She's evil, and she's manipulative," Fitz said firmly. "And her brother is always there. No need to debate hypotheticals. We have enough on our plates as it is."

"Just where is this tent?" Ritchie asked.

Fitz looked around, then saw a single tent further out from the perimeter than all the others. It was positioned between the circular camp and the closest cliff to the south. Just where a good protector would position themselves: between their wards and danger.

"That one," he said, and led the way through the dense snowfall towards the tent.

"You know we didn't get a full upload this morning," Ritchie said as they walked.

"Missing some messages from Guy?" he asked. Too sharply. His teasing tone needed a little work.

"I don't know how there could've been more," she said, completely unbothered, and he regretted saying anything at all. But he just couldn't help himself.

"So you really like this guy Guy?"

"Yeah," she said. "I know what you're thinking."

"I doubt it," he said.

"You think that Guy is just some rich kid spending his parents' money on endless parties, never taking anything too seriously. My total opposite, but not in an 'opposites attract' kind of way. Nothing about the two of us could ever line up. You can't wrap your mind around this at all."

"Okay, maybe you do know what I'm thinking," he said grumpily.

"He reminds me of Moreau," she said. "I had this whole picture of who Moreau was when I met her, but I was all wrong about her. She's far more driven than she seemed at first, and she's the best, most loyal friend I could ever ask for."

Fitz felt like she'd just stabbed him in the heart. Moreau was now her best friend. And she just said it so blithely, not to be hurtful but just stating a fact. He almost staggered before he recovered himself, but given the difficulties they were already having trudging through the snow, he doubted she'd noticed.

Indeed, she just kept on talking, "Guy's sister is the one who adores parties. She has from a very young age. And her parents don't really care to spend all their time throwing bashes for kids. So it's been Guy's job to keep his sister happy. He's so good at it, it's kind of hard to tell he's just not that interested in most of the people that show up for his parties. I didn't, not at first. You know, like with Moreau. I only saw the surface thing. Although he adores his sister. I saw that pretty clearly."

Fitz decided not to volunteer his opinion of Cicey Travert at that time.

"He loves the ocean, but he never swims. It's sailing over it in ships that he adores. He has plans to build his own wind-driven vessel, like the ancients used to sail, you know? His parents say it isn't safe, so he can't do it yet, but he's been studying all the designs. He's mastered navigation using only the equipment the ancient sailors used, and he can tie just about any knot you can name. Actually, a lot more than I could name."

"You like him. That's great," Fitz said. "We're here."

He started to open the tent flaps, but Ritchie put her hand on his wrist. He didn't look up at her, but he waited for her to finish whatever it was that she had to say.

She was clearly waiting for him to meet her eyes, but in the end she gave in with a sigh. "I just wanted you to know I wasn't doing anything underhanded. I didn't know you were there when we said goodbye. I wasn't trying to rub your face in anything. But, in my defense, I couldn't tell you about it before because *you* weren't talking to *me*."

"You really don't need to explain anything to me. It's your life. I mean, it is interfering in our investigation at the moment, but only because you're insisting that we talk about it *right now*."

She let him go, so quickly it was like touching him burned her.

He didn't dare look up at her face. He just pushed his way into the tent.

Ritchie took a moment before following him inside. The red circles on her cheeks were prominent, but she immediately set to work searching the tent to the right of the door.

He took the left side, and they met in the middle at the back of the space. It took less than a minute.

"All of his stuff is gone," Ritchie said. "He gets a cot. Must be nice for him. And a desk. But his personal stuff is all gone."

"Not everything," Fitz said, pointing towards the desk. "He left a pair of gloves behind. As well as the rope."

"The rope he was holding?" Ritchie asked. They gathered around the desk.

He picked up the gloves and turned them over. The palms were blackened and burned, leaving exposed holes clear to the bottoms of the fingers. "No wonder he left these behind. Worthless now."

"The rope is burned too, like you said Wyder's was," Ritchie said, examining the charred end.

"Her gloves as well," Fitz said. He held up one of Hansen's gloves to show her the palm. "When she fell, she had her hand out. It was just like this."

Ritchie brushed the charred edge of the rope delicately with her bare fingertip. "What would do this? We didn't see any fire."

"It smells kind of chemical," Fitz said, sniffing the gloves. "Although I have no idea what it would smell like if you burned a pair of climbing gloves with fire. Its nanotechnology that makes them adhere to the ice, right? Does that have a smell?"

"Wyss would know," Ritchie said. She sniffed at the rope, made a face, and set it back on the desk. "This doesn't help our conundrum at all. Did he take his equipment and leave, or did someone drag him off and take all of his stuff with him?"

"I don't believe that Hansen could kill a cadet," Fitz said.

"Not like that. Not in public with dozens of witnesses," Ritchie agreed.

"I don't believe he would at all. It's just not him," Fitz said. "I know he served in combat, which is rare for a guardian. And it certainly feels like he saw things, did things, he's never going to tell the likes of us. But killing a cadet under his command?"

"You'd think if he were going to, he would've started with the Berwegers," Ritchie said. He knew it was her attempt at a joke, but he couldn't even pretend to laugh.

Then they both froze in place, once more startled by their implants coming to life. Blaser had sent out a message to all of them.

"No sign of Hansen, no surprise," Fitz sighed.

"And we press on in the morning, with or without him," Ritchie said. She gave Fitz a nervous look. "Is that wise?"

"I think so," he said. "I'm with Blaser. The third base camp is in a better position to evacuate us on shuttles if need be. It's also in direct line of sight with the school. That will improve our chances to get through to Wyss. I had no luck at all this morning, and I was trying the minute my inbox lit up."

"I should've thought of that," Ritchie said, clearly meaning contacting Wyss.

But then the rest of what he had said sunk in, and she just stood there gaping at him.

"What? I did the reading. Why does everyone think I skate by without doing the homework?"

"I wasn't thinking that at all," Ritchie said.

"Sure you weren't," he grumbled. He started to head out the door, then changed his mind and went back to the desk, zipping open the large pocket on the front of his parka. "There's nothing we can do with this stuff here, but when we get back down, maybe Wyss can learn something from it," he said as he shoved the gloves inside.

"Good idea," Ritchie said, and coiled up the rope before handing it to him. She wasn't looking at him again when she said, "I didn't get anything useful out of Joosten, but there were five other people in the room. A one-on-one conversation would be better, if I can arrange it. Have you tried talking to Finn at all?"

"No, not yet," he admitted. "I had a conversation with him yesterday. It was aggravating enough without me actually trying to get any information out of him."

"Maybe I—" Ritchie started to say, but he couldn't let her even finish that thought.

"Absolutely not," Fitz said.

"Why?" she asked, getting angry again. "You don't think I can handle him? I don't have your natural resistance or whatever?"

"You don't," Fitz said.

"You really think I'd be swept up into his thrall?" she demanded.

"That's not what I'm afraid of," he said.

"What are you afraid of?" she asked.

She asked twice more before he managed to get through both layers of tent flaps and out into the blinding midday snow.

He couldn't go there. Even dodging that question would involve touching on thoughts and memories he kept locked down for a reason.

But one thing was certain. He wasn't going to be able to avoid talking to Finn. But he really wasn't looking forward to it.

13

THE NEXT MORNING, they were all up before the sun had even risen over the eastern slope of the mountain. It had stopped snowing, and Ritchie was shocked to catch a rare glimpse of a star in the Oymyakon sky through tiny breaks in the ever-present cloud cover.

The snow had stopped falling the afternoon before, and the wind had died away as well. The air was still and so quiet it seemed to make her ears ring, as if she could hear her own eardrums straining to pick up any kind of stimulus.

The lack of wind was welcome, but the air itself was shockingly cold. Ritchie was grateful there would be no climbing that day, just hiking. That meant they were all wearing their warmest gloves and boots, leaving the more flexible but not as insulated climbing gear in their packs.

As she tucked her hair inside her tight-fitting knit cap, then covered it with the warmer lined hat and fastened the ear flaps together under her chin, she remembered when she and Moreau had been telling Sokolov and Wyss about the diving on Epsilon 20.

It was a good thing that diving suits and spacesuits didn't trigger her claustrophobia at all, because this alpine gear was just as smothering as either of those. The layers were bulky, and she couldn't really feel anything with her hands or even see anything that wasn't within the range of the tunnel left by her parka hood directly in front of her. She would be pretty miserable if that was something that bothered her.

But as she stood at the edge of the base camp meadow looking out over the glacier they had climbed two days before and all the valleys and mountains beyond, her spirit felt light. It was a large world all around her. Even the usually oppressive skies were just high, wispy clouds chasing each other across the brightening sky.

She could do this.

She turned away from the edge and trudged back across the snow to where the others were gathered around the supply building. Blaser was gathering the tents and distributing protein bars for breakfast. They'd have to eat and hike both for breakfast and later lunch as well, but it was important to make good time up the mountain. Darkness would be their enemy, particularly for that last stretch of the path before they reached the third base camp.

"No sign of Hansen?" Moreau said to her as she handed Ritchie her protein bar.

"Nothing," Ritchie said.

"Blaser is leaving his tent up. Just in case," Moreau said.

"Good," Ritchie said. "I'm sure he'll be back from wherever he went."

"Wherever he went with all of his equipment without telling anyone where he was going or when he'd be back," Moreau said.

"He must've gone back for Wyder," Ritchie said. "He didn't say anything, because he didn't want to get our hopes up. He might not find her."

"Maybe," Moreau said, but she didn't sound like she remotely believed it.

"Nothing else makes sense," Ritchie said. She didn't add that she'd been up half the night trying to come up with some other theory.

"Whoever killed Wyder killed Hansen and threw his stuff over after him," Moreau said.

Which had been the only other theory, the one Ritchie refused to entertain.

"Time to head out!" Blaser called to all of them. Then he gave orders she couldn't hear to a group of last-year cadets. Some of them ran ahead to lead the way, but others lingered, waiting for the others to go so they could bring up the rear.

"Where's Fitz?" Ritchie asked. With everyone in their parkas, she couldn't tell one cadet from another save for the very tallest and very shortest. Normally she would know Fitz just by his walk, but the deep drifts of snow made that impossible.

"I think that's him up at the front of the pack," Moreau said with a frown. "Is he back to freeze-out mode?"

"No," Ritchie said. "Really, there's no reason for us to walk together. We don't have enough information to come up with any theories, and it's easier to talk to people if we're not together."

"So you two discussed this?" Moreau said sharply.

"Well, no, but it makes sense," Ritchie said.

Moreau had that tight look on her face, one that Ritchie had seen many times during the last few months. As far as Ritchie knew, she had never cornered Fitz to give him a piece of her mind. But she always looked like she was about to run him down like a jungle cat, tackle him to the ground, and do just that.

"I think he wants to talk to Finn, and he doesn't want me there for that," Ritchie said.

"And Frei and Grof were going to sound out Joosten," Moreau said. "Let's get going. I want to stay within earshot of them."

"Sure," Ritchie said.

But she couldn't keep up the pace. Not that the hike was too challenging for her or anything. The path was on the narrow side, not letting the cadets walk more than two abreast, but the last of the winds had been blown it clear of snow.

And the sun as it rose was only barely discernable as a bright disk behind the constant gray cloud cover. It wasn't reflecting with blinding intensity off the ice and snow.

No, the reason Ritchie was dawdling at the back of the line was that she couldn't stop looking back down towards the base camp.

The path they were following up the steep mountain slope was a zig-zag of switchbacks. Each time they passed over the camp again, it was a little harder to see the shapeless lump of snow that was Colonel

Hansen's tent. There was never any sign of him when she looked, but she couldn't stop herself from checking each time they passed.

"We have to keep moving. It really is a race against time, this leg," Heim said to Ritchie when she saw that Ritchie had stopped to shade her eyes and peer down towards the glacier again. But she added, "Colonel Hansen knows where we're going."

"I know. It just doesn't feel right leaving without finding him first," Ritchie said.

"I know," Heim agreed, falling into step beside Ritchie as they continued the hike. "It's strange that he didn't tell Blaser or anyone where he was going or anything. It's not like him at all."

"I'm sure there was a reason," Ritchie said. "I'm just afraid to find out what it is."

"You and Fitz are investigating?" Heim asked.

"Sort of," Ritchie said. "I guess we've gotten a bit of a reputation for poking our noses into things."

"And solving crimes," Heim said. "But he's not here with you now."

"No," Ritchie said, and left it at that.

They had to shift to single file as the path made another narrow switch back. Then the grade was suddenly a lot steeper, and Ritchie had to focus on moving one foot after the other. The ringing in her ears was back, even though she could hear her own breathing and the skittering of rocks under her boots.

"Here is your last chance to look back," Heim said, and the two of them drew to a halt. Ritchie could see that the path ahead of them cut through a narrow gorge before continuing on around a jagged ridge to the far side of the mountain. She turned to try to take one last look back toward the camp, but she could no longer tell which bit of lumpy snow was Hansen's tent.

"Okay, I'm good," Ritchie said, and continued hiking at a swifter pace. "I'll stop dragging my feet now."

"We have fallen a bit behind, but we'll catch up before lunch," Heim said.

They walked in silence for a bit, but the path was leveling out through the gorge, and Ritchie soon had her breath back. "So how's Joosten doing?" she asked.

"Better than Feena seems to think she is," Heim said. "It can be a little hard to tell with Joosten, though. She tends to keep people at arm's length under the best of circumstances."

"She seems close with Finn," Ritchie said.

"Does she?" Heim said with a frown. "Sure, I guess I could see that. She's more open with him than with most people. But I think Finn brings that sort of thing out in lots of people."

Ritchie had to remind herself that most people didn't know what she did about the Berwegers. Or rather, what Wyss suspected was true, about their unnatural power over people. Most of the cadets just thought of it as popularity, pure and simple. "Feena does too, doesn't she?" she said, just to see what Heim thought.

"Yes, she does. I guess it's no surprise they're both opting for diplomat training next year," Heim said.

"Really? I don't know why I thought Finn was going to be a guardian," Ritchie said.

"No, they've both been accepted at the diplomat school, same as me," Heim said.

"What about Joosten?" Ritchie asked.

"Guardian. Wyder was planning on guardian school as well. They were going to continue being buddies there," Heim said.

"They were that close of friends?" Ritchie asked.

"Does it sound mean if I say I think they were just used to each other?" Heim asked, wincing just a bit.

"I suppose better the buddy you know than the new randomly selected buddy you'll be assigned," Ritchie agreed. But then she said, "so are you and Feena still going to be buddies since you're both going to diplomat school?"

"We haven't talked about it," Heim said. "My first buddy dropped out midway through my first year. She just couldn't hack it. I had two more that first year, same thing. I guess I've stopped really trying to bond with any of the new ones since. But Feena is all right. We've been together all year so far. That's a record for me. It's just, no one is ever going to be closer to her than her brother. Believe me. They are tight."

"I definitely believe that," Ritchie said.

They walked together in silence again, and Ritchie just focused on closing the gap between the two of them and the tail of the line of cadets ahead of them. But she started to sense that Heim beside her was wrestling with saying something. She decided, having an entire day's worth of time, to wait for her to be ready to speak.

But it was tough. Ritchie preferred to be more direct. And after nearly an hour's worth of Heim almost opening her mouth to speak and then just not doing it, that she began to suspect it was never going to happen.

But in the end Heim finally said, in a very soft voice even though there was no one remotely close enough to overhear them, "are you sure what happened to Wyder wasn't an accident?"

"Do you think it was?" Ritchie asked, surprised.

"Well, how could it be murder? Who would want to kill Wyder?" she asked.

"That part is definitely a mystery," Ritchie agreed. "But I really don't think it was an accident either."

"I know it's supposed to be impossible for us to fall," Heim said, looking down at her own padded gloves. Ritchie supposed she was imagining the climbing gloves they had all been wearing at the time.

"She was sliding," Ritchie said. "Her gloves weren't holding like they were supposed to."

"So it *was* an accident?" Heim asked.

"No," Ritchie said, but before she could say more, Heim was pouring her heart out.

"Because I'm really afraid that Wyder might've caused her own accident. Not deliberately!" she quickly added, her face even paler than usual. "No, I don't think she wanted to die or anything. But I'm not sure her mind was on what she was doing the way it ought to have been. Ugh! I shouldn't be saying these things out loud." She buried her face in her gloved hands.

"Heim, it's okay," Ritchie said, and stopped hiking to put her arms around Heim.

"She was just so distracted," Heim said. "Something was bothering her, but she wouldn't talk about it. She looked tired and sad, and I was sure something was wrong at home or something. But she wouldn't talk to me."

"Did she talk to Joosten about it, do you think?" Ritchie asked.

"Maybe?" Heim said. Then she pulled herself together in an instant, tugging at Ritchie's sleeve to get them both walking again.

"Fitz saw Wyder when she fell past us," Ritchie said, and now she was the one keeping her voice low for no reason. Respect, maybe.

"How horrible for him," Heim said with sympathy.

"He told me that the rope in her hands had been burned through, and so were the palms of her gloves," Ritchie said. "And we found Hansen's gloves in his tent after he disappeared, as well as the rest of the rope. They were burned as well."

"Burned by what?" Heim asked.

"We don't know. We're hoping to figure that out when we get back to school. The point is, it wasn't an accident, and it certainly wasn't Wyder's fault. She didn't fall because of her emotional state. She did everything she could to keep herself on the ice, but someone really wanted her dead."

"I don't know how to feel about that," Heim said, looking up towards the cloud-filled sky.

"It's okay if you're relieved that not getting her to talk didn't play a part in it," Ritchie said. "I would be relieved to know that."

"It feels kind of selfish," Heim said.

"Kind of selfish to not blame yourself for something you didn't do?" Ritchie asked.

Heim took a deep breath. "Well, if you're going to put it that way."

"I am," Ritchie said. "What happened to Wyder is definitely not your fault."

"If only we knew whose it was," Heim sighed.

Ritchie sighed as well. That was, after all, the real question.

14

FITZ FELT like he was trapped inside some silent version of a children's playground game of keep-away.

Part of it was on him. He definitely didn't want to be near Ritchie if he didn't have to. He told himself that with no new clues in their case, there was no reason he *should* be near her.

But the truth was, he couldn't listen to another minute of her rhapsodizing about Guy Travert. There was a voice in the back of his head that kept whispering that he didn't know Guy at all, not really. But the louder voices in the front of his head were delineating all the ways that what she said didn't fit with the Guy he knew. Not at all.

But she didn't seem to want to be near him either, as he never even laid eyes on her after they left the base camp, so whatever.

But then the silent game got more complicated. Because he *did* want to talk to Finn, but Finn was deftly keeping away from him. Occasionally, Fitz would catch sight of him and would try to fall into step with him. But despite being considerably taller than any of the others, Finn could slip from sight through packs of cadets. He never made eye contact with Fitz, but Fitz knew that Finn knew he was trying to talk to him. And he was avoiding that like the plague.

For his part, Fitz was trying to avoid Finn's sister, but he had far less success. By the time the afternoon was fading into evening, he had given up all together.

So when he reached the bluff before the last stretch of trail before the third base camp, it was with Feena at his side. She was saying something, but he wasn't even pretending to listen.

Her little clingy grabs at his arm were harder to tune out.

Fitz stopped at the edge of the bluff to sip at his water bottle and examine the path ahead. He had no fear of heights, but what lay ahead of them was going to require a certain *respect* for heights. He could see where they would end up was a wide, snowy bluff much like the one they stood on now, if more than a hundred meters higher up.

But the path between the two bluffs was across a thin, stony buttress that looked like the next hard wind was going to blow it down to the chasm below. He took another drink and swallowed hard.

"Fitz! Good," Blaser said as he marched up to where Fitz stood at the edge, Feena by his side. "I'm going to stay here to keep a head count and make sure we're all across. I need you to go on ahead and meet the scout party at the caves at the edge of the base camp above."

"Okay," Fitz said. "What's up?"

"The temperature is dropping, as you've probably noticed," Blaser said.

Fitz didn't quite bark out a laugh. They had all put their face coverings on shortly after lunch. They made vision a bit tricky, but that was a far sight better than the real risk of frostbite to any exposed skin.

"Yeah, but there's also a storm blowing in, and I'm really worried about getting everyone past here in time," he said.

"Ritchie's back there," Fitz said.

"Oh, Ritchie," Feena said as if concerned, looking back down the trail.

"Heim is with her," Blaser told him. "They've been bringing up the rear since we left base camp, but they've been moving faster since lunch. You don't need to worry about them. But I do need you to go ahead and tell the scout group to get the heaters running inside the caves. The temperature is going to be more dangerous than the wind, at least once we're past this point on the trail."

"No tents?" Feena asked with undisguised delight.

"No tents," Blaser said. "Maybe Hansen would've made a different call, but Hansen's not here. I'm going to make sure that no one freezes to death on top of everything else that's happened."

"Got it. You can rely on us," Feena said, grabbing Fitz's arm again.

Blaser lifted his eyebrows—Fitz could just make out this detail through his visor in the fading light—but he said nothing except, "single file."

"Of course," Feena said, but didn't let Fitz go.

Fitz pulled her with him to the edge of the stony buttress. It was wide enough for them to walk abreast, but just barely. A single rope hung at waist height, securely anchored on both ends. The scouting group must've just set it up, as the rope itself showed no sign of weathering.

"I'll go first. You come behind me," Fitz said.

"Do I make you nervous?" Feena asked with a teasing look in her eyes.

"No," he said. "Just give me a little space, all right?"

"Sure," she said, and waited for him to attach his safety line to the guide rope before doing the same with her own.

Fitz walked out onto the rocky prominence, and because he couldn't help himself, he instantly looked down into the chasm below him.

Or tried to. In the growing darkness, he couldn't make out just where the bottom was. But there were a lot of icy and rocky protrusions between him and the eventual bottom, anyway. He doubted anyone would have to fall all the way before hitting something that would kill them.

His steps were not quite as brisk as he had intended, but he kept up a steady pace. There was wind out in the open that he hadn't felt on the bluff tucked against the side of the mountain. He couldn't feel the coldness of it, not through all his warm layers. He couldn't even really hear it through the flaps of his hat and the hood of his parka. But he could feel it, pushing on him.

Pushing on him with the unspoken threat that at any moment, without warning, it could push harder.

He felt Feena's hand on his shoulder, just a squeezing gesture of comfort. She didn't say anything, and she didn't try to draw him back to her or push him to move faster.

He hated how comforting that touch was. But with her hand on his shoulder, he was able to tune out the wind's influence on his mind. He pressed on until they reached the far side and could untie their safety lines from the rope.

He paused there for a moment, looking back at the other cadets below and behind them. They were black smudges on a gray background. More than a dozen were already crossing the rocky bridge. The others were gathering on the bluff near Blaser to wait their turn.

But if Ritchie were among either group, Fitz couldn't tell.

"She'll be okay," Feena said. "We have a job to do."

"Right," Fitz said, looking around the bluff. Feena pointed to the narrow path that climbed steeply up through a gash in the rock and ice, and they followed it as it twisted around a cathedral-sized rocky prominence to another open alpine meadow, now covered in snow.

"Hey!" someone called out as they jogged over to Fitz. It was only when he stopped right in front of him that Fitz realized it was Kung.

"Hey. Blaser says no tents," Fitz said. "He wants everyone inside the caves."

"And to turn on the heat," Feena reminded him.

"Right. Heat," Fitz said.

"Got it. It's this way," Kung said. They followed him to a structure much like the supply building at the base camp below, but this one was set flush with the side of the mountain itself. The first part of the interior was the same as well, pallets of tents and rations as well as a communications console set into the wall. But further in the squared-off walls of the structure became the natural stone formations of cave walls. There were lights strung up everywhere, but the cave took a turn almost at once, blocking the deeper portions from view.

"How deep does this go?" Fitz asked.

"No idea," Kung said, leading them down the narrow cave into a larger open cavern. The lights were attached to the ceiling, but that was so far overhead that Fitz couldn't even see where the fixtures were among the stalactites. The floor was smooth and flat, but showed the signs of stalagmites having been removed to create this even surface.

The stalagmites nearer the walls were still there, and the stalactites above reached down to them, so that the edges of the cavern were impossible to define exactly. But he could make out a few more tunnel mouths behind that stony forest here and there. And closer to the entrance where they stood were fabricated walls, rooms with locked doors but no apparent roofs.

"I can start up the heaters from there," Kung said, pointing to a control console in the center of the cavern.

"Have you tried connecting with the school?" Fitz asked, half pointing back to the communications equipment they had passed before coming down the tunnel.

"That one by the door is useless. But yeah, I tried it," Kung said, his voice echoing through the open space.

Even without the heater running, the air underground was warmer than the air outside. Feena was already pushing off her hood and removing her hat and face covering. She heaved a sigh of relief, then smiled at him.

"I hate being bundled up like that," she said.

"It beats the alternative," Fitz said to her. Then he called out to Kung again, "you made it sound like there's better communications equipment somewhere."

"In one of those rooms, but Blaser has the key codes," Kung said.

"What else is in here?" Fitz asked.

Kung finished adjusting things on the control panel, then looked around as if to refresh his memory. "Cots for all of us."

"Cots. Delicious," Feena said, hugging Fitz's arm again.

"Enough rations for all of us for a month. And it's all the good ones," Kung went on. "Which is going to come in handy because the weather systems on that board there are showing a pretty epic storm blowing in. We're not getting down from here anytime soon."

"Great," Fitz said darkly.

Someone had killed Wyder, and he really didn't think it was Hansen. Which meant they would all be stuck up here together, trapped with a murderer.

And if he wasn't dead already, Hansen was going to be stuck out in the storm all on his own. And not able to help them at all.

"Great," Feena echoed, far more happily.

Fitz extracted his arm. "What about lab equipment?"

"Lab equipment?" Kung repeated. "We don't have any science homework due while we're doing EETT. What do you need lab equipment for?"

"To study evidence, of course," Feena said.

Kung looked to Fitz with a question in his eyes, but Fitz just shrugged. She wasn't wrong.

"I don't think so, but most of those rooms I've never been in," Kung admitted. "Blaser will know."

"I guess I wait for Blaser then," Fitz said. Feena unzipped her parka and started to stroll around the cavern, clearly intending to explore the nooks and crannies.

Fitz quickly slipped away, back up the tunnel and out the door to the snow-covered meadow.

He hadn't taken off a bit of his winter gear, but the cold still sucked the breath out of his lungs the minute he was outside. That, and the whole world had gotten measurably darker in the few minutes he had been below in the bright lights talking to Kung.

He jogged to where the path emerged from the gorge to see it packed with cadets on their way up. He waved the first few in the right direction, and the others fell in behind. Everyone walked with their heads down, just wanting the long day to be over.

Fitz wished he felt the same.

The crowd tapered out to a few last stragglers. Last of all came Blaser, the gold stripe across his parka glowing out of the darkness. Fitz felt a momentary panic. He hadn't seen Ritchie in that herd of cadets. Had he missed her?

But when he grabbed Blaser's arm, Blaser just gave him a thumb's up then dragged him along towards the door to the cave complex. Blaser closed the door, then set the lock.

"Is that necessary?" Fitz asked, as they both pushed back their hoods and pulled off their face coverings. The air was still bracingly cold, but he didn't want to wait until they were below with the others to talk.

"Protocol," Blaser said simply.

"What if Hansen comes back?" Ritchie asked from the top of the tunnel to the cavern below. She had her hat and gloves off already and was unzipping her parka.

"He has the code," Blaser assured her.

"You realize you're locking us in with a murderer," Fitz said.

Ritchie winced. Clearly, she hadn't thought of that yet. But he hadn't been able to dismiss it from his mind.

Blaser took a deep breath, then leaned back against the wall. "Wyder wasn't an accident, then?"

"Did you think it was?" Fitz asked.

"I was trying to avoid thinking about it," he admitted. Then he glanced up at the two of them. "You're on the case, I take it?"

"We have evidence we'd like to examine if there's any equipment here," Fitz said.

"I don't know what all's here, to be honest," Blaser said, rubbing at his hat-matted hair tiredly. "But I can find out for you. This used to be a military installation, a lot like the school below, but a bit more modern. There just might be the sort of thing you're looking for here, somewhere."

"That helps," Ritchie said brightly.

"What else do you need from me?" he asked eagerly. Not so much eager to help as eager to pass on the responsibility, but Fitz decided that wasn't a thought Blaser needed to hear. It's not like he had known he'd be the only one left in charge of two years' worth of cadets.

"We need to ask everyone a lot of questions," Ritchie said, glancing at Fitz for confirmation.

"I can order everyone to cooperate," Blaser said. "I'm not really able to *enforce* those orders, but I'll do my best. Anyone in particular you want to start with?"

"Finn Berweger," Fitz said, then realized that Ritchie had said the same name at the same time.

"I'll open up the officer's quarters. You can interview people privately there," Blaser said.

"Thank you," Ritchie said. She started to follow him down the tunnel, but Fitz caught her arm and pulled her back.

"Just me," he said.

"What do you mean 'just you'?" she asked with a frown.

"I'm the one who's going to question Finn. Just me," he said.

"No way," she said, twisting her arm out of his grasp. "And I'm not going to argue about it. I know what it's like, talking to him. Believe me. I don't particularly relish the idea. But you're absolutely not doing this alone. We're going to talk to him together."

She stood with her arms crossed, her eyes bright, daring him to argue with her.

But he knew that look from when they were kids. Arguing would be futile, and he didn't want to waste the time.

"Fine. Suit yourself," he said, and brushed past her to jog down the tunnel to the cavern below.

There was a real chance his entire life was about to blow up before his eyes.

But the only thing he could feel was just the desire to get it over with already.

15

WHEN RITCHIE REACHED the main cavern, she found it full of cadets all bustling with activity, setting up rows of cots and distributing sleeping bags. The space had already grown so warm that most had started shedding layers. It was a relief, not just to be warm again but to see the others, their hair and faces. To finally be able to tell at a glance who was who.

But Fitz had somehow slipped out of view in the few seconds it had taken her to jog down the tunnel after him. She could see Blaser, still wearing his gold-striped parka, unlocking some of the doors that lined the cavern walls.

And she could see the Berwegers, sitting with some of their usual group of friends on the cots at the far end of the room.

"Hey," Moreau said as she appeared at Ritchie's side. "I set up cots for each of us over that way with Frei and Grof, and Heim and Joosten are one row over. Feena will probably join them. I assume that won't be a problem?"

"Not for me," Ritchie said, still trying to find Fitz in the crowd. If he wasn't with Blaser, and he wasn't heading towards Finn, where could he have gone?

"Everything okay?" Moreau asked.

"Yeah," Ritchie said distractedly. Then she forced herself to look at her buddy. "Not really. Blaser is setting up a room for us to question people in."

"And that's a problem?" Moreau asked.

"We're starting with Finn Berweger," Ritchie said.

"That seems sensible," Moreau said.

"Yeah. It's just, Fitz has been so weird about me talking to Finn," Ritchie said. "And to be honest, I'm not relishing the opportunity to talk to him myself either."

"You've only really talked to him that one time," Moreau said. "In the incinerator room, right?"

"Exactly," Ritchie said.

"You didn't do so badly there," Moreau said. "You're not immune. None of us are. I mean, Fitz says he is, but we really only have his word on that. He handles it better than me, sure, but maybe they just haven't pressed him yet. Finn was definitely pressing you in the incinerator room."

"You're not helping, you know," Ritchie said.

"But you handled that just fine," Moreau insisted. "Come on. Let's go over to your cot and you can stow your pack and parka, get a little more comfortable before you have to go start interrogating Finn."

They walked down the aisle between the two long lines of cots to the very end, as far as they could get from where the Berwegers were holding court. Frei and Grof were stretched out on two of the cots, and Ritchie could see Moreau's stuff neatly packed under another of the cots. She dropped her pack onto the floor and kicked it under the cot beside Moreau's, then dumped her hat, cap, gloves and parka onto the cot itself next to the rolled-up shape of the sleeping bag.

Ritchie toyed with the idea of talking to Frei and Grof about some of the things Heim had said about Wyder. Surely, Heim hadn't been the only one to notice a change in their cadet captain in the last few days? But she wasn't sure how much time she had before she and Fitz started questioning Finn, and she didn't want to start that all distracted by other half-finished conversations.

Not that there was any way for her to be more prepared.

Moreau sat down on the foot of Ritchie's cot and motioned for

Ritchie to sit beside her. Frei and Grof were chatting while sprawled out on their unfurled sleeping bags, both with their eyes closed and Grof with an arm flung across them, as if to block out even more of the overhead light. Neither seemed to notice that Ritchie and Moreau were there, but still, Moreau slid closer to Ritchie to whisper close to her ear.

"You've been through this once before. You know what to expect. He can't possibly catch you off guard this time," she said. "Plus, his sister won't be there. And Fitz will."

"I'm not sure Fitz being there isn't just going to make it so much worse," Ritchie said.

"Fitz will look out for you," Moreau said confidently.

"I think he'll try to," Ritchie allowed. But then she sighed. "This is going to sound terrible, but a lot of what Finn was doing to make me trust him last time was sort of invoking things that made me think of Fitz."

"He was pretending to be Fitz?" Moreau said with a frown.

"No, it was way vaguer than that. I just kept smelling things that reminded me of my childhood back on Buennagel, my time as a kid with Fitz. It was like my brain kept firing off these full-blown memory flashbacks," Ritchie said.

"It sounds overwhelming," Moreau said. "But again, I think you'll be able to handle it. Without his sister there, he's not going to be at full strength."

"We hope," Ritchie said. "We don't know how any of this works."

"I'm not so sure even they do," Moreau said. But then she had another thought and looked all around them before inching even closer to Ritchie. "I don't think he knows what he's doing to you specifically. He's making you think of Fitz, but I don't think he knows that's what he's doing. Do you follow me?"

"Does it matter?" Ritchie asked.

"I think so, yes," Moreau said. "You're worried about what you'll be thinking and feeling, but if you steel yourself, it won't matter. No one else will know what's going on inside your head. Not Finn, and not Fitz."

"I really hope you're right," Ritchie said. Then it was her turn to drop her voice. "But something has still been off since that day."

"Fitz has been a jerk. I'm the last person to argue against that fact. But it's not because of what happened in that incinerator room. I never told him what any of us said. I assume you didn't either," Moreau said.

"I didn't. But what if Finn did? Fitz hasn't been weird since that day. He's been weird since Finn got out of the infirmary," Ritchie said.

"You're right," Moreau said, her eyes brightening. "That is interesting. You know, they've been avoiding each other ever since. Feena has been all over Fitz since the break, sure, but Finn not so much. I wonder what that means?"

"One way or another, I think I'm about to find out," Ritchie said, as she looked past Moreau to where Blaser was approaching her.

"Do you want me to come too?" Moreau asked.

"No, thanks. Finn wanted to do this alone; I just barely forced myself in there," Ritchie said, as she got to her feet.

"You better hurry. Fitz is already taking Finn into that room over there," Moreau said.

Ritchie saw it. Finn ducked inside the low doorway, hands in his pockets, as practiced a casual air as he ever projected. Fitz paused and looked back, holding eye contact with her for only a fraction of a second before disappearing into the office and closing the door behind him.

"Dammit," Ritchie said, running past Blaser to get to the door. She was prepared to knock it off its hinges if he dared to lock it, but the handle turned easily in her hand.

Too easily, she realized as she stumbled into the darkened room beyond. Her hip collided with some piece of furniture before she caught her balance. Then she shut the door, closing out the light and noise from the cavern beyond.

The room wasn't completely dark, as she had first thought, only dimmer than the overly lit cavern. Fitz moved around the desk that dominated the room to settle himself into the chair behind it, situated between two lamps that put out a gentle, almost greenish light. Finn was sitting across from him, his back to Ritchie, although he turned to look at her the minute she burst in.

Her breath caught, but she quickly dropped her eyes away from his and ducked over to the only other chair in the room, off to one side of the desk, but closer to Fitz than Finn.

Had Finn's eyes changed color? Or did they just look different in this strangely soothing light? Whatever the reason, something was different now.

They had reminded her of the sky of Buennagel before; she remembered that very distinctly. But now, as much as they still invoked skies, they brought something else strongly to mind first. The shallows of a sea…

Ritchie just managed not to gasp out loud.

They were the exact shade of Guy's eyes.

"All right?" Fitz asked her. How could he manage to sound concerned and irritated both at once?

"Fine," Ritchie said.

He leaned in closer to her, putting a hand over the side of his mouth as if to hide his words from Finn. "I'll start the questioning, if that's all right. You can jump in if I'm missing something, I guess."

"That's fine," she agreed. Her nervous heart was hammering so loudly in her chest she was afraid he could hear it.

Especially when he didn't sit back in his chair but stayed there, close to her and attempting to shield them both from Finn's curious gaze. He looked like he was about to say something more, but then gave up with a shake of his head and sat back to turn his attention to Finn.

"This is fun for all of us, I'm sure," Finn said sardonically. "I've been doing as you asked, Fitz. I've been a model cadet. I hope this isn't going to involve more threats, because I swear I haven't breathed a word to anyone."

"You're flirting with it just this minute, aren't you?" Fitz asked with an edge to his voice that made all of Ritchie's hair stand on end.

"What's this about?" she asked, and Fitz glared at her.

"Ooh, he does *not* want you to know," Finn said. Now Fitz was glaring at him, and he held up his hands as if pleading contrition. "Sorry. Sorry. Broke the rules. Maybe this would go better if you'd just hit me with your questions. Yes?"

"Blaser told you it was an order to answer all of my questions, correct?" Fitz asked.

Finn shrugged. "As much as he can back up such an order, sure. But we're all friends here. I have no reason not to comply. Ask away."

"I still want to know what you and Joosten keep arguing about," Fitz said. "And if it's a personal matter, I'm going to need some details."

"Why?" Finn asked, and frowned as if genuinely confused. "What's this about?"

"Someone is dead," Ritchie said.

And instantly regretted it, when she found herself making eye contact with Finn again. But he didn't seem to be putting the whammy on her this time. His eyes were blue, but the sensory and memory overload wasn't washing over her like before.

Was he keeping his pheromones in check now? Because of some threat Fitz had made?

"Wyder," Finn said with a nod. "Sure. And she was Joosten's buddy. I can see why you're curious about her. But I don't know what any of this would have to do with me." Then he looked at Fitz. "You know this isn't connected. You were prying into this before Wyder ever even fell. It's almost like I'm doomed to be your first suspect no matter what the circumstances."

"I'm sorry if that hurts your feelings," Fitz said dryly. "But answer the question."

But Finn just sat back in his chair, arms crossed as he regarded them both. "I don't have to alibi myself for the time of the murder. You were both right there. You know I wasn't anywhere near Wyder when she fell. And neither was Joosten."

"We think we know what the mechanism was, and it didn't involve the murderer being right there when she fell," Fitz said.

"Interesting," Finn said, his eyes lighting up. "I thought it was odd that you weren't looking into Hansen."

"We already cleared him," Fitz said, giving Ritchie the quickest of glances. She kept her face carefully neutral, although if this were true, it was certainly news to her.

"I had nothing against Wyder," Finn said. "I have nothing against anyone here on Oymyakon. Not even the two of you."

"Gee, thanks," Fitz said.

"But it's true," Finn said with another shrug. "Wyder seemed a little stressed of late, but this training, EETT or whatever, is the most stressful part of the cadet captain's year."

"And Joosten?" Fitz asked.

"Joosten is hard to get along with. You have to admit that's true," Finn said.

"I don't know her as well as you," Fitz said.

"Well, take my word for it, then."

"Were you two in some sort of relationship?" Fitz asked.

"We were friends. Anything else is not allowed between cadets," Finn said. His eyes were darting between the two of them, and there was a smirk on his face. Ritchie could feel the anger coloring her cheeks and sat back in her chair, further away from the light on the desk.

"Not allowed, but it still happens," Fitz said.

"It's good to see you and Feena are of a mind about that," Finn said with an indulgent smile.

"I'm not looking to get expelled, thank you very much," Fitz said with a scowl. "And please feel free to tell your sister that."

"Don't need to. She keeps insisting to me that she only likes you as a friend," Finn said. Then he glanced over at Ritchie and stage whispered, "but it's lots of touching for friends, am I right?"

"Don't speak to her," Fitz snapped, and Ritchie fought the urge to slug him for saying that. She didn't need a protector.

"Right," Finn said, and to Ritchie's amazement sounded actually chastened. "Look, Joosten wanted something from me that I just wasn't prepared to give. And she was very pushy. She's not very good at taking no for an answer. But no is and always will be my answer. And that's really all there is between us. Now, are we done here?"

Fitz started to nod, but Ritchie leaned over the desk to say, "not quite."

Finn had started to get up from his chair, but sat back down to turn his attention to her. "Proceed, Cadet Ritchie," he said.

Again, inexplicably, he didn't sound sarcastic.

"Do you know if either of them were at the school over the break?" she asked.

"Don't you know already?" he asked, but then shook his head as if retracting the question. "I do, actually. Wyder went home. She had originally been intending to visit the capital planet with my sister, but at the last minute changed her plans. Family emergency, I gather, but Feena didn't pry."

"And Joosten?" Ritchie asked.

"Joosten stayed here. She had not been invited for the trip, and didn't take it well when her attempts to commandeer Wyder's invite were rebuffed. My sister is very selective in her choice of company."

"Really?" Ritchie asked. "Because she's been fawning all over Joosten this trip."

"After Wyder fell, sure," Finn said. "My sister isn't a monster, you know. If anything, her empathy is so large it often overwhelms her."

"I bet," Fitz scoffed.

Finn glared at him. "You've never proven a single charge against my family. I would ask you to maintain a civil tone."

"One last question," Ritchie said before Fitz could respond to that request.

"Of course," Finn said, his attention all on Ritchie again.

"How would you describe the relationship between Wyder and Joosten?" she asked.

He frowned. "Honestly, I really don't know them as well as you think I do. Yes, I'm aware that they sit at the same table as my sister and I at every single meal. I know them to chat with for ten minutes at a time. But neither has ever been a close friend of mine."

"As an outsider, then," Fitz said.

"They were buddies. They were tight. Did they always get along? No. Who does? But they were loyal to each other." Then he gave a humorless laugh. "I don't think I need to explain that to either of you."

"You know, I don't even know who your buddy is," Fitz said suddenly.

Ritchie realized she didn't either.

But Finn just shrugged. "That can be your next mystery to solve. Now, if we're done?"

"Sure," Fitz said after exchanging a glance with Ritchie. "But you can go find Joosten for us and send her in."

"Happy to," Finn said in a voice that made it abundantly clear that 'happy' was far from the actual emotion he felt at being assigned that task.

The minute the door clicked shut, Ritchie was on her feet, hands on her hips as she glared furiously down at Fitz.

"What was that all about?" she demanded. But she kept her voice pitched to a furious whisper. She had no idea when Joosten would be bursting in on them.

"What do you mean? I thought that went well," Fitz said. He got up from the chair so he could be taller than her, but then seemed to rethink the looming and leaned back against the desk.

"I want to know, right now, what happened between you and Finn," she demanded. She only realized she was jabbing him with a finger when he caught her hand to make her stop. "Something happened between you two after we got back from the Julius Henry Observational Center, after he got out of the infirmary. You've both been weird and different ever since then. I've had enough being in the dark. I want answers."

Fitz took a deep breath, but then nothing. No answer was forthcoming from him.

"Fitz," she started to say, edging towards shouting territory.

But then he looked at her with such torment in her eyes that the anger just flowed out of her. But how easily he could make her not be mad just by looking anguished without ever explaining why was infuriating in its own way.

Her feelings were beyond complicated.

"You can't keep doing that," she said to him. "There is something wrong between us, and I don't understand why you can't just talk to me."

"I know you can't," he said.

"So tell me why you can't talk to me!" she said desperately.

"Ritchie, there are things that go on in families like mine and like the Berwegers that it's better for you not to dig into," he said.

"That's not an answer I'm just going to accept," she said.

"I know," he said with a sad sort of laugh. "It's ironic. It's just that attitude of yours, of not accepting the vague answers, that keeps me from talking to you at all. I know you won't stop digging until you know everything. But knowing everything would destroy you, Ritchie."

"That is such a weaselly thing to say," she said, the anger building back again.

"I know it is," he said. "I know you'll never be satisfied with the little I can tell you. Why do you think there's this wall between us? Because I can't tell you more, and I know that's not acceptable to you. So. Here we are."

He looked so bereft when he said it, like their friendship was already dead and gone as far as he was concerned.

And there was nothing she could do about it. He had decided for her what she would or wouldn't accept, and she wasn't ever going to get the opportunity to change that.

Especially not now, as with a brisk knock on the door, Joosten let herself into the room.

16

FITZ HAD TRIED NOT to judge Joosten, especially as it was Finn Berweger that kept telling him how hard to get along with she was. When she came in the door to the office at the worst possible moment, interrupting him and Ritchie, he told himself it was just bad timing, not any malice on her part.

But then she towed an apologetic-looking Blaser in behind her, and it was hard not to find her just a little disagreeable.

"What's going on?" Fitz asked.

"Sorry, guys," Blaser said as he closed the door behind him and looked around for a fourth chair. Fitz raised a hand numbly to point at the far corner where the only remaining chair lurked, still askew from when Ritchie had run into it getting in the door.

"There's no reason to be sorry. I simply don't acknowledge their authority in this matter," Joosten said. "You don't have the right to ask me questions."

Her voice was maddeningly devoid of emotion. Which wasn't in itself a problem. He often found Wyss and even Moreau to have their emotional tells dialed down so low he couldn't easily read them himself.

But her wording was so aggressive. It was hard to tell if she meant it to be. And looking into her watery blue eyes, he still couldn't tell.

"In the absence of Colonel Hansen, Cadet Captain Blaser is in charge," Fitz said as reasonably as he could. "He's asked for everyone to cooperate so we can figure out what happened to Wyder. Your buddy. Why would you impede that?"

"Because you're not the ones who should be investigating," she said, not inflecting any of her words in any meaningful way. "When the school sends shuttles up to retrieve us, and the proper authorities are called, I'll, of course, answer any question that they might have. In the meantime, not so much."

"Aren't you worried that makes you look guilty?" Ritchie asked.

"Not at all," Joosten said. "The two of you twisting everyone's minds to accept your forgone conclusion, that's what would make me look guilty. You surely can't think I would cooperate with that."

"We haven't reached any conclusions," Fitz said. "Why would you think we had?"

"No one thinks this was an accident," Blaser said. He had set his chair next to Joosten's and sank into it with a little sigh of relief. They had all had a very long day of hiking, but Fitz felt a little stab of sympathy. Blaser's day had started earlier and would doubtless run later. Such was the pain of being a cadet captain.

"And for some reason, no one thinks either of you is looking into Hansen at all," Joosten said. "And if you're not looking into him, then everyone assumes that means he's innocent. Never mind no one even knows where he is."

This time she was stressing words, namely "no one" and "everyone." He was pretty sure he got her point, but he opted not to respond to it.

"We're considering the possibility he fell victim to the same murderer who took out Wyder," Fitz said. "Someone is covering their tracks."

"I'm sorry, but I just doubt you have proof for either charge," Joosten said, shaking her head.

"Fitz and Ritchie are very good at this sort of thing," Blaser told her.

Joosten looked directly at Fitz with those emotionless eyes. "You tried to get the Berwegers expelled last semester. Everyone knows you wanted them gone. But they never did anything wrong. Even you couldn't make that one stick."

"You think Weld and Keller were innocent?" Ritchie asked. That flush of color was back in her cheeks, and he could feel the anger that kept bubbling back up in her about to spill over again.

"They were committed to the observational center after a thorough and quite public hearing," Fitz said. "No reasonable person can question that they had both caused the deaths of others and were highly likely to be a danger to society again in the future."

"Why don't you let Fitz and Ritchie ask what they want to know? Maybe when you hear the questions you'll realize no one is trying to entrap you," Blaser said.

"I don't think so," Joosten said. "I don't think that would be wise."

"Finn was fine with it," Blaser said.

"Finn isn't like me," Joosten said, and there was the tiniest flash of an emotion with that statement. And her posture in the chair was ever so slightly stiffer.

She *had* been angry with Finn before. Fitz hadn't been imagining that.

But what had Finn said to push her so far?

"Finn is the actual suspect, right?" Blaser asked.

Fitz gave him a look he hoped conveyed all of his annoyance. "You know, we'd rather not announce all that in front of others."

"He means that I'm a suspect too," Joosten told Blaser.

"Why did you stay at the school over the break?" Ritchie asked. Fitz could tell she was anxious to get the conversation back under their control, but Joosten was having none of it.

"The same reason you did last year," Joosten said automatically.

"I was here to get in extra flight hours before combat glider training," Ritchie said.

"No, you weren't," Joosten said simply.

"Come on," Fitz said, irritated.

"No, you come on," Joosten said. "Not all of us have rich family," she said, pointing to Fitz, "or rich friends to take us places," she said, pointing at Ritchie.

"It sounds like you're feeling hurt about that," Ritchie said. Fitz glanced at her and she shot him the briefest of looks, enough for him to know she knew the irony in her words.

Joosten didn't sound hurt at all.

"You know, on the university world, there are more opportunities for we low-caste cadets during the breaks. Extra work assignments, or travel studies. I'm looking forward to it," Joosten said with no particular relish.

"You were going to still be buddies with Wyder at guardian school," Ritchie said.

Joosten nodded. "That had been the plan. Time for a new plan."

"Such is life?" Fitz asked, but she just shrugged, unbothered.

"Wyder was depressed lately," Ritchie said. "Any thoughts on that?"

"That I'm prepared to share with you? Not particularly," Joosten said.

"But you're her buddy. If she had something going on, you of all people would know it," Blaser said, still trying to encourage her to be more cooperative.

But she was having none if it. "It's a private matter. Show me proof of your authority to ask me such personal questions and I'll consider it. But I'll want legal representation first."

"That sounds like an admission of guilt," Fitz said. He hoped that would provoke that little flash of anger again.

But she only said, "no, it doesn't." And left it at that.

"Any luck getting through to the academy?" Fitz asked Blaser with a sigh.

"Not so far," Blaser said. "The storm down there has never let up, and we've got a sizable blizzard blowing around us up here. I'm afraid we're likely to be cut off from the rest of the world for several days."

"Plenty of time for you to question everyone about their last vacations," Joosten said as she got up from her chair. "Can I go?"

Fitz wanted to say no, but he had no follow up. He just nodded. But he signalled for Blaser to stay. Joosten went out into the growing noise in the cavern beyond, letting in a tantalizing aroma of dinner simmering on a variety of light boxes. Meat in rich sauces, savory/herby smells from some kind of starchy side item, and something sweet and fruity and spicy for dessert.

"Are we feasting?" Fitz asked Blaser as the door closed behind her.

"I guess so," Blaser said with a flush as he moved into Joosten's chair to be closer to the desk. "I told the last-years to bust open whatever looked good. I'll have to keep tighter control tomorrow."

"Or we'll run out of food?" Ritchie asked.

"Not likely. There's tons. But if we come back down the mountain considerably heavier than we went up it, I'm sure to hear about it," he said with a tired laugh.

"Any sign of Hansen?" Fitz asked, and they were all serious again.

"No. What do *you* think happened to him?" he asked.

Fitz had left his parka draped over the back of his chair. He reached into the breast pocket and took out the rope and gloves. "Ritchie and I found these in his tent when he left. He had taken everything else with him."

"What could do this?" Blaser asked as he touched the blackened ends of the rope.

"We were hoping there would be lab equipment here that might help us figure that out," Fitz said.

"Well, maybe not us personally, but someone here must be good with that sort of chemistry," Ritchie said.

"What she said," Fitz said. He shot a smile towards Ritchie, but couldn't quite make himself risk eye contact with her.

"I can find both for you, I'm sure," Blaser said. He had turned his attention to the gloves. "What does this mean, though? What did he touch?"

"The same thing Wyder did, it looks like," Fitz said.

Then, to his surprise, Ritchie added, "or he wanted us to think so. He might have left these behind on purpose for us to find."

"You think it's a lie?" Fitz asked her, not bothering to hide his incredulity.

"Fitz, we both agree that we don't think Hansen could do this," she said. "But the fact remains that he left us all without a word. And he left these behind—"

"Because they're garbage," Fitz said emphatically.

"Where he knew we'd find them," she pressed on, giving him a hard look he quickly darted his eyes away from.

"If he left them behind on purpose, we should definitely test them," Blaser said. "I'll find the equipment and figure out who's best to run the tests."

"Good idea," Fitz said, and pushed the rope and gloves across the desk towards him.

"Do you need to speak to anyone else?" Blaser asked as he got up and started putting the evidence in the pocket on the side of his pants.

"Everyone," Ritchie said with a tired sigh.

"But not in any particular order, I don't think," Fitz said, fighting the urge to sigh himself.

"Right," Blaser said. "I'll just catch the closest. We have a local network up in the caves, so if you need me just send a signal to my implant."

"Will do," Fitz said.

He wished there were more he could say to keep Blaser there with them if just for a minute longer, but there was nothing. The door closed with that little click he was starting to hate, and Fitz braced himself for another barrage of Ritchie's anger.

But nothing was forthcoming. At last, he had to look over at her. She was sitting back in her chair, tugging at her bottom lip as she stewed in thought.

"What's between us and Finn isn't part of this. So we can just focus on this and forget about the other. Okay?" he said.

She looked up at him as if surprised to find him still there with her. "Agreed," she said and nearly lapsed back into thought before adding, "for now."

"Ritchie, there are always going to be things I can't tell you. That's just the way it is," he said.

She huffed out a breath, not quite a laugh. "Whatever, Fitz. I mean, have it your way. Your and Finn's way, I guess. It's not like I ever needed someone to tell me straight out what was going on before. I always find out in the end, don't I?"

"Some things you can't unknow, no matter how badly you want to," he said. She started to scoff again, but he stood up, pulling her up from her chair to stand close to him. They both had their backs to the door, but he looked back over his shoulder to be sure it was still closed.

"You're not actually about to tell me something?" she asked with a gleam in her eye.

"No," he admitted. "Look, I'll say this much. Finn and I both know something we'd really rather not know. Now we're all bound up together, whether we like it or not. I promise you, I do not. But there's no putting this mess back inside the box. We're stuck together, and even when he and his sister are gone, we'll still be bound together in this inextricable way."

"If this is about the conspiracies we're tasked to investigate, why have you never told us or at least Colonel Hansen?" she asked suspiciously.

"Because it's not about that. But please stop asking me questions about it. I will burn the whole Union of Free Worlds to the ground before I'll see you stuck in this mire with me and Finn Berweger."

"Why do you get to make this decision for me?" she asked.

"Because there's no way for you to make it, and you know it," he said. "Please, please, just trust me."

"I'm sorry, Fitz. I just really don't think I can," she said.

Then there was another knock at the door, and she turned around to sit back down in her chair just as the door swung open and Feena Berweger poked her head inside.

"I volunteered to be next. I hope you're ready for me," she said as she slipped inside.

Fitz pinched the bridge of his nose and asked the universe for strength. But he had managed to muddle through an interview with Finn. Surely his sister would be easier.

Or, at least, a very different sort of challenge.

17

RITCHIE SETTLED back into her chair and watched Fitz as Feena stepped into the room and closed the door behind her. He had his hand to his face as if Feena's sudden presence was immensely stressful. But when he lowered his hand and gestured for Feena to sit across from him, his expression was carefully bland.

"I'm not sure we're quite ready to question everyone just yet," Ritchie said to Feena.

"That's okay. You can practice on me," Feena said. Fitz had moved to sit forward in his chair, hands folded on the desktop, and Feena quickly mimicked his pose. "Ask me anything."

"Ritchie is right; the two of us need to come up with a standard set of questions first. For investigative purposes," Fitz said.

"I want to help," Feena said, reaching across the desk to grasp his folded hands. "I was a big help in finding out who was messing around at your parents' dinner party, right? Even Wyss had to admit I helped you both out. Let me help again." Feena clutched Fitz's hands tighter, desperate for him to make eye contact with her. He didn't look up, but he didn't pull away either.

"How did you help specifically?" Ritchie asked, since Fitz didn't seem like he was ever going to speak.

"Oh, I assumed you knew the whole story," Feena said, turning her attention to Ritchie. Her eyes were the same carefully crafted shade of blue as her brother's, but the effect wasn't the same. She wasn't trying to win Ritchie over. She wasn't even trying to put a whammy on Fitz that Ritchie could tell, although she was still holding his hands.

"Not really," Ritchie said. "Do you want to fill me in?"

"Well," Feena said, giving Fitz the briefest of glances before returning her focus to Ritchie. "You know there was a dinner party on our last night on the capital planet, right? Fitz's parents threw it together rather last minute. My uncle and aunt were invited. They are very close friends with Fitz's mother, and my aunt has served under Fitz's dad since forever. Very close. And since I was staying with them, I went along to the party."

"One of the other guests was trying to get her husband to notice her by pretending that she was having an affair with my father," Fitz said, finally extricating himself from Feena's grasp to sit back in his chair. "She sneaked into his office to send a message to herself, supposedly from him, declaring his love and all that."

"Fitz! You ruined my story," Feena said with a dramatic pout. Then she turned back to Ritchie. "He's telling it all out of order."

"I was skipping to the end," Fitz interjected.

"We were still at the table enjoying dessert when Fitz's father discovered someone had been inside his office and using his equipment. All the adults were separated by the house staff and questioned one by one. It was a real evening of intrigue," Feena said to Ritchie.

"I bet," Ritchie said.

"Maybe you're used to it, but it was fun for me," Feena said.

"I'm quite sure you attend far more dinner parties thrown by prominent officials than I do," Ritchie said.

Feena smiled demurely and her cheeks pinkened, as if Ritchie had paid her the highest of compliments. And Ritchie really didn't think she was faking any of it. Either she was a very good actress, or she sincerely wanted Ritchie to think well of her.

"You and Fitz are best friends, right? I figured you had been to his house before me," Feena said shyly.

"We fell out of touch before we were old enough to attend parties with the grownups," Ritchie said. "And since then we've been here, at the academy."

"Oh, I didn't realize," Feena said. "Fitz, you brought Wyss home with you, but not Ritchie?"

"This really isn't relevant to the task at hand," Fitz said.

"He's not wrong," Ritchie said.

"But it is," Feena insisted. "You don't know what a help I was that night. When the grownups were being questioned, Fitz brought Wyss and I up to his room and we decided to investigate it ourselves. Wyss had the technical know-how, of course. And Fitz knew the house and all of its secrets. But I was the one who knew all the parties at the table. I was the one who suspected the young officer's wife first, and I was right."

"I'm sure we would've got there in the end," Fitz said. "Wyss broke the encryption on the message before my father's people did, but only by a matter of twenty minutes or so. It was just a way to pass the time, really. Not a proper mystery."

"Not like what you did over vacation," Feena said to Ritchie, her eyes bright.

"You know about that?" Ritchie asked.

"Cicey Travert was also at the party," Fitz said. "She told us a very garbled story of pirates and jewels and a daring rescue of the crew, which she had to admit she wasn't even there for in the first place."

"It doesn't sound too far off, actually," Ritchie said. He raised his eyebrows at her, but she waved the subject away. "A story for another time. We're here about Wyder."

"Poor Wyder," Feena agreed. "She was a good cadet captain. So organized, a natural leader, but still approachable. She would've made a fine officer some day."

"You were in the same tent as her. Do you share a barracks back at school?" Ritchie asked.

"No, as cadet captain, she and Joosten had a private room. Heim and I bunk with two cadets a year behind us," Feena said.

"So you really wouldn't know if she was meeting anyone or had issues with anyone in particular, then," Ritchie said. Not a question.

"I know, I'm not much help," Feena agreed. "I don't know anything helpful yet, but that doesn't mean I can't find it out. People like to tell me things. All I need to know is who and what to ask."

"Is that all?" Fitz said blandly.

"Actually, it could be a lot," Ritchie said. He shot her a questioning look, but she ignored him. She leaned over the desk towards Feena. "Here's where you can start. See if you can find out who was still at the school over the break."

"But why would that be important?" Feena asked with a frown. She seemed genuinely confused.

"It doesn't matter," Fitz said before Ritchie could reply. "If you want to help, we'll take it, but information is given out on a need to know basis only." His tone was unnecessarily harsh. Apparently, he had forgotten he was supposed to be wooing Feena, winning her over.

"For now," Ritchie said gently, "just figure out who was here and who wasn't. If we have followup questions after that, we'll tell you more."

"I'm on it," Feena said. She stood up and gave them both a quick salute, then disappeared out the office door.

Fitz slumped forward over the desk, burying his face in his hands. "Why did you do that?" he moaned.

"Do what?"

"Trust her," Fitz said. "We can't trust her."

"I thought we agreed she'd be a useful tool for us," Ritchie said. "I thought that's why you were being nice to her in the first place."

"I can't stand her. And what's the point, anyway? This is their last semester here. There isn't enough time left for me to *use* her for anything," he said bitterly.

"What we're digging into is bigger than this academy," Ritchie said. "I assumed we'd still be investigating what we can even after we leave, let alone after the Berwegers leave. That's why we went to talk to Keller and Weld, right? Because this is bigger than one planet."

"We're not officially sanctioned to do anything, you know," Fitz said. "We're Hansen's little private project, and I know he's spun it to his own superiors as a way of keeping us in check. It's almost a sanction against us, like a punishment that doesn't go onto our permanent records."

"I don't think it's that bad," Ritchie said.

"You're missing my point," Fitz said. "We don't know where Hansen is. He might be dead. Or if he's not dead, he might really be guilty of whatever he's been accused of back at the school. Either way, without him in charge, our task force is done."

"No, it isn't," Ritchie said. "We were a team before that. We'll be a team after. All Hansen did was give Wyss permission to access things he could hack into, anyway."

"That's not all Hansen does," Fitz said bitterly.

"You're really that mad about being pushed to befriend Feena Berweger?" Ritchie asked.

"No. I mean, yes, but that's not what I'm talking about," he said.

"Tell me what you mean," Ritchie said after too long of a silence.

"He shields you," Fitz said. "He kept you out of trouble over what happened with Weld, and then again with Keller. It would've been far easier to dismiss you in both cases out of an abundance of caution, you know."

"Believe me, I don't need you to explain to me how my background makes me easy to throw away," Ritchie said. Now she was the one who sounded bitter. Well, she felt pretty bitter. She was tired of being reminded of her low social standing.

"The problem is, we don't know who is on what side," Fitz said. "We don't even know if there are only two sides."

"It feels like more than two," Ritchie said with a sigh.

"I know. But the point is, the one thing we do know, is that Hansen is on our side. We can agree on that, right?"

"Yes," Ritchie said. "How long do you think it will take to figure out what burned that rope and gloves?"

"I don't know. It could end up being something so commonly available it tells us nothing, you know," he warned her.

"I know," she said.

Suddenly, her implant started pinging her as message after message dropped into her inbox. "Blaser connected with the school," she said.

"I'm an idiot," Fitz said, hitting his own forehead with a loud smack. Ritchie gave him a confused look. "Wyss gave us both tablets to contact him. I haven't tried since we got here. Have you?"

"We've been busy," Ritchie said. But she shared his urge to smack herself on the forehead as well.

"I'll go get mine," Fitz said.

"I've already sent Moreau a message to come join us," Ritchie said. "We can all call together."

"Right. Blaser should be in on it too. I'll see if I can find him," Fitz said.

Ritchie nodded, but she was already distracted, her eyes unfocused as she scanned through the contents of her inbox. Nearly two dozen new messages from Guy, but a lot of them were flagged as corrupted downloads. So Blaser had managed to connect the local network to the school, but the signal wasn't stable.

She could only hope that Wyss' communications equipment worked a little better, or this would be a very short call.

18

BLASER HAD SET up an office of his own and stationed another last-year cadet outside the door to screen those who went inside. Fitz had to wait for three other cadets to get their time alone with him, but, as anxious as he was to get back to the other office and talk to Wyss, he could see that Blaser wasn't jerking him around. He was summoning reliable cadets, and each came out of the office with a clear mission to sort something out for Blaser.

Even so, when it was Fitz's turn to go into the office, he found Blaser looking a little frazzled. He had been scrawling notes by hand on the surface of his tablet, but the handwriting was beyond anything that Fitz could decipher.

"Sorry, I'm a little disorganized," Blaser said as he scrolled through his notes.

"There's supposed to be another cadet captain here," Fitz reminded him. "And a colonel. I'm sure you're doing fine."

"Thanks," Blaser said distractedly. "Okay, I found the two cadets with the highest qualifications in chemistry. One of them is my buddy Kung. You know him, right? They've taken the rope and the gloves to the facility lab. It's down the south tunnel, around a bend. It feels like you're walking too far, too deep, but it's there."

"The local network is up, so I have a map," Fitz said, tapping his forehead.

"Right," Blaser said. Then he grimaced. "I don't know how long it's going to take. Or even if they'll find an answer."

"Don't worry about it," Fitz said. "Look, Ritchie and I are about to call down to the school. We're going to compare notes with Wyss and Sokolov. Did you want to sit in?"

"I got the local network up, but the signal with the school is too wonky for me to speak with anyone. I sent some text messages, but I haven't heard back." He sounded distracted, like he hadn't quite heard what Fitz had said.

"We have some other equipment that seems to work better," Fitz said as vaguely as he could. "It calls direct to Cadet Wyss, but he can get a message to the administration if you need him to. If you don't want to wait, that is. And it's always assuming that *we* can get through."

"I suppose I should be there," Blaser said, scrolling back to the top of his notes. "Yes, I think I've done all I can for the minute here, anyway. Let's go."

They headed out of the office, then across the open space of the cavern to the office on the far side that he and Ritchie had been using. A few cadets tried to approach Blaser directly, but the other last-years deftly headed them off.

"You delegate really well," Fitz said, amused.

"Have to," Blaser said with a shrug.

When they went into the office, they found Moreau and Ritchie sitting at the far side of the desk already attempting to use their tablet to connect with Wyss. They both had a tense look on their faces, and he didn't think this was the first time they'd tried. But slowly the connections lined up and Wyss's face appeared, blurred and distorted, on the screen.

"There you are," he said, although he could only see Ritchie and Moreau at the moment. "I was starting to worry when I didn't hear from you or Fitz."

"I'm here too," Fitz said, and Moreau and Ritchie tucked closer together so that he and Blaser could get in front of the camera.

"This connection isn't stable," Wyss said, frowning at something just off camera.

"No, the storm is getting worse up here," Blaser said. "I'm surprised we got through at all, actually. I haven't been able to reach the administration to let them know about Hansen."

"What about Hansen?" Wyss asked with a frown.

"He's missing," Blaser said. "And Cadet Wyder had a fatal accident. We need shuttles up to the third base camp as soon as they can be sent."

"I'm letting them know now," Wyss said, and Fitz could tell from the angle of his head that Wyss had shifted his attention to another of his computers. "Tell me more about what happened to Hansen."

"We don't know," Fitz said. "Two mornings ago, when the rest of us got up, he and his equipment were just gone. We don't know if he left us or was taken. He didn't leave any kind of message behind."

"You know what he's been accused of?" Wyss asked, presumably of Blaser.

"Rumor says treason," Blaser said. "But that's just a rumor, right?"

"Sokolov and I have uncovered more information," Wyss said, a very careful wording if Fitz had ever heard one.

"So it *is* treason," Fitz said, his stomach sinking.

"He's been accused of that, yes," Wyss said. "At the beginning of the intersemester break, he attended a conference with certain other key military figures. At some point at that conference, he had access to confidential intelligence, which he acquired copies of. After returning to the school, still during the break, he went into the communications room in the middle of the night to transmit that intelligence to a specific point outside of the Union of Free Worlds, presumably for a passing ship to pick up, as there's nothing normally there at those coordinates. He was seen by a cadet who, for unknown reasons, waited several days before reporting what she saw."

"Allegedly?" Ritchie asked anxiously.

"It's hard to say exactly what happened. The official authorities are still working on it. It's an open case," Wyss said. Then he glanced up and nodded, and Sokolov joined him on screen.

"Hey, everyone," she said with a little wave. "We've been busy down here, as I'm sure Wyss has told you."

"Working on it," he said.

"So Hansen is a traitor?" Blaser asked.

"I don't think any of us believes that," Sokolov said.

"But there's an investigation," Blaser said.

"They let him take you all up the mountain while they finished up the last few details," Sokolov said.

"The people in charge of the investigation are suspicious of the witness, to say the least," Wyss said. "That was why they opted not to keep Hansen in custody. It looks like someone is trying to set him up."

"And failing," Fitz guessed.

"Not as much as they should be," Wyss said. "The use of an unreliable eyewitness is... inelegant."

"Compared to?" Fitz asked.

"The encryption on the outgoing message. None of us have been able to crack it yet. And it's not the encryption our intelligence services use, for sure. Someone stole that file, added this extra layer of encryption that it no way concealed Hansen's digital fingerprints, and sent it out."

"Like they wanted Hansen to get caught as the sender, but they didn't want this actual information out in the universe for anyone else to use," Sokolov said. "It's all very strange."

"It gets stranger," Wyss said to her. "They told me that Cadet Captain Wyder is dead."

"No!" Sokolov said, putting a hand over her mouth. This felt like more than the shock and sympathy of hearing about a fellow cadet's fatal accident to Fitz.

"What's going on?" he asked.

"Well, the witness on the official reports, the ones that the authorities find unreliable on several details, was Cadet Captain Wyder," Wyss said.

"At first they considered her highly reliable because of her rank and the regard the instructors here hold her in," Sokolov said. "But the details of her story don't hold up. Some things she is very sure on, but other little details didn't stay consistent when she was questioned more than once."

"But why would she accuse Hansen at all?" Ritchie asked. "She always struck me as someone with a lot of integrity. She must've had what felt to her like a very good reason."

"Wyss, did Hansen know who his accuser was?" Fitz asked. He hated saying those words, and he could feel Ritchie gaping at him, appalled, but they had to be said.

"I don't think so," he said, looking to Sokolov, who also shook her head.

"If he didn't know, how do you two?" Blaser asked.

Wyss flushed. "We've been digging into things since you all left," he said. Totally true, as far as it went.

"Well, if he didn't know, it's a very weird coincidence," Blaser said, folding his arms angrily.

"What's he talking about now?" Wyss asked.

"When Wyder fell, Hansen was there," Moreau said.

"He tried to save her," Ritchie said. "I know that's what we saw. And the equipment was tampered with. We all know that's true, right?"

"Someone is trying to frame him *again*?" Wyss asked skeptically.

"But if it was Wyder who framed him the first time, who would be doing it now?" Blaser asked. "No, the simplest answer seems to be that Hansen is guilty of treason and he's removing the witness against him."

"No, that doesn't make any sense," Fitz said. "If he knew it was Wyder that reported him, he'd also know that they were discrediting her story. All he had to do was wait, and this would all go away."

"It looks that way to me," Wyss agreed.

"Whatever. I still feel safer with Hansen not here," Blaser said.

"Do you? Because if he wasn't the one who killed Wyder, and I don't think he was, that means we're all trapped down here until the storm passes with a murderer in our midst," Fitz said.

Blaser frowned back at him, but finally relented. "I'll set watches," he said. "I'm not saying I think you're right, but I'll set watches."

"And keep people from wandering off in murderer/victim pairs," Fitz added.

"I suppose that's sensible, too," Blaser sighed. "Tricky, though. Even if we keep all these side rooms locked, there are a lot of tunnels everyone has access to. And you don't have to walk far to be out of sight of anyone up here in the cavern."

"So we have more frequent roll calls," Fitz said. "It's not like you have to explain yourself to anybody. You're in charge."

"The way you say it, it sounds like fun. I promise you it isn't," Blaser said.

"Wyss?" Ritchie said, but she was waving her hands in front of a blank screen. "The call dropped."

"Probably the storm," Blaser said. "It's going to get worse before it gets better. Let me know if you need any more from me."

Ritchie was tapping at the tablet, trying to restore the connection, but Moreau was sitting back in her chair, arms crossed as she glared at Fitz.

"Actually, there is one more thing," Fitz said, hopping up from his own chair to chase after Blaser. "Can you show me where this lab is? I'd like to see how they're coming along."

"Sure," Blaser said tiredly.

He didn't even remind Fitz that his implant would guide him there now that the local network was up. Which was just as well.

Fitz wasn't prepared to admit that he just didn't want to be left alone with Moreau and Ritchie. Particularly Moreau, who was still shooting daggers out of her eyes.

                                    19

RITCHIE EXPECTED that Fitz leaving with Blaser would dissipate the stifling tension in the room. It was only after the door shut behind him, cutting off the furor from the cavern full of giddy cadets beyond and leaving the darkened office in pleasant silence, that she realized the tension remained.

It was coming from Moreau. And it hadn't just been directed at Fitz. She had something she wanted to say to Ritchie as well.

But Ritchie kept her attention focused on the tablet. She was about to try reconnecting a fourth time when Moreau gently reached across the desk to pull the tablet away from her hands, closing the top and setting it aside. She wasn't angry, but she had a very intense energy. Ritchie knew there was no ignoring her when she was in this state.

"Catch me up," Moreau said. "I know you talked to Finn. I think I saw Feena come in here as well. How was that?"

"Weird," Ritchie said. "No one seems to know anything, except possibly Joosten, but she's not talking. She's rather combative, isn't she?"

"She has boundaries," Moreau said after a moment's consideration. "If she was evasive, it's possible she knew about Wyder."

"That Wyder was the witness, or that she wasn't considered reliable?" Ritchie asked.

"Either. Both," Moreau said with a shrug. "If she's protecting her buddy, that could be why she's cagey with your questions."

"That, plus she's always kind of prickly, I think," Ritchie said.

"What about the twins? You and Fitz make it through being alone with them, okay?" Moreau asked. Ritchie could see how nervous Moreau got at just the idea of being alone with the twins. Ritchie belatedly realized that those feelings had likely been why Moreau had never pressed to be part of the interrogation process.

"You still feel the effects of them being inside your head?" Ritchie asked. "You never described to me what that was like for you. I guess it was bad, though."

"I didn't enjoy getting shot either," Moreau said. "But you're right. I much prefer when neither of them notices me. And I really don't want to describe what it feels like in detail, because the whole experience is just so intrusive. I mean, I know Finn did a number on you in the incinerator room, but you've never had both of them working you at once."

"No," Ritchie admitted. "Finn all on his own is trouble enough. And there is definitely something going on between him and Fitz that I just don't understand."

"Wyder isn't the only unreliable witness to things," Moreau said.

"Fitz isn't lying to us about anything," Ritchie said.

"He isn't telling us everything either," Moreau said. "I don't have your boundless depths of patience. Not with him, not with anybody."

"If you're saying his protectiveness feels a little condescending, I'm not going to argue with you," Ritchie said.

"I wasn't saying that at all, but it's nice to hear that's what *you're* thinking," Moreau said with a wry grin.

"Ugh, I don't know what I'm thinking," Ritchie said, and rested her head on her arms folded on the desktop. "Is it bedtime yet? It feels like bedtime."

"Just barely dinnertime," Moreau said, patting her on the back fondly. Most of her killer intensity had faded away, but Ritchie still sensed the rest of it lurking, waiting to flare up again without warning.

"If someone is trying to frame Colonel Hansen, I would suspect the Berwegers long before I would suspect Wyder," Ritchie said. "And yet we have no evidence to point to either of them. Just my gut feelings."

"Using Wyder to frame Hansen does sound like their sort of thing," Moreau said. "They like keeping their hands clean and manipulating others. If they knew she was failing to be compelling enough to the authorities, that could be reason enough to eliminate her. Only, why so publicly?"

"To try another frame job on Colonel Hansen," Ritchie said. "That has to be what happened. We need to question more people about what happened on the top of the ice cliff. Who had access to the rope?"

"Anyone who climbed up that side had access to that rope," Moreau said. "Dozens of cadets, and it's already so long ago that everyone's memories are bound to be faulty."

"They can recreate their own positions with their implant histories," Ritchie said.

"We aren't authorized to compel anyone to share those," Moreau said. "And if we asked everyone to self-report their histories, the guilty party would surely lie. No, the actual authorities might be able to work the case from the implant memories, but that's beyond us. And I really don't want to do anything remotely like encouraging Wyss to try."

"Nor I," Ritchie said. "I've had it rubbed in my face enough that these things aren't as secure as we've always been told they were." She rapped her knuckles on her forehead, a location nowhere near her implant.

"So, what *do* we have to work with?" Moreau asked.

"Someone put something on the rope, and it burned through Wyder's gloves as well as Hansen's," Ritchie said thoughtfully.

"Or someone put it on Wyder's gloves somehow and she contaminated the rope when she started back down," Moreau said.

"That makes more sense," Ritchie agreed.

"I thought so," Moreau said.

After a long moment's silence, Ritchie forced herself to sit back up in the chair. She opened the tablet and started trying to connect with the school again.

"Missing Guy?" Moreau asked.

Ritchie flushed, not wanting to admit she hadn't even been thinking of Guy. "I haven't played his messages back yet. I figured I'd wait until we were back in the barracks. I don't need random cadets looking over my shoulder, you know?"

Moreau shrugged. "Plenty of privacy here. I could even step out, if you like?"

"No, even if I tried to record a message for him now, I'd just be all distracted." The connection to the first satellite failed, and Ritchie closed the tablet again. "What is it about what Finn and Feena do? I mean, what does it feel like to you when they're doing it?"

Moreau bit at her lip. "Like I said, I really don't want to talk about it. If that's okay." That last was more of a challenge than a question.

"Sure, I get it," Ritchie said. But then she went on. "It's just, Finn used to make me think of Fitz, even though he looks nothing like Fitz. Now, today, he was reminding me of Guy. You know how Guy smells like the ocean, and feels warm like the sun just being near you."

"I'll take your word for that," Moreau said with just a hint of a smile.

"I don't like it. It's like he's hijacking my feelings for others," Ritchie said.

"You can't talk to Guy until that feels less tainted?" Moreau guessed.

Ritchie felt her cheeks flush, but she just nodded.

"It'll pass," Moreau said. "It always does. Until they come around again, anyway."

"It passed for you?" Ritchie asked.

Moreau said nothing, her lips a tight line. She wasn't going to say again that she didn't want to talk about it, apparently.

But Ritchie couldn't let it go. "I don't think Feena has ever tried to influence me the same way," she said. "I get sensations from her, but nothing specific to anything."

"That makes sense," Moreau said. "She could be trying just as hard as her brother but failing because there's no connection she can piggy-back on to reach you."

"Is that it?" Ritchie asked. There was a smudge on the desktop, a long greasy thumbprint, and she found herself rubbing at it. "Because

Fitz says neither of them trigger him at all. And I just wondered what that meant."

"It means Fitz is an unreliable witness," Moreau said. "I already told you that."

"He says they don't affect him. I don't think he's lying to us about that," Ritchie said.

"No. Lying isn't his problem. Secrets are his problem," Moreau said.

"Right. Like whatever is between him and Finn," Ritchie said. The greasy thumbprint was refusing to buff away, and she pulled the cuff of her shirt down to use it as a cloth. "But I watched him while we were talking to Feena. And he really does seem like she doesn't affect him that way."

"Sure," Moreau said noncommittally.

"I mean, she's always touching him. Have you noticed?"

"I have."

"So what do you think that means?" Ritchie asked, looking up from her work cleaning the desktop to see Moreau gazing at her intently. There was that intensity flare-up.

"Do you really want to know what I think?" Moreau asked.

"Of course," Ritchie said, and forced her hands to stop moving.

"Because I think I know why Fitz isn't swayed by the twins, but I don't think you're going to like it."

"Try me," Ritchie said.

"Fine," Moreau said, leaning forward in her chair to take Ritchie by the hand. "These are my thoughts on the matter. I'm going to speak them now and forever hold my peace."

"No jokes," Ritchie said.

"No jokes," Moreau said seriously. "Ritchie, I think Fitz is a very broken person. I think he walled off parts of himself and left them to die, and that's why the twins don't affect him. They are hijacking our feelings, and Fitz cut himself off from all those years ago."

"Fitz has feelings," Ritchie said, pulling her hands away from Moreau angrily.

"I told you that you wouldn't like it," Moreau said.

"It's not true," Ritchie said. "I mean, *years ago*? He was fine until we got back from interviewing Weld and Keller. Something happened after we left that shuttle, and he's been weird ever since. But he's not dead inside."

"I will concede he is very good at hiding it," Moreau said.

"Well, you would know all about it, I suppose," Ritchie grumbled. "Any of us could take lessons from you on not showing undue emotion. It wouldn't be *proper*."

"No, it wouldn't," Moreau said.

Ritchie took a deep breath. "Sorry. You're right. I didn't want to hear what you think. But I asked you to tell me anyway. Now you've said it, and we'll just let it drop."

"What do *you* think it means, that Fitz doesn't respond to Feena?" Moreau countered.

"Well..." Ritchie trailed off. Her cheeks were flushing again. She could feel their heat.

"Something is weighing on your mind. Spill it," Moreau said.

"It's just, I wonder what would have happened with me if I'd met Finn before Sokolov said..." she broke off again.

"Right," Moreau said with a laugh. "I remember. You had to chase Sokolov away from Fitz."

"That's not what happened!" Ritchie said.

"Close enough," Moreau said. "But after that conversation with Sokolov, you started noticing Fitz. In, shall we say, ways that Finn could exploit."

"Exactly!" Ritchie said. "And now he's doing the same thing with my feelings for Guy."

"Which just brings me back to my original point," Moreau said.

"That's not what I meant at all," Ritchie said, giving up with a sigh.

Moreau sat quietly for a long moment, her face unreadable. Then she softened and said, "I get you."

"Do you?"

"You think Fitz still sees you like the girl he used to know back when you were kids. Like you saw him until Sokolov made you look at him properly," Moreau said.

"Isn't it possible?" Ritchie asked.

"I don't think that's why Feena isn't getting a response out of him," Moreau said. "She's Feena. Even when she was twelve, she was still

Feena. She was never really a little girl like that. If you know what I mean."

"Fine," Ritchie said, throwing up her hands. "I guess you must be right about Fitz, then."

"It's not just me, you know. Wyss and I have compared notes," Moreau said.

"Great," Ritchie said through her teeth. "Because if there's anybody that knows more about human emotions than you, it's Wyss."

"Now you're just being mean," Moreau said and got up from her chair. But she turned back before opening the door. "Look, why don't you take a minute now that you're alone in here and play back your messages from Guy? If you're not ready to answer him because Finn made that weird, that's fine. But I really think you need to hear Guy's voice again. He pulls you out of the Fitz vortex, and that's really where you need to be just now."

"I'll think about it," Ritchie said, more sullenly than she intended to.

"In the meantime, I'm going to wade into that vortex myself," Moreau said with a sigh. "I doubt there's anything more we can do here without more evidence to work from, but the idea of trying to sleep tonight in one big room with at least one murderer and potentially a bunch of coconspirators trying to destroy our whole way of life just freaks me out."

"We'll be together," Ritchie said, reaching out a hand. Moreau took it and gave it a squeeze, and that was all the apology they needed to leave the argument behind them.

Moreau wasn't wrong about Guy, either. The minute Ritchie linked her implant to the tablet and started the first message, she heard "Hey, Murdina!" in that voice so full of affection and she just felt at ease.

Everything was confusing and wrong, but he was the one thing in the universe that felt absolutely right to her.

The next time she was alone with Moreau, she'd be sure to thank her again for that vacation.

20

THE LAB WAS JUST where Blaser had told Fitz it would be, past the point where he'd thought he'd walked too far. But that was probably a good thing. He didn't want random cadets going in and out of that space, potentially interfering with the testing. He was a bit disappointed not to see a guard outside the door. He sent a quick message for Blaser requesting one.

Then amended it to two, not buddies. It was really hard to work around conspiracies when the players were unknown.

He pushed open the door to find himself inside another natural cave, only the wall the door was set into was fabricated. The floorspace still had a squarish feel because of the various pieces of equipment lined up to form walls of sorts. Stalactites descended just behind all of them, some of the backsides of the machines even having been pressed up against them for so long they were becoming one with the rock.

He really didn't like the look of the equipment. It was clearly far older than anything down at the school. But he could see several were running already, indicator lights illuminated and screens showing streams of data he couldn't make heads or tails of.

But given the lack of a guard outside the room, he couldn't exactly be surprised to find more cadets inside than he had been expecting. Fitz had known that Kung was working in the lab, but not that Imhof and Stucki were in there with him.

"Hey," he said. He had been feeling flustered all evening, and more irritated by the minute. Now he got to add confused to the list.

"I'm just observing," Stucki told him. "Imhof is the chemistry guy here."

"Kung's had more classes than me," Imhof said.

"I bow to your raw talent. I'm more of a mechanical kind of guy," Kung said.

Fitz took a deep breath. "Can you tell me anything?"

"Not just yet," Kung said, waving an arm towards the banks of equipment behind him. "We can do more here than I had thought, but it's going to take some time. The equipment isn't what you'd call state of the art."

"How optimistic are you of finding an answer?" Fitz asked.

Kung looked to Imhof, who shrugged.

"Tell him about the DNA, at least," Stucki said.

"Right," Imhof said, and waved Fitz over to a large, flat table in the center of the room. He touched the surface, and it came to life, opening windows of text in front of each of them and also projecting a hologram over the center. At first, the hologram was only the academy emblem, and an older design of it at that. Then Imhof touched something on the window in front of him and threw it up onto the holographic field.

Fitz was disappointed to see it was just more data visualization, nothing he remotely understood.

That must have shown on his face, because Stucki said, "it was my idea to look. It occurred to me when Kung and Imhof were examining the gloves that there are two possible scenarios to explain the burns. That Hansen grabbed a rope coated in whatever and burned through his gloves, or that he had it on his gloves in the first place and used them to burn through the rope."

"I didn't see what was happening well enough to tell," Fitz said. "Where does DNA come in?"

"If he was going to burn the rope on purpose using his gloves, he would've put a protective layer underneath it, right? So he wouldn't burn himself, just the rope?" Stucki said.

"Good thought," Fitz said. "What'd you find?"

"Hansen's DNA," Imhof said, gesturing at the hologram. "He burned his flesh and bled quite a bit. Like, a lot. He felt the pain but didn't let go."

"Allegedly," Kung put in.

"You know, we usually say that when we're accusing someone of wrongdoing. Not trying to save others," Fitz said.

Kung just shrugged.

"We've also eliminated the most obvious caustic agents, if you need a list of things that weren't on that rope and gloves," Imhof said, tossing up another graphic. This one Fitz could understand. They'd tested for dozens of things already.

"I might need that. Go ahead and send it to my implant," Fitz said.

"We'll keep you updated, then," Imhof said, tapping commands on the tabletop.

"Did you guys eat?" Fitz asked, suddenly realizing he had missed dinner himself. Two protein bars after a day of climbing and hiking were nowhere near enough. He was getting downright lightheaded.

"I brought them food," Stucki said. "I was going to go back for our cots. It seems like we'll be here waiting for a bit."

"Sounds good," Fitz said. "I've asked Blaser to put guards on the door, but until then, don't let anyone in here that isn't me, Ritchie, Moreau or Blaser."

"Got it," Kung said. "No one's tried to come by, but we'll keep them out if they do. At least until the testing is done."

"Thanks," Fitz said. "Ping me if you need me. I have to go find some food myself. Then maybe a cot."

Stucki walked with him back out of the semi-lit depths of the winding tunnel to the warmer, even drier air of the cavern. He could smell dinner on the air, but not so fresh as before, and about half of the cadets were already collapsed on their cots, fast asleep or well on their way to it.

"There's stew left on that light box there," Stucki pointed out to him. "Do you want me to haul a cot down for you too?"

"No, I haven't decided where I'll be yet. But thanks," Fitz said, carefully picking the stew container up by one corner. It was more than half gone, but what was left smelled divine. Bits of beef, potatoes cooked to creamy perfection, brown gravy that smelled like the choicest bits of a fresh herb garden had been added to exacting proportions. When he found a spoon and dug in, he found the stew thicker than he expected after simmering for so long on the light box, but that only made it that much more warm and filling.

"Fitz. I need a minute," Moreau said, suddenly at his elbow.

Fitz took another bite and swallowed before saying, "about what?"

But she didn't answer his question. She just said, "someone wants to talk to you," and walked away. She must have been pretty confident he was going to follow her, as she never once looked back.

Curious, he put another large spoonful of the stew in his mouth and followed her, ration container still in his hand.

She went into another one of the doors at some random point between where he had left her and Ritchie and where he imagined Blaser was still working on Blaser things. Inside was another office, smaller than the other two. Here the desk was pushed up against one of the side walls, and there was only a single chair. Moreau had crossed to the far side of the room and was leaning against the wall, arms folded.

On the desktop stood one of Wyss's tablets. And Wyss was on the screen, although he seemed to be working on something else at the moment.

"I hope you don't think I'm going to sit there," Fitz said, as he kicked the door shut behind him. The chair was lined up with the tablet, which wasn't really a problem, but Moreau had taken a position where, if he sat down, she'd be looming over him.

As much as a girl her size could loom over him, at any rate.

Fitz took another bite of the stew. "Wyss is who wanted to talk to me?" he asked as he chewed. "Why so mysterious about it, then?"

"Oh, good. He's here," Wyss said, and furrowed his brow as he finished whatever else he was doing.

"Sit in the chair. If it makes you more comfortable, I'll move," Moreau said, pushing off the far wall to lean her hip against the desk.

Not exactly an improvement, but at least she wouldn't be out of his field of view if he was facing Wyss.

"What's this all about?" he asked as he sat down. "Why do I feel like I'm about to be interrogated? I'm pretty confident I'm not a suspect. Wyss knows where I was all break, and everyone knows where I was when Wyder fell."

"This isn't about that," Moreau told him. He looked at her, but as usual the expression on her face was giving him nothing.

He scraped the last of the stew into the spoon and ate it, then set the ration pack and utensil aside to sit back in the chair. "Fine. What *is* this about?"

"Fitz, I don't know how long this line will stay up, so I need you to cooperate," Wyss said, glancing out of the tablet screen at him. Fitz just nodded. "This is what Moreau and I know so far."

"About what?" Fitz asked.

"Don't interrupt," Moreau said. "The line *will* cut out. When is the only variable."

"Go ahead," Fitz said. "I'll hold my peace."

"We know that you and Ritchie were close as children. And that your fathers were also close. Your father, a lieutenant general at the time, worked closely with Ritchie's father, who was a diplomat but also a master linguist." Wyss took a deep breath. "They were both dealing with the yuffids, separately and together."

"We can jump over the details of that," Moreau said, not to Wyss, but to Fitz. Fitz was starting to feel like he was in a scene the two of them had rehearsed carefully, and that wasn't a comfortable feeling. But he said nothing.

"Ritchie's father was meeting with the yuffids, an important step towards their people becoming allies of the Union of the Free Worlds. The language barrier was a large problem, but things were looking very optimistic. Right up until the minute it all fell apart."

"I'm not talking about this," Fitz announced, and tried to get up from the chair, but to his surprise, Moreau forced him back down.

"We're talking about it," she said. "Now let Wyss speak."

"Most of this is common knowledge, that Ritchie's father was abducted by the yuffids and never seen again. Missing, many presume dead. And Ritchie and her mother went back to the space station where her mother was from originally, and you never saw her again until you both came late to this school, last year."

"You had a weird energy," Moreau said.

Fitz glared at her, wanting to ask why she was allowed to speak while he was to remain silent. But he could see that Wyss' signal was starting to glitch and break up. This would all be over soon.

"What Ritchie doesn't know, I don't think, is how hard your father worked to keep her out of all the foreign service academies. Despite her high scores on all aptitude tests, she kept getting rejected. She shouldn't have been."

"It wasn't about you," Moreau told him. "Even you, as much as you moved around, were only going to one school at a time. Keeping you two apart is one thing. Keeping her away from foreign service entirely is quite another."

Fitz was shocked by this, and yet he could see the sense in it. He had always assumed it was because of him, to keep Ritchie away from him, but Moreau was right. That didn't make sense. Not even his father was that thorough to the point of overkill.

"Another thing that Ritchie doesn't know, but is beginning to suspect, is that Finn knows your big secret," Wyss said.

"Which is?" Fitz asked, unable to hold still any longer.

"We don't know that exactly," Moreau admitted.

"But we know it has something to do with what happened between her father, your father, and the yuffids," Wyss said.

"And we're fairly certain whatever it is, if Ritchie knew it, she would be heartbroken," Moreau said.

"Oh, it's so much worse than that," Fitz said with a humorless laugh. "So much worse."

"Tell us," Moreau said.

Fitz looked at Wyss on the tablet screen. For a second he thought the image had frozen, that the signal had gone down. But then he saw Wyss blink, waiting for his answer.

"If Ritchie knows what I know, it will be very dangerous for her," Fitz said. "Yes, she'll be heartbroken, but then she'll be angry. And then she'll be unstoppable. And then she'll be dead."

"Can you just tell us?" Wyss asked.

Fitz was about to say no, when a sudden feeling washed over him, so overwhelming it paralyzed his mind.

Could he just tell them? After all, Finn already knew. And if Finn knew, Feena likely knew as well. Those two might not have all the details, but he knew in his bones what little they had pieced together they would find a way to use for bad ends. All they needed was the opportunity.

He couldn't tell Ritchie. That hadn't changed.

But maybe he could tell Wyss and Moreau? They would understand why Ritchie could never know. They could help protect her.

He just had to be sure they understood why the secret itself had to be protected, not just for now but for all time.

"Only if you swear not to tell her," Fitz said at last. "You can't. You just can't."

"Finn already knows?" Moreau asked.

"Yes," Fitz said resignedly.

"Then tell us," she said.

"Ritchie's father spent months working on what he was going to attempt to say at that meeting with the yuffids. Months. He studied every example of their speech he could find, searching for nuances. And Ritchie, just barely twelve but kind of a genius at noticing things, was right there with him. Helping."

"Oh, no," Moreau said, putting a hand over her mouth in horror. "She did something that led to what happened to her father? That's—"

"—not what happened," Fitz finished the sentence for her. "It is what Ritchie *thinks* happened, however."

"I'm lost," Wyss said from the tablet screen.

"Ritchie was still working on aspects of their nonverbal communication, studying the videos and that, long after her father had started his journey to where the meeting was taking place. I remember that time well. There was no distracting her from it at all. Then, just before the meeting was scheduled to begin, she saw something important. A little gesture, like three fingers fanned under one's chin." He demonstrated it for them briefly. "The yuffids use it to soften requests for information. Without that gesture, questions are rude. And every question without it becomes exponentially ruder."

"She figured it out too late?" Moreau guessed.

"Not that either," Fitz said, raking his fingers through his hair. He hated these memories. The gesture, the look on Ritchie's face when she'd come to him telling him what she'd found.

The look on his father's face when he'd passed on the information.

"Fitz," Wyss said, calling him back to the moment.

Fitz sighed. "She told me, and I went straight away to my father's office and told him. And he swore to me that he would tell her father. He swore it."

"But he didn't," Wyss said. His gaze was slightly offscreen again, and Fitz just knew he was watching one of the most famous pieces of video in the last decade play on another computer.

"No. If you're watching the video, her father never does the gesture. And the yuffids grow more and more enraged, and he doesn't know why."

"But surely Ritchie knows?" Moreau said.

Fitz laughed far too shrilly. "You'd think so, right? But she's never seen it. Not even once. Not even when Keller kept asking her about it over and over again."

"No one but Ritchie and you and your dad would even know there was anything to notice about it, right?" Wyss guessed.

"My only hope," Fitz said quietly, "is that if she ever sees that video and knows her father never got her message, that she blames me. She can't blame my father. She just can't." He barked out another laugh. "Well, you've figured out for yourselves what lengths he'll go to against her when she's not even trying to work against him. Imagine if she threatened his career."

"Frankly, I'm more worried she'd go after the yuffids," Moreau said.

"That's my second biggest worry," Fitz said. "Welcome to the hellscape of my mind."

"Finn knows, but he's not talking?" Wyss asked.

"Because of my father," Fitz said. "And before you ask, I have no idea why my father never told Ritchie's father what she learned. I suspect he didn't take her seriously. Her own father would've. But not mine."

"I'm not sure this is enough of an explanation for me," Moreau said. "You've been a huge jerk this entire year."

"Finn has threatened to tell her," Fitz said helplessly. "He'd do it. Maybe even despite his fear of my father, he'd do it. If he thought it would get to me. So I have to stay away from her. There'd be no point in using that to destroy our friendship if we weren't friends anymore. Tell me you get it."

"No," Moreau said. "That's not what you're afraid of."

"I don't want her to hate me," Fitz said. "But she will. When she thinks this is my fault, she will. I've been waiting for that blade to fall for a really long time."

"You have to tell Ritchie," Wyss said.

"No," Fitz said. "You guys, you have to swear—"

"No, you aren't getting me," Wyss said, leaning into the camera on his end. "*You* have to tell Ritchie. Before Finn does. Before she finds out on her own. You have to tell her."

"And stop assuming you know better than she does how she's going to react," Moreau said. "Trust her a little."

"I *do* trust her," Fitz said.

But Moreau just put her hand up. "Stop. I don't need to hear it."

"We won't tell," Wyss said. "We'll wait for you to find the right time, I guess. But Fitz, it only gets more dangerous the longer you wait."

"Guys, I really don't see any path to 'less dangerous.' Not at all," Fitz said.

Then he picked up the remains of his dinner and left the room. Just one more little conspiracy he hadn't known enough to avoid stepping into.

But he knew he was right. There was no safe path ahead of him. Not at all. But if he kept his wits about him, he might still find a path that led Ritchie to safety.

Or so he hoped.

21

RITCHIE PLAYED every single one of Guy's messages, making the most of the privacy of the office while she still had it. They were short and breezy, and while she wasn't quite in a place to laugh out loud at his stories of campus life, he did manage to bring a smile to her face that lingered after the last message ended.

She recorded a response of sorts. She didn't want to tell him about the murder or the missing instructor. She definitely didn't want to get into anything about the conspiracies that felt like they were always closing in on them. She didn't even really want to tell him about the storm that had driven them down into the caves. Any of that was just going to make him worry.

But that didn't leave much else to talk about except the actual climbing. Once she got into it, it felt like it went okay. She knew he would be interested in the equipment they had used, and when she described the view from the alpine meadows, she was sure her enthusiasm came across.

She quickly ran out of things to say and signed off, then hesitated with her finger over the playback button. No, if she watched herself talk she'd be tempted to keep recording it over and over again, and it was never going to get any better. She knew she looked exhausted, and her tan was already fading. If she forced herself to confront her own image and then record again, the result would just be sadder than the first.

No, he just needed to know that his messages were getting through —or most of them, anyway—and that she was okay.

Alas, while her implant was connected to the local intranet, there was no signal to send the message out to the academy or the rest of the universe. She tried a few times, but there was nothing.

She looked at the tablet in her hands. She had connected her implant to it to use it to view and record, but that wasn't its primary purpose. She extended the antenna and tried connecting to Wyss again.

It took forever, each connection taking longer than the last. And when the screen changed from the connection information to a face, she was surprised to see Sokolov looking out at her.

"Hey," Ritchie said. "It's you."

"Yes, Wyss is occupied," Sokolov said, her eyes shifting to something out of frame then back again. "He's talking to Fitz at the moment, actually."

"Fitz? Why is he talking to Fitz without me?" she asked.

"Oh, nothing bad!" Sokolov assured her. "Kung and Imhof wanted Wyss's assistance with the tests they are running on the rope and gloves you found in Hansen's tent. So Fitz brought his tablet down to them. You can find them both there if you need them. Or I can help you with something?"

"I was just trying to send a message from my implant, but the official communications equipment at this base camp isn't doing anything at all. Can I send something down to you through the tablet and you can forward it for me?" Ritchie asked.

Sokolov frowned. "I think so? But I don't really know how it works for anything besides calls. I can grab Wyss—"

"No, don't interrupt him if he's working on something for the case," Ritchie said quickly. "It's not important. It can wait."

"Are you sure?" Sokolov asked.

The image on the screen was grainy and distorted, and it kept freezing then skipping, so it was really hard to tell for sure. But Ritchie sensed something in Sokolov's eyes, some unspoken but profound sympathy. For Ritchie. But why?

"I'm sure," Ritchie said. "How's everything down there?"

"Same," Sokolov said. "No updates yet. I've been helping Wyss run searches on Thecla Joosten. Since you and Fitz are treating her as a suspect, we want to see if there's anything in her background that might be relevant."

"That's a good idea," Ritchie said.

"Yeah, but nothing so far," Sokolov said. Then her face froze for several seconds, the last word hanging half-said before the signal dropped completely and the tablet switched back to its home screen.

Ritchie closed it up, then stood up and stretched her back. She was so ready for bed, but she should really find some food first.

She stepped out of the office to find the cavern in a twilight state. Safety lights glowed dimly from unseen places among the stalactites, and the doorways and tunnel entrances were marked by bluish light strips, just barely illuminating the shapes of the cadets inside their puffy sleeping bags.

The last of the food had been put away, every light box now on night mode with nothing left simmering on its surface. Ritchie sighed. She had no idea where the food was kept, or even who to ask besides Blaser. And if he was sleeping, there was no way she was going to wake him back up.

Her protein bar breakfast and protein bar lunch were about to be followed up by a protein bar dinner.

She really missed the cookouts on the beaches of Epsilon 20.

It took a moment for her to remember where the cot with her stuff was, but before she could take more than a single step towards it, she heard a beeping sound. It was faint, and no one sleeping around her stirred, but she was sure she wasn't imagining it. She tipped her head to get a sense of its direction, then found herself walking towards the bottom of the tunnel that led up to the door out to the meadow above.

The beeping was coming from the door. But what could it mean?

She looked around the cavern behind her. Blaser had said he would set watches, but she saw no sign of any cadets standing guard anywhere.

She decided not to wake anyone until she knew what was going on. If she had to, she could roust everyone at once with a communications blast from her implant.

She jogged up the tunnel, the air around her getting decidedly colder by the second. There were no heaters within the utility building at the end of the tunnel, but it hadn't been this cold when she had come in. By the time she reached the last turn before the door, she was shivering from the breeze blowing past her.

Then she rounded that turn and realized where the breeze was coming from. The door was standing wide open, and the blizzard winds outside were filling the air with a blinding snow. She ran towards the panel to shut the door.

She was sprawled out on her butt on the cold concrete and stone floor before she quite realized she had collided with somebody hidden in that snowy haze. Someone had broken into the base camp.

She started to send out a general alarm, but the shadowy figure standing over said, "hold, cadet."

"Colonel Hansen?" Ritchie gasped.

The figure turned and slapped the control panel beside the door, the one Ritchie had been trying to reach. The door slammed shut with a booming thud, and the wind instantly fell away. It took another second for the snow to settle out of the air. But it was definitely Colonel Hansen standing over her. She recognized him even with his hood pulled low over his masked face.

And there was a large object wrapped in tent plastic draped across his shoulders.

"You found Wyder?" Ritchie asked.

Hansen pushed back his hood, then removed the shield covering his face. He rubbed the back of his gloved hand over his forehead, particularly at the deep indent in his skin where the top of the shield had been resting. Then he looked down at her. "I have."

"Do you know who killed her?" Ritchie asked.

"No. I was rather hoping you and Fitz would've figured that out by now," he said. He extended a hand to help her back to her feet.

"We're working on it, sir," Ritchie said.

"Of course you are. Come. There's a lab down one of the side tunnels with rudimentary forensics equipment. I'm going to bring Wyder there," he said.

"I believe Fitz is there right now, sir," Ritchie said. "Kung and Imhof are running some tests on the rope and gloves you left behind. I think they might be close to something since they've been talking to Wyss down at the academy. Although," she added with a frown, "the signal just dropped. I'm not sure they had enough time to get any answers."

"Only one way to find out," Hansen said, then led the way down the tunnel, through the cavern of sleeping cadets, and then down a deeper, narrower tunnel.

No one in the cavern stirred as they passed by. And she still saw no sign of anyone on guard. If Blaser had set watches, they were terrible at their jobs.

They reached a closed door, and Hansen pushed it open. Over his shoulder, Ritchie could see Imhof, Stucki, Kung, Fitz and Moreau all gathered around a data table in the center of the room. They jumped when the door banged open, then lit up when they realized who had just burst in.

"Still no guard out there, sir?" Fitz asked.

"No guards anywhere," Ritchie said. Hansen was still in the doorway, looking around the room. He finally saw what he was looking for and crossed the room to lay his burden down on a wheeled metal table. He touched a gloved hand to what must have been Wyder's face under the plastic, but made no move to uncover her. "No watches were set. We need to wake everyone up and get a head count right away."

"What's going on?" Hansen asked, turning away from the body to look at the five of them.

"Well, sir, we cleared your name a while ago as being responsible for what happened to Wyder," Fitz said.

Hansen gave him a dry smile. "Thanks for that, cadet."

"Yes, sir," Fitz said. "The problem is, that leaves an unknown murderer among us. Possibly with coconspirators."

"Which was why we asked Blaser to set watches," Ritchie said. "We know this was murder, and we suspect it was another attempt to frame you. But we're not certain enough of that as the motive to feel safe assuming no one else is going to be a target."

"Frame me?" Hansen said with a frown.

"We know Wyder is the witness against you, officially," Fitz said. "But we also know she isn't actually the person who saw anything. We think that's why she's dead."

"Of course," Hansen said. "The Berwegers."

"It does seem like they are trying to remove you from the board. So to speak. Sir," Fitz added belatedly.

"Some of this is news to some of us, you know," Stucki said from the far side of the data table. He made a gesture of something flying over his head.

"You three," Hansen said, pointing to Kung, Imhof and Stucki. "Go find Blaser. Have him take a head count and set the watches. Then I want him to report to me. Go."

Ritchie started to move out of the doorway to let them pass, when a sudden thought struck her. She caught Imhof's sleeve. "Did you learn anything?"

"Something," he said vaguely. "Fitz can catch you up." Then he brushed past her to head up the tunnel at a fast walk. Stucki just grinned at her before following his buddy. But Ritchie was glad to see she wasn't the only one who felt better now that Hansen was back among them.

"Blaser must've fallen asleep before setting the watches, sir," Fitz was saying to Hansen. "He's been very helpful to us in our investigation, but being the only one in charge here, I think he got a little overwhelmed."

"Rest easy, cadet. I'm not planning to ream anyone out," Hansen said, resting a hand on Fitz's shoulder. "He brought you up here into the caves, just like I ordered. That was the main thing."

"You ordered, sir?" Ritchie asked.

"Didn't Blaser tell you?" he asked. "That is why you're here, isn't it?"

"Blaser phrased it like this was his own plan. Even like you might not like it if you knew, but as you weren't here..." Fitz trailed off with a shrug.

Hansen said nothing, but his confusion was clear on his face.

Then Ritchie had a horrid thought. "Sir, it wasn't you that snoozed all of our implant alarms the morning you left us?" she asked.

"Certainly not," he said, sounding offended at the very idea.

"But you *did* tell us to stay inside our tents," Moreau said.

"Because of the storm. Which I trust you all did. I give orders, I expect that they will be followed. I do not expect I need to tamper with everyone's implants to make my orders happen."

"It must be connected, then," Ritchie said. "Someone snoozed all of our implant alarms and deleted any trace of the message you left for Blaser."

"I sent a message to the two of you as well," Hansen said, looking from Fitz to Ritchie.

"We never got it, sir," Fitz said.

The scowl on Hansen's face grew deeper, his pallor darkening.

"Well, we know who can do such a thing," Moreau said. "Means and motive and opportunity. We have them all."

"The Berwegers are close with Wyder and Joosten both," Fitz said. "We've been looking for anyone who was here over the break, who had the opportunity to try to set you up, but that almost doesn't matter. The Berwegers are clearly behind this. They didn't even need to be here to get it done. They have enough other cadets in their thrall to do the dirty work for them."

"Why do you mention Joosten?" Hansen asked with a frown.

"We think she's the one who convinced Wyder to speak against you. I mean, we know Wyder wasn't there. But Joosten was," Ritchie said.

"You're forgetting just one little fact," Hansen said darkly. "I didn't do anything. So it really doesn't matter who was here or not here, since there was nothing to be witnessed."

"Damn," Fitz said with a dry laugh, and slapped a hand to his forehead. "We've been going about this all wrong."

"Not *all* wrong," Hansen allowed. "I'm certainly pleased the two of you found what I left for you even though you never received the instructions to pick them up. Did you learn anything from the rope and gloves?"

"We isolated something," Fitz said. "But—"

Ritchie interrupted him with a gasp as the tablet she still held clutched to her chest started to vibrate. She set it on the data table and opened it up, but the screen only displayed its home settings.

"What's going on?" Moreau asked her.

"It vibrated. I didn't even know it could do that," Ritchie said. "I thought we were getting a call, but there's nothing here."

"Not *nothing*," Fitz said, and pressed one of a serious of unmarked buttons on the bottom of the screen. Green text filled the screen at a rate too fast to follow.

"What is it?" Ritchie asked.

"The chemical signature we sent down to Wyss to look up," Fitz said, as the text finally came to an end. He glanced at the last few lines of text, then looked up at Hansen with a grin. "Ever heard of Bemtic acidic compound, sir?"

"It sounds familiar," Hansen said. "Brand name?"

"A brand name so proprietary, no one knows exactly what's in it. Well, except Wyss now, apparently. It's not for sale to the public. In fact, it's very hard to acquire for any but the richest or most connected of families," Fitz said.

"So, the Berwegers," Moreau said, folding her arms over her chest. "Everything always comes back to the Berwegers."

"Only circumstantially," Hansen said. "Unless we find either of them in possession of it, we can't even attempt to hold them for this."

"We'll get more evidence," Ritchie said.

She hoped she sounded more confident than she felt. But in truth, she was afraid the twins were going to slip away again.

She could almost hear Finn laughing at her already.

22

FITZ LET Ritchie give Hansen the full story of everything that had happened since he had left the last base camp. She was meticulously thorough, but Fitz could tell that Hansen was only half-listening. He had the slightly dazed look to his eye of someone who is trying to communicate through their implant at the same time as listening to the person in front of them. Fitz was sure if Ritchie said anything he deemed important, it would snag his attention. And he supposed Ritchie was sure of that as well. There was no way she didn't notice Hansen's distraction.

Moreau had wandered off to the far corner of the cave. Fitz assumed she was just looking at all the machines that Imhof and Kung had left running, hoping for clues as to what they were finding. But then the smell of brewing coffee filled the air, and he was instantly, if silently, grateful for what she had really been up to.

"That's all good work, cadet, but this is far from over," Hansen said to Ritchie. "First thing I need is to get in contact with the academy."

"The administration knows we're in need of rescue, and that Wyder is dead. The last time we reached them, you were still missing, though," Fitz said. Then he picked up Wyss's tablet from the tabletop and held it out to Hansen. "Wyss built this. It works better than the native equipment up here. The storm has been blocking the signal, but this will break through at the first opportunity. Either Wyss or Sokolov are always on the other end when we call. They can fetch anyone else for you."

"Thank you, cadet," Hansen said, taking the tablet and turning it over in his hands as if to admire it from every angle.

"We've been using the officer's quarters as a private place to call down there," Ritchie told him. "And Blaser commandeered one for himself."

"Yes, Cadet Captain Blaser," Hansen said in just the sort of tone Fitz never wanted to hear his own name in. "Clearly that boy is not coming to me. I shall have to go in search of him."

"We can find him for you," Fitz offered.

"No, I need you to stay here and guard this space. The evidence, the body, and the machines that are still running all need to be kept secure and confidential. No one save Kung, Imhof, Stucki and yourselves are to be allowed inside this room."

"Yes, sir," Ritchie said.

"If Blaser hasn't already assigned guards, I will see it done myself. In the meantime, ping my implant if you need me. And take turns sleeping on those cots over there. You need to stay sharp. This storm will last for days, easily. You're no good to me sleep-deprived and physically exhausted from the hike up here."

"Yes, sir," Fitz said.

Hansen gave them one last nod, then went out the door.

Leaving Fitz standing there awkwardly with Ritchie.

She seemed preoccupied with her own thoughts, for which he was grateful. He wasn't sure what he would do if she tried to talk to him or even look at him now.

He had told Moreau and Wyss everything. He still couldn't believe that had happened. He had just... told them. And now he was terrified. His secret had only been safe so long as he was the only one who carried it. Moreau he could at least keep an eye on, but Wyss was out of his reach and would be for days.

Although maybe it *was* Moreau he should be more worried about.

She was the one sharing space with the Berwegers. And he knew just how susceptible she could be to the two of them.

So he was terrified, and as exhausted as he was, he knew sleep would be impossible.

And yet, at the same time, his heart felt lighter. He was sharing his burden with others, others who unlike Finn would actually try to help him carry it. After five long years of going it alone, the relief to finally have someone in it with him was so profound it almost hurt.

"Here," Moreau said, handing him a cup of the freshly brewed coffee. He looked up to thank her, but the words died on his lips. Her face, usually so blank to his eyes, was unusually expressive. Like she knew what he was feeling, particularly how he felt about standing so close to Ritchie, who still didn't know what was really going on between them.

She clutched his hand briefly as he took the cup from her. Then she turned to give the other to Ritchie.

"Ugh, that's strong," Ritchie said, after taking a sip.

"Were you planning to try sleeping?" Moreau asked her, raising a single eyebrow.

"No, that's not happening," Ritchie said. "It's just that I've not eaten yet. This much caffeine on an empty stomach is never a good thing for me."

"I'll go find you some food," Moreau said, but Ritchie caught her arm before she could head towards the door.

"Maybe we should both go," she said, setting her coffee on the data table. Which was absolutely not good for the equipment, even if it never spilled. Fitz picked it up and brought it over to one of the tall workstation desks against the cave wall, where it would be safe.

"Why should we both go?" Moreau asked.

"Fitz can watch the room on his own until Imhof, Stucki and Kung come back," Ritchie said.

"I suppose he can, but why?" Moreau countered.

Fitz was curious to know the answer to that himself, but he said not a word.

"I think we should find Feena," Ritchie said. She shot a little glance at Fitz that fell away before quite landing on him.

"To?" Moreau prompted.

"First of all, she had volunteered to compile a list for us, only she's never reported back. So that's what we'll open with," Ritchie said. "But really I want to see what she knows about this Bemtic acidic compound."

"So she can lie to you about it?" Fitz asked, despite his intentions to not draw attention to himself.

"I want to hear what she has to say. The first thing she says, unprepared, when we ask her about it," Ritchie said. "It might be a lie, but she might also reveal something when she hears the question."

"I don't know. The Berwegers are pretty good at masking their responses, and even better at fabricating whatever they want you to see," Moreau said.

"I think you two should stay here and I'll go out," Fitz said.

"To do what?" Moreau asked.

"Search Finn's pack," Fitz said. "I guess I'm thinking along the same lines as Ritchie. I want to know what he has before he knows we have anything in particular we're searching for."

"As much as we've tried to lock down the number of people who know this information, I have to admit the cadet grapevine is not a force to be taken lightly," Moreau said. Then she took half a step closer to Fitz. "Ritchie does need to eat, though. I think we two should go. But when Kung and Imhof get here, you should definitely check that pack out."

"Then you and I go out and Ritchie stays here," Fitz said. Now that he'd said it, he realized that was really the best plan. Moreau had not yet been alone with Ritchie since hearing Fitz's secret. The idea of watching the two of them walk off together, heads together as they whispered to each other, twisted his stomach into anxious knots.

But Moreau took another step towards him, tipping her head just enough so that her face was out of Ritchie's view. "It's going to be fine, Fitz. It won't take long for us to talk to Feena, and then we'll be right back. There's nothing to worry about."

He could see in her eyes that she knew just what he was feeling. But it really didn't ease any of his anxiety.

"I like the first plan. It gets me to food faster," Ritchie said. She clearly wasn't sensing any subtextual conversation happening around her. She was just hungry and getting cranky.

"Fine. Go," Fitz said. "I'll wait here. Alone."

Moreau gave him one last sad little smile, and then she and Ritchie were gone. The door clicked shut behind them, and Fitz was alone with the frozen body of Wyder, nothing but the soft humming of the machines to keep him company.

He finished off his coffee, then started sipping at Ritchie's as he toured the room, watching the data flicker over the screens on the front of the machines. He didn't know what most of it meant. They probably already had the only answer they were going to get, the identity of the chemical compound used to burn the rope and gloves. That and the presence of Hansen's DNA. Fitz doubted there was anything more to find.

He drained the last of the coffee from Ritchie's cup, then carried it along with his own empty mug back to the coffee machine. He was just pouring another cup when the door clicked open again. There was nothing sneaky about the click, and he assumed one of the team was back to join him.

But when he put the pot back on the warmer and turned towards the door, he saw it was Finn closing the door behind him.

"Sorry, you can't be in here," Fitz said, not sorry at all.

"Blaser is posting guards. Maybe I'm one of the guards," Finn said.

"If that were true, you'd have a partner," Fitz said. "I don't see a partner."

"You got me," Finn said with a shrug, then crossed the room to where Wyder's wrapped body lay slowly thawing on the stainless steel table. "So he went back for her."

"You're here to hold a wake?" Fitz asked, setting his coffee aside before walking over to Finn. He might have to wrestle the other cadet out of the room, and he wanted his hands free. That, and the caffeine he'd already had was enough to make his hands shake. Ritchie wasn't wrong. Moreau liked her coffee beyond strong.

"Don't you know why I'm here?" Finn asked. His voice wasn't quite the purr of his sister's, but it was unnervingly close.

"You tell me," Fitz said, putting himself between Finn and the body.

"As usual, you're looking for something you think I have. And as usual, I'm here to tell you it has nothing to do with me."

"Way to be vague and wait for me to fill in the blanks for you," Fitz said, as blandly as he could. But his heart was pounding, and not just from the coffee. The cadet grapevine was running faster even than they'd feared, if Finn knew already.

But there was always the chance he was guessing. He was good at it. But it didn't always mean that he knew what he pretended to know.

"Bemtic acidic compound," Finn said, articulating every syllable distinctly as if to be sure there was no mistake. They were both talking about the same thing.

"You have some," Fitz said. Not a question.

"I have some," Finn admitted, but he was grinning. Fitz didn't like that grin. But he said nothing, so Finn was forced to speak again. "I acquired some over the break to use for a science project I'll be working on later this semester. I did some research ahead of time, and I'm all prepared for what I intend to do. Which involves acid."

"Nice story," Fitz said.

"It really doesn't matter if you believe me, because—and listen up well, because this is the important bit," Finn said, raising an admonishing finger that Fitz just barely controlled the urge to grab and force out of his face. "I don't have any of it here with me. It's all in my locker back at school. In the barracks, with the appropriate paperwork. It's a highly controlled substance, you know."

"So highly controlled, most of us can't even get it," Fitz said.

Finn just shrugged. "Like you never use your family's connections to acquire things."

"Actually, I don't think I ever have," Fitz said.

"Well, you should try it sometime. It makes life so much simpler," Finn said. His face morphed from wistful to serious, and he said, "it's all there in my locker. The amount in the container will match the amount on the paperwork down to the microgram. Once we get back to the academy, I'll be sure to present it to the proper authorities. But if you want to see it first, between friends, I'll happily show you."

"What I'd really like to see is everything you have with you on this mission," Fitz said. "Your pack, to start with. All your clothes, so I can check the pockets and search for hidden compartments. You know the drill."

But Finn didn't seem to hear his request. He was studying Fitz closely, with a strange look on his face.

"What?" Fitz asked, annoyed. He wiped at his face, but there was nothing there. No coffee moustache, nothing.

"There's something different about you," Finn said.

"I'm less patient and more cranky than usual," Fitz said. "Lack of sleep will do that to me."

"No, that's not it," Finn said, rubbing at his chin as if in deep thought.

"Did you hear me about the pack?" Fitz asked.

But Finn still ignored him. "Yes, there *is* something different about you. You look like a mountain of stress has been lifted off your shoulders."

"Hansen is back. That's a relief," Fitz said, but his stomach was starting to knot up again, tighter than ever.

Then Finn grinned at him, a slow grin that kept growing and growing. It was deeply creepy.

"Hey, Fitz!" Stucki called out as he and Imhof all but slammed their way into the lab. "We're here to relieve you." Then he saw Finn standing there, too close to Fitz. "What's he doing here? Colonel Hansen has a very short list of cadets who are authorized to be in here, and he's definitely not on it."

'We were just leaving," Finn said, turning away from Fitz to face Stucki and Imhof. That almost-a-purr was back in his voice, and Fitz could swear that Stucki rocked back on his heels when Finn turned his attention onto him.

"You were?" Stucki asked, almost sounding disappointed.

"Yes. Fitz here wants to search my pack and the like," Finn said.

So he had been listening.

"All right, then," Stucki said dazedly.

"Ping me if you get any more results," Fitz said to Imhof. Imhof just nodded, unbothered by the state his buddy was in. Well, he'd probably seen it before. The Berwegers used their powers of persuasion at the drop of a hat, and after more than a semester at the academy, everyone was getting jadedly used to it.

"I'm this way," Finn said, and Fitz followed him back into the main cavern. Most of the cadets were still sleeping, but not everyone. He could see a pair of cadets standing at the base of the tunnel that led up to the door to the meadow, and another flanking one of the office doors. Another pair was walking among the cots, using a red light to count the number of sleeping cadets in each row of cots. And one last pair passed Finn and Fitz on their way back down the tunnel, presumably to guard the lab.

"Do you mind if I unpack it myself? I have a system," Finn said. He wasn't even attempting to keep his voice down despite the dozens of cadets sleeping around them. A few of them stirred, but none of them sat up.

"Whatever," Fitz whispered back.

Finn's sleeping bag was still in a tight roll at the head of his cot. He pulled his pack out from under the cot and set it next to the bag, then began opening pockets, one after another, and arraying the contents in neat rows and columns on the rest of the cot. When he was done, he stepped back, and Fitz touched everything. He opened the bottles and sniffed the contents, and ran his fingers over every centimeter of the pack itself in search of hidden compartments.

"Okay, you can repack it," he whispered to Finn when he was done. Finn did so with brisk efficiency, then set it back under the cot. Fitz untied the sleeping bag and shook it out over the cot, but nothing was hidden in its folds either.

"Satisfied?" Finn asked, again speaking ever so slightly too loudly.

"Clothes," Fitz said with a sigh. "We can use the office—"

"No, it's fine," Finn said. He was, in fact, already shedding layers. Fitz ran his fingers over every item as Finn handed them to him. Soon he stood in only his boxers, both eyebrows raised high. "Shall I?"

Fitz didn't need to look around; he could hear the squeaks of cots as several cadets, not remotely bothering to be subtle, sat up to see what would happen next.

"I trust you," Fitz said, handing Finn his clothes back.

"How kind of you," Finn said.

"Yeah," Fitz grumbled under his breath.

But then he did glance around at the other cadets, and the looks he was getting back were suspicious and far from kind. A few looked like they had been about to leap to Finn's defense if Fitz had asked him to strip all the way down. Others looked like they kind of wanted to jump Fitz anyway.

Clearly, Joosten wasn't the only cadet who thought that Fitz and Ritchie were targeting the Berwegers and treating them unfairly.

He thought a few bitter thoughts about mind-controlled zombies, but he forced a smile to his face and said, "thank you for your assistance, Cadet Berweger. I regret it was necessary, but your cooperation is very much appreciated."

"Happy to help, Cadet Fitz," Finn said as he hopped back into his pants. "Happy to help."

This seemed to placate the cadets around them, who one by one tucked themselves back inside their sleeping bags. But Fitz could still feel a miasma of menace radiating all around him, following him as he walked away.

He just kept walking. He had no goal in mind but one.

To put as much space as possible between him and Finn Berweger.

23

RITCHIE AND MOREAU started at the part of the cavern they were sure was where they had seen the Berwegers hold court, but there was no sign of them now. Ritchie silently motioned that the two of them should split up and take opposite sides of the cavern, and Moreau nodded her understanding.

Ritchie crept from cot to cot, trying to get a good look at each cadet's face without risking waking them up. This wasn't easy to do, as most of them were still wearing their caps and were buried deep within the folds of their sleeping bags. On more than one occasion, she had to gently pull back the top layer to be sure she wasn't looking at a Berweger. A few half-woke with a murmur of protest, but none of them were either Finn or Feena.

"Cadet?" someone whispered to her. She turned to see two of the last-years standing behind her. She followed them to a corner of the cavern where there were no cots. "Can we help you?" the male cadet asked.

"You're on watch?" Ritchie asked. He nodded. "I'm looking for the Berwegers. Feena, actually."

"They were bunking right where you were," the other last-year cadet said. But there was a puzzled frown on her face. "Did they move?"

"We're supposed to do a head count," the first cadet said, brandishing a light equipped with a red filter. "Why don't I ping you if I find her?"

"That sounds like a plan," Ritchie agreed. Mostly because she was starting to doubt either twin was in the cavern now. If these two cadets were going to be checking every cot anyway, she'd be free to search some of the tunnels and caves that branched off of the main cavern.

"Great. Are you Ritchie or Fitz?" he asked. She almost thought he was joking, but his face was completely sincere.

"I'm Ritchie," she said, touching the name tag on the breast pocket of her uniform.

"Got it. Ritchie," he said. The other cadet gave him a joshing slug to the arm, then they left to get to work.

Ritchie had gotten used to the cadets outside of her circle of friends as thinking of her and Fitz as a matched set. It had been nice at first, less so since Fitz stopped talking to her.

But this thing where they were a set of indistinguishable parts was new. And a little disconcerting.

Ritchie looked around for Moreau, but couldn't see her anywhere in the cavern. Ritchie crossed to where she had seen her last and poked around among the little forest of stalactites and stalagmites that took up most of that corner of the space. There was no sign of her, but just beyond it was a small cave opening she hadn't noticed before. It didn't have lights running down the sides like the tunnel down to the lab, but at some point dozens of meters in a single dim light was illuminating what looked like a turn in the cave.

Ritchie headed for that light, digging another ration bar out of her pocket. She had refused Moreau's insistence that she eat proper, hot food. The idea of sitting down at a table with cutlery and everything while the case just sat there, not being solved, had no appeal to her. So Moreau had ducked into the supply room and come back with a fistful of bars instead.

The first had been a protein bar like she'd had for breakfast and lunch, but she realized on the first bite that what she was eating now was a very different thing. It was sweet and creamy, tasting of dark chocolate and thick peanut butter. The rush of sugar made her brain sing, and the fat content soothed her belly. She didn't even know such things existed, but trust Moreau to find the best possible thing and just hand it to Ritchie like it was nothing.

"Hey, Ritchie!" someone whispered to her. The voice was coming from behind her, back towards the cavern. She turned to see Feena Berweger making her way slowly through the cave. Ritchie knew her body was probably blocking the dim light from Feena's view, but it still seemed odd the way she was moving like she was blind. Didn't she have her implant on night vision mode?

"I was looking for you," Ritchie said.

"And *I* was looking for *you*," Feena said. She stumbled over nothing Ritchie could see, then caught herself to pull up close enough to Ritchie to have a proper conversation. Ritchie turned to rest her back against the side of the cave, and the light from the bottom finally illuminated Feena's face. She gave a smile of deep gratitude.

"Did you compile the list for us?" Ritchie asked as Feena continued to bathe in the light from the dim bulb as if it were a beach sun.

"Yes, but I wanted to say first I'm sorry if I made you uncomfortable before," Feena said.

"Uncomfortable when?" Ritchie asked.

"Before, with Fitz. You know," she said with a conspiratorial grin. Then she remembered she was meant to be contrite and quickly rearranged her expression to match. "I know you're not together or anything, but it's still probably unkind of me to be so open about my feelings in front of you. It wasn't my intention to upset you."

"Did I seem upset?" Ritchie asked.

"Oh, of course not," Feena said with that grin again. "You can play it close when you want to. Not so well as your buddy Moreau, but better than most. I'm something of an expert in the area, you know. Reading people."

"I think I've heard something like that," Ritchie said. She considered bringing up just what she had heard, that Feena's parents had used not only their own finest DNA but selective bits taken from a universe worth's of species. That those species were often still on the Union of

Free World's list of species of unknown sentience so that their consent to being used that way was not required. That Feena and her brother were capable of all sorts of things, of which reading people was only the beginning.

But she said nothing. It felt unwise, bringing all that up when it was only the two of them.

And no one knew where they were at the moment.

Ritchie sent a quick message to Moreau with her location, just in case.

"Perhaps you think it presumptuous of me to assume that you'd have protective feelings regarding Fitz," Feena said. "I mean, everyone knows you have another boyfriend now."

"Fitz was never my boyfriend," Ritchie said.

But if she was hoping that would steer the conversation away from Guy, Feena had no intentions of following her lead. "I've known Guy Travert nearly as long as I've known Fitz, you know. Say what you will, I'm not going to deny that you have very excellent taste."

Ritchie didn't say anything. She was waiting for the next bit, where Feena would subtly or not so subtly suggest that Ritchie's aspirations were far outside her social range. Not acceptable. Laughably naïve, even.

"Cicey likes you too, you know," Feena went on. "I think that's so important, don't you? That your paramour's family accepts you? And especially a sister. There's nothing closer than a sister."

"Yeah. So, the list?" Ritchie said, and turned her attention back to the remains of her bar. Because Feena was sounding like she was about to try match-making her brother with Ritchie, and the very idea made Ritchie's flesh crawl.

"The list, yes," Feena said, gamely letting the conversation get back on track. "I have the list of names. I'll send it to your implant, if that helps."

"Thanks," Ritchie said. She already had the official list from the school from Sokolov. It had been one of the many messages her implant had received during the brief window when the signal was up. But it would be interesting to compare that list to Feena's. A name on one but not the other could be a clue.

"Can I confess I'm really only worried about one of these names?" Feena asked, wrinkling her nose as if the question bothered her to ask.

"Which name?" Ritchie asked.

"Thecla Joosten," Feena said. Ritchie almost choked on the last bite of her bar and had to clear her throat several times. Which gave her time to process that declaration.

She ran the interview she and Fitz had had with Feena earlier, and she was certain they had never mentioned Joosten in any way that would make her seem like a suspect. So maybe Feena really was suspicious and not playing a game.

On the other hand, they had grilled Finn extensively on his arguments with Joosten during his interview. And it was pretty much guaranteed that he shared everything with his sister.

"Why?" Ritchie finally asked.

"She and Wyder were very close, you know," Feena said. "But I don't mean like most buddies are close. They weren't like friends or sisters or anything. It was more like they shared a bond, like they'd been through combat together. Do you know what I mean? My parents are with the military now, so I've seen that relationship in some of their colleagues."

"I know what you mean," Ritchie said. "I'm not sure why that's worrying. That's not the sort of bond that usually ends with one killing the other, is it?"

"No, no," Feena said quickly. "No, I guess my suspicions are more vague than that. I just know that Wyder would do anything for Joosten, anything at all. And Joosten knew that. Only with Joosten... well, I don't think she was above using other people to fulfill her own ends."

Ritchie was glad she had finished that bar, or she'd be choking again.

"Maybe I'm not being clear," Feena said. "Wyder wasn't at the academy over the break, but Joosten was. And I guess we all know the rumors about Wyder. Only they couldn't possibly be true if she wasn't even there, right? But Joosten was."

"Okay," Ritchie said, a bit disturbed that Feena had followed her and Fitz's thinking so closely. "But maybe you're only saying this because suspicion on Joosten is suspicion that's not on your brother."

"I swear that's not what I'm doing," Feena said. She put a hand on her heart and held the other up as if taking a vow.

"It's a big ask for me to just take you at your word on that," Ritchie said.

"I know. I'd do anything for my family, anything for my brother. Everyone knows that. You more than others, maybe," Feena said. "But you also know, or at least suspect, that our parents have told both of us we absolutely, positively must keep our noses clean. We have to finish this year without giving anyone any reason to suspect us of anything at all. Which is tough since some people are going to suspect us no matter what we do or don't do."

"Come on," Ritchie said, annoyed. "When it's just the two of us, we don't have to pretend that you or your brother has ever been accused of anything we don't both know you're guilty of."

"Perhaps," Feena said and grinned at her again. "I like you, Murdina Ritchie. I really do."

"Thanks," Ritchie said dryly. "But I'm going to need a little bit more than that."

"All right, then how about this," Feena said, and despite the fact that no one could possibly overhear them, she stepped close enough to whisper in Ritchie's ear. She even put her hand on Ritchie's arm. Ritchie jumped at her touch, certain she was about to be whammied hard.

But it was just a hand. A warm touch, no more. And the lips close to her ear were just to convey a whisper in a normal, nonenhanced voice. "Joosten always hated Hansen."

Then she stepped back, but gave Ritchie a significant look. "I never understood why. Lots of cadets hate certain instructors. That's not weird. But her hatred of *him* was so intense, so personal. I really think you and Fitz ought to look into it."

"I guess we will, but I have to tell you Feena, it still feels to me like you're trying to distract us from your brother. Neither of you were in your cots with the others just now," Ritchie said.

"Neither were you nor your friends," Feena said. "Perhaps we all had things to do."

"Can you give me anything like proof?" Ritchie said, sure that the answer would be more vagueness.

But Feena licked her lips, then smiled. "You know, actually I can. But first you have to trust me."

Ritchie didn't like the sound of that at all. But when Feena waved for Ritchie to follow her back up the cave to the main cavern, she came along behind. Just like a good whammied cadet.

A cadet who had never remembered to ask her about the Bemtic acidic compound to note her reaction.

Feena was probably playing some form of misdirection on Ritchie, if not an outright trap, but Ritchie was too curious about what she intended to do next to just walk away. Just what proof could Feena possibly provide?

24

IT HADN'T SEEMED like there were so many places a cadet could disappear to, but as Fitz wandered the cave complex, he had to revise that opinion.

The two cadets on cot watch had given him the head count, so he knew *most* of the cadets were where they were supposed to be. He, Ritchie, and Moreau were three of the missing, as were Stucki, Imhof and Kung. Blaser was still in Colonel Hansen's office.

But that left two still unaccounted for. The two Berwegers. Finn was back in the cavern now, so that was one missing cadet who could be crossed off the list.

Which left only Feena. The cadet on watch had mentioned that Ritchie and Moreau were looking for her, but no one had seen any of the three of them since.

And Fitz had just burned the better part of an hour walking up and down dimly lit caves, trying to find any of them.

The tunnel down to the lab area was smooth-walled, evenly floored, and well lit. But the other caves were... well, cave-like. The walls were gritty and damp when he touched them, and the floors were worn in ruts from water long-since gone. Most annoyingly, the lights were incredibly widely spaced. And yet every time he reached a light, he saw another just at the farthest point he could see, deeper still under the mountain.

There was no way Ritchie was down here. But he couldn't quite make himself go back without being sure.

Suddenly, his implant received a summons from Hansen to report to his office. Fitz turned and jogged back up to the main cavern and past the rows of sleeping cadets. The two on guard duty outside the door saw him approach and silently opened the door to let him pass inside.

"Good, we're all here, then," Colonel Hansen said. Fitz looked around to see Ritchie and Moreau leaning against the back wall behind Hansen. Moreau gave him a little wave, but Ritchie appeared deep in thought.

Joosten turned in the hot seat across from Hansen to look up at Fitz, then turned back as if dismissing him from her mind.

But while Fitz had expected to see Blaser also there, when he came around the desk with its glowing lamps, it was Finn and Feena who were also there in the shadows, not Blaser at all.

"What's going on?" Fitz asked the colonel.

Hansen looked up at him from his chair, his lips drawn in such a tight line they were turning white. "The Berwegers have offered their services, and I've taken them up on it."

"What?" Fitz asked. "We have to talk about this first. Make them wait outside."

"Cadet, I've made my decision," Hansen said with a dangerous edge to his voice.

"Well, I object," Fitz said recklessly.

"Fitz, Joosten has agreed to be cooperative and answer all of our questions, provided that the Berwegers are the ones asking the questions," Ritchie said. But she didn't sound like she liked it any better than he did.

"Seriously?" Fitz said, turning to stare at Joosten.

"Seriously," she said primly.

"You do realize they can make you say whatever they want," Fitz said.

"Don't be ridiculous," Joosten said. "No one has that kind of power.

And even if they did, I'd certainly feel it happening to me. I wouldn't allow it. I wouldn't speak."

"I don't think you understand what's happening here," Fitz said. "Finn Berweger here is our chief suspect. It's not even ethical for him to be the one interrogating you. It just isn't."

"And yet that is the only way I'll agree to speak here and now," Joosten said. "In the presence of the colonel who is also a suspect in this, as well as in something far more."

"Joosten has agreed that my sister and I are the ones best able to protect her interests. We will ensure that the colonel remains correctly impartial," Finn said.

Fitz scoffed.

"We have skills at this sort of thing, you know," Feena said.

Fitz scoffed again. Louder.

"Fitz, this is out of our hands," Ritchie said. Fitz gaped at her, but she was pointing with her gaze towards the back of the colonel in front of her.

Oh. So *his* hands were tied. Somehow.

"We'll all be witnesses to everything that happens in this room," Moreau told him, then motioned for him to join her and Ritchie at the back wall.

But he turned back to Joosten instead. "I just want you to say for the record that you understand that Finn Berweger is a suspect, and that, as he and his sister have *special skills*, they are both capable of positioning you to take the fall for him."

"I swear to you I'm only here to confess what it is that I've actually done," she said. She folded her hands on her lap and gazed up at him steadily.

"I believe you," Fitz said. As much as he hated to say it, it was true.

He moved to the back to stand with Ritchie and Moreau.

"All right, Thecla," Finn said. He and his sister moved around the desk to flank Joosten in her chair. They both leaned back against the desk, not quite blocking the colonel's view, but Feena also bent forward to give Joosten's hands a quick squeeze.

"Where do you want me to start?" Joosten asked calmly. "With the Bemtic acidic compound that I stole from your locker?"

Fitz swore under his breath, but Ritchie and Moreau on either side of him dug their elbows into his ribs, and he fell silent.

"Yes. Tell us about that," Finn said smoothly.

"I knew you had it. You had been talking about your project for your final assignment for some time, and I knew you had both stressed over acquiring it and then rejoiced when you succeeded. In short, I knew you had it and where it was," Joosten said. Her voice was as dully monotonous as ever.

But Fitz had to admit there was nothing in her voice, body language, facial expression or even eyes to suggest that she wasn't telling the plain and simple truth.

"When did you take it?" Finn asked.

"When did I take it?" she repeated, and for a split second Fitz was sure she was asking Finn what the correct answer was. But he said nothing, and finally she went on. "The morning we left on the shuttles. After you left your barracks, I went in and stole it. I mean, some of it."

"Why did you take it, Thecla?" Feena asked, sounding almost pained. Like Joosten had hurt her somehow by taking it.

"To kill Wyder, of course," Joosten said with a shrug. "She is the cadet captain. I knew she would be spending time apart from the other cadets, watching over us and backtracking to help stragglers. I knew there would be many opportunities."

"How did you do it?" Fitz asked. Joosten pretended like she hadn't heard a thing until Finn repeated the question.

"I was wearing two parts of gloves," she said. "I had hazardous material handling gloves on under my climbing gloves. When I saw that Wyder was going to double back down the side of the glacier, I went to help her get over the side. I put all that I had taken from Cadet Berweger's locker on my hands as I walked behind Wyder, and then made sure to clasp both her hands when I helped her get down to the guide rope. She gave me a funny look, like she thought that was a strange thing to do. But I guess if she really suspected anything she wouldn't have started to climb." Joosten shrugged again.

"What happened to your gloves?" Feena asked.

"I threw both pairs over the side right away. But air resistance being what it is, they took a lot longer to reach the bottom than Wyder did. Oh, and I had brought spares."

Ritchie sucked in a breath and put a hand over her eyes. Fitz didn't much like the sound of Joosten's dead voice relating these events either.

"Why Wyder?" Moreau asked.

"Yes, why Wyder, Thecla?" Finn asked.

"She was going to turn me in," Joosten said.

"For what?" Feena asked.

"She had done what I asked her to because that's just who she was, loyal, but afterwards it didn't sit well with her. The more she thought about it, the less she liked it. It was just a matter of time before she told on me. She had to be stopped," Joosten said.

"Can you tell us about that, Thecla?" Feena asked, leaning forward to put her hand on Joosten's knee.

Joosten blinked at the touch, but when she spoke again, her words were as carefully chosen, her tone as steadily robotic as ever. "I told Wyder that I had seen Hansen committing treason. Sending classified information to our enemies, specifically. But I told her I was sure no one would believe me if I said so. But they'd believe her. Wyder, with her perfect record, so beloved by all the instructors. No one would doubt her for a second."

"Except they did," Fitz said. Joosten ignored him.

"But Wyder believed you were right? That Colonel Hansen was doing something treasonous?" Feena asked, still touching Joosten's knee.

"She believed enough to agree that it should be looked into," Joosten said. "I don't know what changed. Maybe something came up during all the interrogations she was put under, when her story started to fall apart. I should've coached her better. But the past is past, right? All I know is that when she finally was back in the barracks with me, she was no longer on my side."

"How could you tell?" Finn asked.

"She was just cold. Sullen. She wouldn't even look at me. She told me she needed time and space to think things through," Joosten said.

"Well, I could see what time and space were going to lead to. But I already told you that part."

"You stole my chemical compound," Finn said.

"Yes."

"Framing the colonel a second time was just a bonus?" Fitz asked. He expected her to ignore him again; he knew the twins were never going to repeat that question. But to his surprise, she looked up at him.

"Indeed. Not planned. Just a happy little coincidence. It was like the universe had my back."

The words sounded delusional, but her voice was all cold rationality.

"Let's back up," Ritchie said, pushing away from the wall to walk over to stand by Finn. Fitz started to reach out and pull her back, but Moreau put a hand on his arm and gently shook her head.

"What do you want to know more about?" Finn asked her in his most melodious voice.

Ritchie nodded as if to acknowledge what he'd done there, then folded her arms over her chest. "I want to know what she did to frame the colonel in the first place. We know there was a message that was supposed to be stolen intel, but the encryption on that seems to be unbreakable. But this was within a larger file that was very easily broken, which yielded metadata that pointed to Hansen as the sender, and a coordinate in empty space as the destination."

"What's the question?" Joosten asked with a slow blink.

Finn was still looking at Ritchie, quirking a single eyebrow. "Wyder testified to seeing the message being sent, but that doesn't seem like it was even necessary. The nesting encryption ensured that once the message was found, Colonel Hansen would be framed."

"I don't know anything about that," Joosten said, not bothering to wait for Finn to phrase it into a question.

"Don't you? Thecla?" Finn asked. Now he too was touching her, his hand on her shoulder. Moreau, beside Fitz, gave a small pained moan.

"I saw him send the message. I don't know anything about encryption or the rest of it," she said, lifting her chin defiantly.

"Seriously? You want us to believe you were a witness caught up in somebody else's attempt to frame the colonel?" Fitz said. "Come on.

You were just on about the universe having your back. Did the universe set up this encryption?"

"It's not my skill set," Joosten said firmly. Then she glanced ever so briefly at Feena. Joosten wasn't prone to blushing, but her cheeks did tinge ever so slightly.

Fitz glanced over at Moreau and she nodded. She had seen it too.

But so had Finn, apparently. He cleared his voice twice before finding another question to steer the conversation away from this dangerous territory. "This was all your work, though, right?" he asked. Then added, "Thecla?"

"My work," she repeated.

"Maybe make them stop touching her, sir?" Fitz hissed at Colonel Hansen.

"Step back, cadets," Hansen said with a sigh. Then he came around the desk to loom over Joosten, who stared coldly back up at him. "No one will ever believe that you acted alone, cadet," he said.

"I did. I acted totally and completely alone." Her eyes did that little dart over to Feena before she added, "except for Wyder, who was my patsy."

"But you just admitted you know nothing about the encryption," Hansen said.

She looked to Finn now, who made a little gesture of support and encouragement. She turned her attention back to Hansen. "I knew nothing about the message that I saw you send. But I saw where it was going because after you left, I examined the comm records. And I surmised the intended recipient."

"Thecla, be honest," Finn said. He didn't touch her, but he did lean in close and made sure to hold her gaze. "You were framing the colonel. It's all right. We all know it already. You can admit it to us."

"What's the legal phrase for how this is wrong?" Fitz hissed to Moreau, but she ignored him.

"Thecla, we just want to understand what happened," Feena told her. "We're not mad."

That *we* clearly meant the two of them and no one else in the room. Least of all the colonel.

Then, to Fitz's great surprise, Joosten started to sniffle.

"It was all me," she said, looking down at the hands folded on her lap. "I knew someone who would be at the conference. They stole what I needed and sent it to me among the colonel's own files. When he got here, I used the desk in his classroom to retrieve it myself. I knew how to unlock his system from there, you know. I really don't know what was in it, only that it would be compromising. I put the second layer of encryption on so that the metadata would be easily retrieved. I wasn't sure at that point if I could get Wyder to cover for me, so I wanted to be sure if I wasn't trusted as a witness, there was something else to back me up."

"Oh, Thecla," Feena said sadly.

"Where did you send the message, Thecla?" Finn asked.

"A random point in empty space," she said and sniffed again.

"Thecla," he said reproachfully.

"A point I knew was patrolled by yuffid ships," she said. Her shoulders slumped. More than that, she appeared to be collapsing in to the chair. "I knew they would receive it. I timed it so they would."

"You stole intelligence and sent it to a species we are not allies with?" the colonel said sharply.

Joosten straightened up in the chair again, but didn't quite look up at him. "I knew they would never hack it. They would get the metadata, but so what? They'd never get the real intel. *I* never even saw the real intel."

Fitz looked over at Ritchie. She had taken two steps back away from Finn and the entire conversation, stopping only when her back collided with the wall behind her.

Just hearing that species named out loud still crushed her. And he could see that Joosten had a lot more to say.

"Finn," he said. Just that, just his name.

Finn glanced back at him, then turned three-quarters the other way around to look at Ritchie. Ritchie didn't notice him this time. Her hand was over her eyes again. But Finn made a gesture over his shoulder to Fitz, a little wave of acknowledgment.

"I'm sure the authorities will have more to ask about that later. It's not really what concerns us here," he said. "Thecla?"

"Yes?" she said, looking up at him. The normally carefully blank quality to her face was crinkling just a bit. That, plus the sniffles, was quite a show of emotion from her.

"Why does she hate Hansen so much?" Fitz asked.

"Can you tell us that, Thecla?" Finn asked. "We just want to understand."

Fitz could see Hansen's body tensing up even further. All his muscles had to be as tight as they were able to get by now, but he found just a little more. But he said nothing.

"My father was Sergeant Henri Giger," Joosten said, then looked straight at Hansen to see how he reacted to that name.

He didn't.

"You changed your name, then?" Finn asked blithely, as if he hadn't noticed a bit of that interaction.

"I used my mother's family name. So I could work in secret. I thought it would take years and years to get my revenge, but then he was transferred here. Here, of all places. I couldn't believe my luck."

"That universe, always looking out for you," Fitz said.

"I gather your father was under my command," Hansen said quietly.

"You know he was," she said. Her eyes narrowed ever so slightly, another show of emotion.

"Where did he die? The Battle of the Seven Stars?" Hansen guessed.

Joosten made a sound of pure rage. This sudden show of emotion was startling. Fitz almost wondered if she was possessed.

"Thecla," Feena admonished, but Joosten just turned those narrowed eyes on to her. Feena flinched back as if hurt.

"It was during the Night Comet Maneuvers. As you well know!" she shrieked at Hansen.

"Ah. That was a tough campaign," Hansen said. He touched his face. Only briefly. But Fitz couldn't help noticed that it was only the scar tissue that his fingertips brushed over.

"You killed him!" Joosten screamed. She screamed this over and over again, not letting anyone else get a single word in. She fisted her hands and screwed her eyes shut and shrieked it towards the ceiling. After a lifetime of repressing her emotions, she was going all in now. It was more disturbing than Fitz was prepared for. He wished he could just leave the room.

But it looked like they all felt that way.

Feena pushed away from the desk and fell to her knees at Joosten's feet. She put her hands on Joosten's hands until the fists untensed. Then she touched Joosten's cheeks, brushing back her tear-soaked hair, until slowly, slowly, Joosten's screams became sobs.

Those sobs were almost more horrifying to bear witness to than the screams. But it was like they were all frozen in place, unable to flee no matter how uncomfortable everything had become. Ritchie had both hands over her eyes now.

But Feena just kept murmuring to Joosten, stroking her cheeks, then finally pulling her into a tight embrace. And the sobs faded to a more tolerable level of grief. At least for Fitz.

"Cadets, let's give her a moment," Hansen said, gesturing for the others to step outside of the office with him.

"But, sir? Murder? Treason?" Fitz said.

"She's not going anywhere, cadet," Hansen said.

Moreau followed him first, with no hesitation. Fitz looked to Ritchie, who still had her hands on her face. But Finn was closer, and when he touched her shoulder, she jerked upright, then pushed away from the wall to follow Moreau.

Finn looked back at Fitz and gave him a little shrug. Like Fitz was going to abrade him for touching Ritchie.

Well, on a normal day, he probably would. But this was far from a normal day.

Fitz followed Finn out of the office, then gently shut the door, leaving Joosten alone with Feena's tender ministrations.

Finn lifted his eyebrows as if waiting for whatever Fitz was going to say next.

But all Fitz could find to say was, "thank you. Not for Joosten. For the other thing."

"Well, we don't speak about the other thing, do we?" Finn said. "But you are, of course, welcome. I'm not a bad guy, you know."

"You're totally a bad guy," Fitz said.

Finn just shrugged, then walked away, hands in his pockets.

He couldn't be projecting innocence any harder without whistling a jaunty tune, but Fitz knew it was all an act.

Finn had never answered the one question Fitz had been asking him the longest. And if Joosten had stolen the compound without his knowledge after he left his barracks for the trip up the mountain, just what *had* they been repeatedly arguing about?

Someday he hoped to get Finn Berweger in a room with interrogation tools to match Finn's natural abilities, but until that day came, there were things he would just have to accept not knowing.

But he didn't have to like it.

25

IN THE END, they never got to climb to the summit of the mountain for extreme environment tactical training. But Ritchie kept her disappointment to herself. She was pretty sure she was the only one feeling it. Except maybe for Colonel Hansen.

Instead, all the cadets huddled together in the cavern, only sporadically able to connect to the academy and receive messages from home. It might have been a recipe for cabin fever, but the colonel knew just how to keep them all busy. Everyone was constantly either on guard duty over the cell where Joosten was being kept or over Wyder's body, or walking a watch duty through the cavern day and night, or climbing ever deeper through the cave network around the cavern. Hansen told them this was a mapping mission, but Ritchie knew for a fact all those caves had been thoroughly mapped years ago.

And she really hated when she drew mapping detail. She'd rather be out in the storm of blinding snow and blood-freezing cold than creeping through small spaces under more tons of rock than she cared to imagine. Aside from missing the training she had wanted in the thin air of the highest elevations, she was once more spelunking caves, something she had already had more than a lifetime's worth of. Not a good trade at all.

Days and nights were only measured by the lights in the cavern being dimmed, then brought back up to full brightness. But by the twelfth turning of that pattern, the storm outside finally blew itself out. The signal from the academy was clear, and they'd be heading back down soon.

Most of the cadets fell to packing with a vengeance, but Ritchie found herself in Colonel Hansen's office instead, along with Fitz and Moreau.

"Cadet Joosten will be on the first shuttle out of here," the colonel told them. "She won't even be returning to the school. They are taking her directly to the nearest intelligence site to be debriefed."

"Debriefed?" Fitz asked skeptically. "She hasn't said a word to anyone in all the days since she cried on Feena's shoulder. She's practically catatonic."

"I assure you, cadet, when they are done debriefing her, she will have told them everything. Several times over. You need have no worries in that regard," he said.

Ritchie remembered the scars on the arms of Cadmar Weld, and the way she could feel things squirming under his skin when she'd touched those scars. He had called them worms, and he said they caused him great, ever-present pain. They had been put there to make him talk about how he had blocked Ritchie's implant.

She wondered if Joosten was about to find herself exposed to something similar. Or possibly even worse. Weld, after all, wasn't technically considered a criminal. He had been declared insane and sent to the Julius Henry Observational Center to be studied.

Surely, the actual intelligence forces of the Union of Free Worlds had access to things beyond what the doctors at the center had. She wasn't sure how she felt about that. It felt wrong, hurting someone like that. Perhaps Joosten would tell them everything, and her time of pain would be short.

But Weld had told them nothing. And so his torture continued, perpetually.

"They know we think she's been influenced by the Berwegers and will lie to cover for them, right?" she asked.

"I've told them," Hansen said. "I recorded the entire interrogation for their review. But I don't know if they will believe us."

"Are the intelligence forces under the sway of the Admirals Berweger?" Fitz asked.

"I don't think so. I hope not. Certainly, officially, they have no purview over that department," Hansen said.

"That's not likely to matter much," Fitz said glumly.

"They're going to get away with it again," Ritchie said. Then she had an even more frightening thought. "Are we sure you're in the clear, sir? If they're trying to get rid of you, isn't it possible that something in the case against Joosten is going to implicate you?"

"In the clear," Hansen said musingly. "No, I don't think I shall ever again be in the clear. I've declared my side. I'll always be a target. But I don't think it was the admirals acting against me this time. It's entirely possible it really was Joosten acting alone. But I think it more likely that she was the patsy for the twins. Even so, I don't think they would've moved against me if Joosten hadn't presented them with such a perfect opportunity. No, for the time being, I think I'm as safe as I can be."

"But what happens when they decrypt the rest of the message?" Ritchie asked.

"That's already been dealt with," he told her. "The intelligence forces reclaimed it. I thought I told you? Well, Wyss got a message through to me some days ago, telling me that every copy he had made of it had just disappeared in the middle of an afternoon. Even the copies that were on backups not linked to the network. I think they gave him quite a scare. Which is good. A little healthy paranoia will make him more cautious when he's digging into things he's not supposed to be digging into."

"He's not in trouble?" Fitz asked.

"No. They never said a word. They just took what they wanted and made everything disappear."

"If they weren't aware of him before, they are now," Moreau said. Ritchie shot her a questioning look, and she explained, "you know you can't apply for a position in the intelligence forces, right? They have to recruit you. And the first several levels of entry happen without the recruits' knowledge. They test you, and you don't even know it."

"Rumors," Fitz said. "No one knows how intelligence works but intelligence."

"They're going to want him," Moreau insisted.

"His test scores were beyond high enough to be admitted to a foreign service academy," Hansen said, "but as you know, if you come from a space station community, that's often not enough to get you here."

"Are you saying he's already being recruited, but he's still in the 'doesn't even know it' level?" Ritchie asked.

"It's possible," Hansen said.

"By that argument, *I* could be an intelligence recruit," Ritchie said, horrified.

"They'd be fools not to take you," Fitz said automatically, but Hansen was shaking his head.

"Come on," Ritchie insisted. "I barely made it in here, at the last minute, despite my own very high test scores. What else explains that?"

Hansen didn't answer. Moreau sat back in her chair and brushed her fingertips over her jawline, intrigued by the thought.

But Fitz turned to look at Ritchie like she was crazy. She raised her hands in surrender, not catching his meaning at all. He rolled his eyes, then tipped his head to Hansen, still leaning back against the edge of his desk with his arms folded and his eyes closed.

"Sir?" Ritchie asked.

Hansen opened his eyes. "Sorry, cadets. Got distracted there. Where were we?"

"You were going to tell us about this meeting you were at over the break," Fitz said, clearly bursting out with anything to keep Ritchie from asking her question first.

"No, I was not, cadet," Hansen said. "That meeting was under the highest level of security. The fact that you even know that it happened is a breach. I'm not telling you more."

"Are we going to war?" Ritchie asked. She knew that was technically a question about his meeting, but it was also a general question he still might answer.

"Not that I'm aware of," Hansen said.

"Against the yuffids?" she asked. Her heart clenched tight just saying that word, but she had to know.

"No, cadet," Hansen said gently. "The military and the foreign service branches are both moving to a higher level of preparedness, that is true. But war is not imminent."

"But things are moving that direction, though, right?" Fitz asked.

Hansen sighed. "They seem to have been doing so all my life. Perhaps they will continue at that slow pace for all your lives as well. That would be my fondest wish. War is inevitable, I fear, but perhaps we can work to delay it."

"Are the Berwegers going to be questioned about the Joosten affair at all?" Moreau asked.

"I imagine they will be asked for witness statements, but they won't be pressed hard," Hansen said.

Ritchie wasn't surprised. In the last message they had received from the academy, Wyss and Sokolov had said they had found the Bemtic acidic compound in Finn's locker, along with the receipt. The amount on the receipt was slightly larger than what remained in the container. The difference between the two was easily explained by the little Joosten still had in her possession when they searched her pack, plus the amount that had likely been used to contaminate Wyder's gloves.

And she doubted the official investigators would find that too convenient the way Ritchie and her friends did.

"I can just imagine how handily they'll wrap the interrogators around their fingers," Fitz said with a dry laugh. "Even in separate rooms, they'll dominate the questioning, no problem. I almost wonder why they'll even bother."

"Because they don't know what we know," Moreau said.

"I remind you that we don't know anything, not for a fact," Hansen said. "If we did, things would be different."

"They wouldn't be sending the wrong person to jail," Ritchie said.

"That's not it," Moreau said. "They're only sending one guilty party to jail, but Joosten *is* guilty. No matter how she was manipulated into doing it, she still chose to do it. In the end, it's on her."

"You're right," Ritchie said. "I just wish the Berwegers were going away too."

"Next year," Fitz said wistfully.

Hansen stood up with a suddenness that told them all he had just received a message over his implant. "Cadets, I'm going to have to adjourn our meeting here. The intelligence shuttle is about to land, and I need to get the prisoner up onto the meadow. All other cadets will be confined to the cavern for the time being, but once she's gone, we'll be leaving ourselves."

"Not having done what we came for," Ritchie said glumly. She had only been grumbling to herself, but Colonel Hansen heard her.

"I promise to make up for it next year," he told her. "I'm always harder on the last-years. Your class will be getting two years' worth of training at once. I promise it will be brutal enough even for your tastes."

"Thank you, sir," Ritchie said, but stopped grinning when she saw Moreau scowling at her.

"I suppose we should go pack," Moreau said, but none of the three of them stirred from their chairs. Ritchie figured Moreau was stewing over next year's training, but she had no idea why Fitz was so quiet.

"Fitz, if you knew something I didn't know, like about the yuffids, you'd tell me, right?" she asked.

Moreau bit her lip, a strange reaction from her, at least in Ritchie's experience. But then she looked to Fitz who hadn't answered her question, and she saw the old carefully bland expression back on his face.

"Sure I would, Ritchie," he said with no warmth at all. "But I really have to start packing. And you should too. We can talk about whatever once we're back at the academy."

"Yeah. Okay," Ritchie said, but he was already out the door.

The wall was back up. She definitely hadn't done anything this time to deserve that. Their case was closed, and that was the end of their partnership again, apparently.

"Don't take it so hard," Moreau said, which startled Ritchie. Usually this was the point when Moreau started calling Fitz all sorts of unspeakable names. Then she'd describe in great detail what she'd like to do to him.

"Why are you being so weird?" Ritchie asked.

"I'm not weird," Moreau said as if offended.

"You're not *you*," Ritchie said. "Are you on Fitz's side now? What's going on here?"

"No one is picking sides," Moreau said. "It's just, I think I can see why Fitz might be feeling out of sorts."

"Is that what it is? He feels out of sorts?"

"He doesn't hate you," Moreau said, leaning in to make sure Ritchie was looking at her. "He doesn't. He's just... carrying a lot."

"A lot of what?" Ritchie asked.

"His father works at a very high level of the military, right?" Moreau said. Ritchie nodded. "But he's not what you'd call emotionally available?"

"Never has been," Ritchie said. Her childhood memories of General Fitz might be vague, but that label definitely fit them all.

"So, put yourself in Fitz's shoes. I know he was never close with his dad, but even so. Can you imagine what it must be like every day, wondering if your own father is a traitor? That maybe a day will come when you will realize that the two of you are on opposite sides of an uncrossable line? What must that be like?"

"That can't be what's going on here," Ritchie said. "This is about me somehow. And maybe Finn. I don't know. But it's not about his dad. Believe me, I've known him longer than you."

"You have," Moreau conceded. "Just, think about it. Maybe cut him a little slack."

"How can I cut him slack in any meaningful way when he's shutting me out?" Ritchie asked.

"Well, like I said, you could just not take it so hard," Moreau said. "Just be patient. Things will change."

"When the Berwegers are gone?" Ritchie asked.

"When the Berwegers are gone," Moreau said.

Ritchie sighed. That day was so far off into the future, she'd be seeing Guy again before she saw a Berweger-free Oymyakon Foreign Service Academy.

Well, when she phrased it like that, it did take the edge off.

"Come on," she said to Moreau and pulled her buddy up out of her chair. "Let's go pack. Time to get off this mountain."

26

CADET CAPTAIN BLASER had refused to budge on his orders that every cadet flew down on the same shuttle that they flew up on. Fitz decided that, pressures of the job or not, he just really didn't like Cadet Captain Blaser.

And so he found himself climbing on board a shuttle with Finn and Feena Berweger his only companions.

"Sit by me, Fitz," Feena said. But she wasn't oozing anything like her usual levels of charm. She sounded just like she looked.

Exhausted.

"Fine," Fitz said, stowing his pack then sitting down at Feena's left side. Finn, sitting between her and the door, appeared to be napping. But Fitz was pretty sure that was a sham to avoid conversation.

He could respect that.

"So she's really gone, isn't she?" Feena said as Fitz strapped into his seat.

"Joosten? Yeah. She's way out of Oymyakon's orbit at some intelligence forces site, probably not on any map or directory," Fitz said.

"I feel bad for her," Feena said.

"Do you?" Fitz asked as neutrally as he could.

"What she did was wrong, but it's hard not to have sympathy for her, isn't it?" Feena asked. "I can't imagine what it's like to lose your father at such a young age. And what stories she must've been told to lead her to believe that his death was solely entirely Colonel Hansen's fault."

"You think she believed a bunch of lies?" Fitz asked, not sure she would appreciate the irony if he pointed it out to her.

"Joosten didn't share much about her home life, but there was a reason she never went home for breaks, and it wasn't financial," Feena said. "I don't think she got on with her mother."

"I don't think she got on with anybody," Finn said, loud enough to carry to Fitz over the growing sound of the engines warming up.

"She had no siblings. I can't even imagine what that's like," Feena said. Then she slapped a hand over her mouth, looking appalled. "I'm sorry! I didn't mean anything negative about that. I know you're an only child. I just really can't imagine going through life like that."

"Well, when you've never known anything else, it's not exactly weird," he said.

"I suppose," Feena said. Then she put her hand on his arm and leaned over as far as her restraints would let her. "I guess you and Ritchie had that in common. And you were childhood friends, right? That's a lot like siblings."

Fitz didn't know how to answer that, but in the end, he didn't have to. Finn laughed out loud, then said, "it's not the same thing at all."

"She's avoiding you again, isn't she?" Feena asked with concern in her eyes. "You've been alone for days down in the caves. I noticed."

Fitz suppressed a laugh. The very idea that from any perspective it could look like Ritchie was avoiding him just really struck him as funny. But if he started laughing, he'd probably end up collapsed from hysteria. Better to keep that feeling tight in his chest.

The shuttle lifted off from the ground and was immediately tossed about by the prevailing winds. Feena still had her hand on his arm and she was clutching him in a death grip. He put his hand on hers with the idea of prying her off him, but when the shuttle plummeted down through an air pocket, he found himself gripping her back just as tightly.

Normally he didn't mind that sort of thing, air turbulence. At least, not when he was at the controls. Being at the mercy of some unknown pilot was another experience all together.

As they left the mountain on the horizon behind them, the flight grew smoother, but Feena kept a hold of his hand. He decided not to fight it.

At last they descended over athletic fields that were dusted with snow, the skies overhead gray as ever but storm-free. They landed with a soft bump and Finn at once threw the door open as if anxious to get out of the shuttle. Fitz pulled his hand away from Feena's to unstrap Finn's pack and toss it out to him. Finn gave him a nod of thanks, his face stony blank, then jogged off towards the library doors.

"Are you busy?" Feena asked as Fitz handed her pack to her.

"I am, actually," he admitted. He hoped she didn't press. He doubted he would be able to hide how much he was dreading meeting up with the others in their study room in the library. It was going to be awkward enough seeing Wyss again for the first time after all the revelations. Seeing him and Moreau together, knowing what they both knew, but the others didn't... ugh.

Seeing them and Ritchie all at once, hoping no one let anything slip? And knowing it was only a matter of time before they did, because Ritchie noticed everything, especially when something about her friends was off?

It was all hopeless.

And yet he could see no path before him except the one he was already walking. Alone. Through a veritable maze of potential traps that would end him.

"I guess you probably are," Feena said. "But come find me after. I still have a little of my personal blend of coffee left in my locker. We can share one last quiet moment before we get back to the academy grind."

"Sure," Fitz said with a smile he hoped didn't look too forced.

Her smile back at him certainly felt genuine.

Someone out on the field was calling her name, and with one last little wave she hopped out of the shuttle to join up with whomever it was.

Fitz pulled on his pack, then jumped down to the frozen ground and made his way across the field to the library. But stall as he might, he reached the study room door all too soon.

The others were already gathered inside. Sokolov, Ritchie and Moreau were in a tight huddle, whispering frantically to each other. Wyss was at his usual spot in front of all the computers, but he got up to shake Fitz's hand in a rare demonstration of warmth when he came in the door.

"How's it?" Wyss asked.

"I think I have a date with Feena Berweger," Fitz said, and pulled a face.

"Man on a mission," Wyss said, and went back to his computer.

"So Joosten is really gone?" Sokolov asked in a way that made Fitz guess it wasn't for the first time.

"We didn't get to watch her go, but Colonel Hansen did," Ritchie said. "She's definitely gone. And who knows when anyone will ever see her again."

"There'll be a trial?" Sokolov asked.

"It depends on how much she knows," Fitz said.

"There will definitely be a trial," Ritchie said confidently. "Whether it's public or not will depend on how much she knows."

"It's sweet you think that's true," Fitz said. He actually kind of meant it. What must it be like to still think so well of the government systems they kept seeing the darker side of? It was admirable in its own way. Still, he leaned in hard on the sarcasm when he said it.

"Fitz," Sokolov chastised him. "I'm sure she's right."

"If only there were a way for us to know what she tells them," Moreau said, giving Wyss a significant look. It took him a minute to register it, distracted as he was.

"What? No. I'm definitely not poking into any networks connected to the intelligence forces," Wyss said. "I'm lucky it was very clear I never managed to break that message's encryption or I'd be getting debriefed right beside Joosten." He shivered at the thought.

They all fell silent for a moment, each lost in their own thoughts. Then Ritchie sat up straighter, as if she'd just gotten a message over her implant.

"Hansen has us scheduled for a meeting tonight after dinner," she said as she stood up and reached for her pack. "If you don't mind, we can pick up the rest of this then?"

"Important message?" Fitz asked. It didn't take much effort to make that drip with disdain.

He hated how easy it was, in fact.

"Guy?" Moreau asked, the hands folded together in front of her mouth in no way hiding her smile.

"No, actually, from Sidonie Keller," Ritchie said, and Fitz could see the hand holding the strap of her pack on her shoulder was shaking.

"You're upset," he said.

"No, I'm just tired," she said.

"No, you're not," he said, ignoring the warning look Moreau was directing his way.

"I am," Ritchie shot back. "I haven't even opened it yet, so I don't know what she has to say. Probably nothing. Most of them are nothing. I'm just not ready to deal with it right now, okay? Not that it's any of your business."

"It's kind of my business," Fitz said. Then he held up a hand to block Moreau from his view before adding, "It's task force business, isn't it?"

"If it is, you'll know soon enough," Ritchie said. "Honestly, Fitz. Another semester of this? Really?"

Moreau leaned over to make eye contact with him around his still-raised hand. Wyss was looking down at his tablet but not touching it, a sure sign he was only avoiding an awkward moment and not actually reading anything.

Sokolov looked like a parent who was about to tell him she wasn't mad, just disappointed.

"Another semester," was all he said.

Ritchie fumed for a moment, but in the end she just gave him a curt nod, then slammed her way out of the room.

"That's not acceptable, Fitz," Moreau said.

"You can't keep doing this, Fitz," Wyss said.

"It really doesn't become you," Sokolov said. "It's not you, I know it isn't. You can do better."

Fitz wanted to scoff at that, but then he realized all the things she wasn't doing, like asking what they were all talking about.

"You told her?" he asked Wyss.

"She's on the task force," Wyss said.

"This couldn't be less of a task force matter!" Fitz raged.

"We're keeping your secret," Moreau said.

"Even from Ritchie, but that absolutely breaks my heart," Sokolov said.

"*You* weren't even supposed to know," Fitz grumbled.

"We're keeping your secret, but only because you have to be the one to tell her first," Wyss said. Wyss was never as meek as his slight appearance might lead some to suspect, but he was seldom as firm as he was just now.

"I can't," Fitz said. "I can't risk it."

"You have to find a way. Her finding out on her own is the risky path," Moreau said.

"We have to be patient, I guess, until you find the right time," Sokolov said, "but we can't be patient if it means watching you repeat last semester. Fitz, it's too hard. It's too hard to watch you both suffer."

"Ritchie isn't suffering," Fitz said, and flinched as all of their expressions turned stormy at once. "Much," he quickly added. "She has Guy now. Surely that takes the edge off."

"Guy is her boyfriend," Moreau said.

"That couldn't be less clear," Fitz grumbled.

"But you're her best friend," Moreau went on.

"I thought that was you," Fitz said, and hated how petulant that sounded out loud.

"Oh, not remotely," Moreau said. "You two have a history that's on a whole other level."

"Yes," Fitz agreed, rubbing at a blemish on the tabletop. "You know someone just told me that old childhood friends are practically siblings."

Moreau laughed out loud. "I don't know who told you that, but you're an idiot."

"Wait, don't you mean *they're* the idiot?" Fitz asked.

"No, it's definitely you," Moreau said. "Now, if you don't mind, I think I'm going to catch up with my buddy."

"I'll go with you," Sokolov said. She gave Fitz a look that made clear she didn't want to spend one more second in his company, and she held that look until she and Moreau were out the door.

"I thought she liked me," Fitz said.

"You've been hard to like for a while now, you know," Wyss said.

"Well, then, I guess I should really appreciate you," Fitz said.

"You should," Wyss agreed. "Did anything we said sink in?"

Fitz sighed. "I can't be as close to her as I was. She already knows something is going on, and if I'm alone with her, I'm going to let it slip."

"Is that so bad?" Wyss asked.

"Yes," Fitz said firmly. "Maybe if I can figure out what side my father is on, why he did what he did. I mean, there can't have been a *good* reason. I don't know. Maybe his reason would make some sense, if I only knew what it was. But for now, Ritchie can't know. And I don't know when that changes."

"There's a big gap between not as close as before and the meanness you've been displaying."

"I have to keep her away," Fitz said. "And she has Guy's shoulder to cry on."

"Remotely?" Wyss said.

"Whatever. She'll be fine. She's made of sterner stuff than the rest of you seem to think she is. She doesn't need me."

"Does it change next year, when the Berwegers are gone?" Wyss asked.

"I hope so," Fitz sighed. "But I think this semester might be tougher than the last."

"Why? Because you're buttering up Feena at Hansen's request?"

"That, but also Finn."

"What about Finn?"

"Finn is watching her, more than before," Fitz said darkly. "And he's not bothering to hide it from me."

Wyss set his tablet down and folded his hands over it, giving Fitz his full attention. "I thought that Finn considered Ritchie unworthy. Beneath him."

"He did, before," Fitz said. "Something's changed."

"He's seen her value?" Wyss suggested.

"I wish I thought that's what it was," Fitz said as he got up from his chair and picked up his pack.

"What is it, then?" Wyss asked.

"I think he's seeing a way he can make use of her. He'll never see her as an equal, but she can be a very handy, but ultimately expendable, tool."

"We can't let that happen," Wyss said.

"I certainly don't intend to," Fitz said, heading for the door. "I just don't know if we'll be able to stop it."

Then he went out into the library, about half-full with cadets chatting together in little clusters. No one seemed to be studying, not even the cadets who had been attending regular classes the entire time the rest of them had been up the mountain.

He emerged into the main hall to see Ritchie still there, standing with Moreau, the two of them talking with Frei and Grof just outside the cafeteria doors.

Then he saw Finn on the far side of the hall, leaning against the wall of the corridor that led to the administrative wing, just watching her. His eyes were intent on her in a way Fitz really didn't like. He was just hoisting his pack higher on his shoulder to march over there and demand that Finn stop when Feena was suddenly standing in front of him, a gleaming thermos in her hands.

"You haven't dumped your pack yet?" she asked with a little frown.

"I told you I'd be busy," he said, but she was already pouring a measure of steaming coffee into the stainless steel cup part of the thermos. He expected her to hand it to him, but instead she held it to his lips.

He had a momentary impulse to swat it away. What if it were poisoned? But the smell was too tempting. He took a sip.

"Amazing, right?" she said, pleased at the look on his face.

"It is very good," he admitted.

"No one is down the science corridor," she said conspiratorially. "Let's grab a lonely bench and finish this coffee, what do you say?"

He licked the last of the taste of the coffee off his lips. It had hints of chocolate and cinnamon, a perfect complement to the very strong coffee. And he realized he was smiling at her just as warmly as she was smiling at him.

No coffee was that good. Was she finally using her power on him? But he didn't feel like he was in her thrall either.

Assuming he could know the difference. Maybe he had been deluding himself about that.

Over her shoulder, he could see Finn was now looking at them and not at Ritchie. Finn met Fitz's eyes and gave him a wink, then pushed off the wall to head towards the barracks.

"What if I told you that I'm supposed to be friendly with you for reasons of espionage?" Fitz found himself asking.

She laughed, then leaned close to his ear. She didn't have to get up on tiptoe to do it; she was nearly as tall as he was.

Her warm breath tickled his earlobe as she said, "what if I told you... ditto?"

"Then I'd say it looks like we're about to have a very strange but interesting time these next few months," Fitz said.

She fake-pouted at him. "Months?"

"Days?" he countered.

She laughed. "You know what I meant."

"Hours, then," he said.

"Come on," she said, taking his hand and dragging him toward the science corridor. "We'll start with this one hour and see where we go."

"Lead the way," Fitz said.

He was well aware of the moment they passed by Ritchie, still standing at the cafeteria doors, but he couldn't bring himself to look at her. He'd see her soon enough at the meeting. And Moreau and Wyss along with their glowering disapproval.

And he'd remind them all that this was the mission he had been given over his own very strenuous objections.

If he was lucky, no one would notice what he was really feeling, like all the anxiety and stress in his life were just gone.

Not that she was a calming influence. Far from it.

No, as much as he could feel her effect on him like an intoxicating beverage giving him a warm, blissful feeling, he always knew that that feeling was completely an illusion. He was aware that he was just rolling with her flow. She wasn't whammying him on any deeper level.

He knew that for a fact, because on that deeper level all he was really thinking was that being with Feena was the perfect excuse for not being close to Ritchie. Being with Feena, Ritchie wouldn't even *want* to be close to him. It was a total win-win.

And on another yet deeper level, he knew he deserved it. If he were Feena's automaton, or even if everyone else just thought he was her automaton, he deserved it. All their disdain. The loss of everyone's respect. Whatever else followed. He deserved all of it.

Because he knew he was still too much of a coward to confront his own father. He hoped someday to change that, but that hope was a flickering candle, always on the verge of being gutted out. Until he found a way to transform that candle into a bonfire, trapped in Feena's web of love and intrigue was the only place he belonged.

CHECK OUT BOOK FIVE

The Ritchie and Fitz Sci-Fi Murder Mysteries will continue with Book Five, An Undiplomatic Murder.

Cadets Ritchie and Fitz finally face their last year at the Oymyakon Foreign Service Academy. Which means decision time for what comes next. The golden wings and ivory robes of a diplomat? Or the crossed spears and navy blue uniform of a guardian?

Before they decide, they and the other last-year cadets first spend a week on the university planet, visiting both of the colleges. A single day at the guardian school exhausts even the most highly trained of the cadets.

But the first night visiting the diplomat school ends in a very undiplomatic murder. One of the guests at a mock state dinner dies in the middle of the dessert course, a victim of a very gruesome poison. And the only suspect? Cadet Shackleton Fitz IV.

So Murdina Ritchie finds herself alone on a strange planet with its own set of rules, desperate to prove her partner's innocence. Hard enough under any circumstances, made harder still by the presence of two former Oymyakon cadets: Finn and Feena Berweger.

Can Ritchie defeat her old nemeses one more time? Maybe. Can she do it with her best friend and close partner in crime-solving trapped in police custody?

She has to.

An Undiplomatic Murder, book five in the Ritchie and Fitz Sci-Fi Murder Mysteries.

An Undiplomatic Murder, book five in the Ritchie and Fitz Sci-Fi Murder Mystery series.

NEW SERIES: THE FORGOTTEN PLANET

Coming soon from Ratatoskr Press Books, the new YA sci-fi series *The Forgotten Planet* starts with book 1: *Raiding the Forgotten Derelict.*

History sleeps beneath them all, but only she sees it.

Lafayette Eloi always knew her parents thought differently from others. They kept their books buried beneath her mother's house. They spoke an old language in the dead of night, whispering behind closed doors and bolted shutters. She grew up in a village where no one was related to her, and she never knew why.

Then, after her mother died, her father came to fetch her. Now she and her mother's dog assist her father in his work. The work discussed in whispers in the dark. The work that had cost Lafayette so much all her young life.

But now she learns just how much her father's work means to their entire world. Only no one knows anything about it. Only her father. And only Lafayette.

Because the work that consumed her father's entire life and her mother's too now nibbles at the fringe's of Lafayette's own life. And she cannot refuse its call.

Raiding the Forgotten Derelict, first book in the new YA sci-fu series *The Forgotten Planet*, available in September 2024 from Ratatoskr Press Books.

COMPLETE SERIES: THE RITCHIE AND FITZ SCI-FI MURDER MYSTERIES

The Ritchie and Fitz Sci-Fi Murder Mysteries starts with *Murder on the Intergalactic Railway*.

For Murdina Ritchie, acceptance at the Oymyakon Foreign Service Academy means one last chance at her dream of becoming a diplomat for the Union of Free Worlds. For Shackleton Fitz IV, it represents his last chance not to fail out of military service entirely.

Strange that fate should throw them together now, among the last group of students admitted after the start of the semester. They had once shared the strongest of friendships. But that all ended a long time ago.

But when an insufferable but politically important woman turns up murdered, the two agree to put their differences aside and work together to solve the case.

Because the murderer might strike again. But more importantly, solving a murder would just have to impress the dour colonel who clearly thinks neither of them belong at his academy.

Murder on the Intergalactic Railway, the first book in *The Ritchie and Fitz Sci-Fi Murder Mysteries*.

COMPLETE SERIES: THE TRAVELS OF SCOUT SHANNON

The complete six-book series *The Travels of Scout Shannon* begin with book one, *Under Falling Skies*.

Scout Shannon's whole family died the day the Space Farers dropped an asteroid on their domed city. Now she lives alone, out in the wild with only her dogs for company. She prefers it that way.

But Scout finds herself at a crossroads. One road leads back to a quiet life snug under the protective dome of a city. The other road leads to a life in the rebellion, a life of adventure and excitement but also danger. Dare she try to find the rebels hiding in the hills?

Then a chance encounter with a stranger from the other side of the galaxy threatens to derail what remains of Scout's life. The entire galaxy awaits her, if she survives the next four days.

Under Falling Skies, a young adult science fiction novel, set on a remote planet with a distinctly Old West feel. For fans of gunslinging women and young girl assassins. And dogs.

Under Falling Skies, the first book in *The Travels of Scout Shannon,* available everywhere now.

SCI-FI SERIAL PODCAST!

Check out my new monthly podcast of serialized science fiction: THE TALES OF THE CHAI MAKHANI TRIO!

Elyot loathes the massive Commonwealth ships that hover menacingly over his home world of Adghal. He hates the Commonwealth enforcers who harass the populace even more. But with his mother missing and presumed dead, Elyot keeps his head down and strives to avoid notice. And he succeeds until the day two strangers enter his life...

New episodes of this sci-fi serial drop every 1st of the month.

Now streaming on all major podcast platforms. Also available in eBook and print everywhere books or sold. For a complete episode listing, check out the page on my website.

ALSO FROM RATATOSKR PRESS

Also from Ratatoskr Press, *The Witches Three Cozy Mystery Series* by Cate Martin, a mix of mystery and magic that begins with Book 1: *Charm School*.

Amanda Clarke thinks of herself as perfectly ordinary in every way. Just a small-town girl who serves breakfast all day in a little diner nestled next to the highway, nothing but dairy farms for miles around. She fits in there.

But then an old woman she never met dies, and Amanda was named in her will. Now Amanda packs a bag and heads to the big city, to Miss Zenobia Weekes' Charm School for Exceptional Young Ladies. And it's not in just any neighborhood. No, she finds herself on Summit Avenue in St. Paul, a street lined with gorgeous old houses, the former homes of lumber barons, railroad millionaires, even the writer F. Scott Fitzgerald. Why, Amanda can practically hear the jazz music still playing across the decades.

Scratch that. The music really, literally, still plays in the backyard of the charm school. Because the house stretches across time itself. Without a witch to protect this tear in the fabric of the world, anything can spill over. Like music.

Or like murder.

The complete series is out now, and it all starts with *Charm School*.

FREE EBOOK!

Like exclusive, free content?

To get two prequel short stories to THE RITCHIE AND FITZ SCI-FI MURDER MYSTERIES as well as a bonus prequel novelette to the completed six-book series THE TRAVELS OF SCOUT SHANNON, signup for my monthly newsletter at KateMacLeodWrites.com.

Thank you!

ABOUT THE AUTHOR

Photograph © 2016 Jonathan Conklin

Kate MacLeod has written stories which have appeared in *Analog, Strange Horizons* and *Mythic Delirium,* among other places. She is also the author of two young adult science fictions series: *The Travels of Scout Shannon,* and *The Ritchie and Fitz Sci-Fi Murder Mysteries.* She also contributes to a serialized science fiction podcast called *The Tales of the Chai Makhani Trio.* She currently lives in Minneapolis, Minnesota.

Find out more about the author and sign up for her newsletter at KateMacLeodWrites.com.

ALSO BY KATE MACLEOD

Novels

The Slums of the Solar System:

Mitwa

The Mars of Malcontents

The Whole World for Each

Books 1-3 Box Set

The Travels of Scout Shannon:

Under Falling Skies

In Quaking Hills

Among Treacherous Stars

Against Impassable Barriers

Over Freezing Altitudes

At Galactic Central

The Travels of Scout Shannon Books 1-3

The Travels of Scout Shannon Books 4-6

The Travels of Scout Shannon Books 1-6

The Ritchie and Fitz Sci-Fi Murder Mysteries:

Murder on the Intergalactic Railway

Murder in the Skies

Body in the Catacombs

Death on the Summit

An Undiplomatic Murder

A Lethal Betrayal

The Forgotten Planet

Raiding the Forgotten Derelict (Forthcoming September 2024)

Sci-Fi Novellas

The Intergenerational Tree

I Rise into a Daybreak

Caper Novellas

The Third Pole Job

The Twelve Days of Christmas Job

10-Story Collections

Tales of Blood and Ink

Tales of Old Gods and New

5-Story Collections

Tales from Heian-Kyo and Others

Tales from the Edges and Ends

Tales from Forgotten Days

Tales from Ancient and Future Times

Tales from Across Space

www.ingramcontent.com/pod-product-compliance
Lightning Source LLC
Chambersburg PA
CBHW050839190726
48286CB00007B/2151